NAUGHTY HOLIDAYS

2015

By Nicole Edwards

The Walkers Of Coyote Ridge

Kaleb

Zane

Travis

Holidays with The Walker Brothers

Ethan

Braydon

Sawyer

Brendon

Curtis

Jared

Hard to Hold

Hard to Handle

Beau

Rex

A Coyote Ridge Christmas

Mack

Kaden & Keegan

Trey

Rafe

Violet

BRANTLEY WALKER: OFF THE BOOKS
All In
Without A Trace
Hide & Seek
Deadly Coincidence
Alibi
Secrets
Confessions
Bounty
Off Course
Chain Reaction
To Have and To Hold
Missing Pieces
Smoke and Mirrors

THE JAMESONS OF COYOTE RIDGE
Hot Chocolate Wishes
Rough & Dirty

AUSTIN ARROWS
Rush
Kaufman

CLUB DESTINY
Conviction
Temptation
Addicted
Seduction
Infatuation
Captivated
Devotion
Perception
Entrusted
Adored
Distraction
Forevermore

DEAD HEAT RANCH
Boots Optional
Betting on Grace
Overnight Love
Jared *(a crossover novel)*

DEVIL'S BEND
Chasing Dreams
Vanishing Dreams

MISPLACED HALOS
Protected in Darkness
Salvation in Darkness
Bound in Darkness

OFFICE INTRIGUE
Office Intrigue
Intrigued Out of The Office
Their Rebellious Submissive
Their Famous Dominant
Their Ruthless Sadist
Their Naughty Student
Their Fairy Princess
Owned

PIER 70
Reckless
Fearless
Speechless
Harmless
Clueless

PRIMAL INSTINCTS
Chase (Volume 1-3)
Capture (Volume 4-6)
Claim (Volume 7-9)

HEROES & HAVOC
(Sniper 1 Security, Devil's Playground, Southern Boy Mafia)

Wait for Morning
Beautifully Brutal
Without Regret
Never Say Never
Beautifully Loyal
Without Restraint
Tomorrow's Too Late

STANDALONE NOVELS
Unhinged Trilogy
A Million Tiny Pieces
Inked on Paper
Bad Reputation
Bad Business
Filthy Hot Billionaire
RULE

NAUGHTY HOLIDAY EDITIONS
2015
2016
2021

NICOLE EDWARDS

NAUGHTY HOLIDAYS 2015

COVER DETAILS:

Image: © julietange (21200578) | © beholdereye (32286910) | © salamatik (160259075) | 123rf.com   *Design:* © Nicole Edwards Limited

INTERIOR DETAILS:

Image: © kotoffei (46416182) | © kanate (22764858) | © soniaeps (154862457) | 123rf.com

Formatting: Nicole Edwards Limited

ISBN: (ebook) 9781939786555 | (paperback) 9781939786562

Check out these five-star reviews for *Naughty Holidays:*

"As always Ms. Edwards gives us a lovely little holiday treat."
~BookBub reviewer

"Heat up the winter cold with this amazing collection of holiday short stories for the Nicole Edwards characters you love and can never get enough of." ~BookBub reviewer

"Such fun to get to catch up with some of our favourite characters. Perfect little snippets into their lives." ~BookBub reviewer

Nicole Nation voted, and the winners for the 2015 holiday have been chosen! Come and see how they are heating up the holidays this year!

Alluring Indulgence: Travis, Kylie, and Gage

The Walker brothers are at it again...

Travis Walker recognizes his competitive nature, and this year, with his brothers going all-in on holiday decorations, he is determined to come out on top in this showdown.

Sniper 1 Security: RT and Z

What's the best gift you can get for the man you love?

Ryan Trexler is determined to find his husband the perfect Christmas present—something that will make Z think of him throughout the year. The only problem is that he has no idea what to choose.

Club Destiny: Luke, Sierra, and Cole

Spend New Year's at the hottest fetish club in town.

Known for hosting great parties, Luke McCoy aims to make this year's New Year's celebration at Devotion his best one yet.

Dear reader,

Back in July of this year, I asked the readers to vote on which three sets of characters they would want to see in holiday novellas. The enthusiastic responses were overwhelming. I had so much fun spending time with previous characters and seeing what they were up to. I hope you enjoy spending time with them as well.

Much Love,

Nicole Edwards

Walker Brothers Free For All

Travis Walker, Gage Matthews, and Kylie Prescott

from *Travis*

CHAPTER 1

TRAVIS WALKER WAS UP EARLIER THAN HE'D planned, far earlier than was appropriate on the rare occasion he took a day off, but he had no one to blame but himself. These days, it wasn't easy sleeping alone, and the instant he'd felt Gage crawl out of bed, he'd known Kylie wouldn't be far behind. And she hadn't been.

Yep, Travis's husband and wife had left him by himself, as they'd done many times before when he would've preferred them to remain right where they were so he could block out the coming day for as long as possible.

There was a reason he had a penchant for caffeine—mornings were not his thing.

So, this morning, when they'd disappeared to get their day started, Travis had stared at the ceiling for all of ten minutes before dropping his legs over the side of the bed and forcing himself upright.

The day wasn't going to wait for him and they had plans. Sort of. If heading over to his parents' house for Thanksgiving dinner and then coming back to decorate their Christmas tree counted, then yes, they had things to do. Not to mention, Kylie had volunteered to help Travis's mother cook, as she'd done the past couple of years, and when she volunteered, it actually meant they all did.

On unsteady legs, he managed to walk to the bathroom, still in a fog. Through blurry eyes, Travis stared at himself in the mirror above his sink. There was definitely more gray in his hair than there had been last year. And although his youngest brother, Zane, liked to give him hell about it, Travis didn't mind it. According to Kylie, it was sexy, so who was he to complain? Granted, he seriously needed to shave. Rubbing his hands over the three-day-old scruff on his cheeks, he debated for a minute. Before he could decide whether or not he wanted to put forth the effort, Travis watched as Gage stepped into the bathroom behind him, closing the door.

"Mornin'," Gage greeted, his voice gruff and sexy, brown eyes scanning over Travis's back as he moved closer.

Travis grunted. It was too early for a lengthy conversation, so…

Gage wrapped his thick arms around Travis's waist, warmth infusing him instantly. While his dick absolutely enjoyed Gage's touch, he was still wary of what was expected of him this early in the morning. When Gage's palms flattened on Travis's chest, he relaxed. But when Gage's lips pressed to Travis's naked back, an electrical current shot straight to his groin, making his cock pulse with anticipation.

Well. It certainly wasn't too early for *that*.

"What're you doin'?" Travis smirked, looking at their reflections in the mirror.

"What my wife instructed me to do," Gage replied slyly, his mouth leaving a blaze of fire across Travis's skin. "She told me to take a shower while she fed Kate. When I mentioned you were probably about to do the same thing, her eyes sparkled. So, I'm doing as I was told."

For the past two weeks, the three of them had been so busy that moments such as this had been few and far between. Sleep was rare these days, thanks to all that was going on with the resort due to the holiday season in full swing. And when they weren't at work, the three of them were alternating with Kate—not entirely out of obligation, more so because she was the highlight of their lives, and spending as much time with her as possible had become their top priority.

That meant moments like this didn't happen all that frequently, so when the opportunity presented itself…

"Anyone mention our wife's the smartest woman in the world?" Travis asked, reaching back and cupping Gage's head, sliding his fingers through the cool strands of his hair, and holding Gage close.

"We're lucky like that," Gage admitted, his lips trailing up to Travis's shoulder before he stepped away to turn on the shower.

All thoughts of shaving disappeared entirely when Gage shucked the sweatpants he had on, leaving him naked and beautiful, his hard cock bobbing out from his body, beckoning Travis to take him in hand. He didn't hesitate, moving toward Gage while shoving his boxers down his hips and allowing them to pool on the tiled floor as he followed Gage into the shower enclosure, closing the door behind them.

The water was warm, but Travis doubted that was what caused the steam. At least not after Travis pressed Gage up against the slate tile, his hand easing between them as he wrapped his fist around Gage's erection and fused their mouths.

"Trav," Gage groaned, their lips fumbling together.

A little more than two years since they'd gotten together, Travis still couldn't get enough of Gage or Kylie. They could tease him with a few well-timed words, make him hard with a mere look. So, when he had the opportunity to get his hands on one or both of them, he didn't waste any time.

He stroked Gage's cock firmly, sliding his free hand into Gage's hair and pulling his head back so he could look in his lover's eyes. "I wanna feel your mouth on me."

"That right?" Gage grinned.

"Fuck yeah," Travis huffed, sliding his thumb over Gage's lower lip, thinking about sliding his dick into the warm cavern of Gage's mouth, feeling Gage's lips wrap around the sensitive head… He growled again, unable to hold back.

And when Gage's grin turned into a full-fledged naughty smile, Travis knew the man he loved was going to relent. Which was one fucking hell of a way to kick off the day.

NOW THIS WAS HOW EVERY DAY SHOULD start, Gage Matthews thought as he nipped the end of Travis's thumb. There weren't many things he enjoyed more than Travis's sexually assertive side. Unfortunately, he'd missed that in recent months. It seemed work had become so busy that they'd somehow lost sight of the important things, like one another.

Oh, sure, Travis was still just as forceful when it came to certain things like business, but this... It seemed as though it had been too long since Travis had taken what he'd wanted from him, and Gage loved this side of the man he loved.

Here, cocooned in the shower, just the two of them, Gage wanted Travis to take control. And he wasn't disappointed.

Travis tightened his hand in Gage's hair, urging him down. Knowing Travis needed a little defiance to fan that flame, Gage resisted, reaching for Travis's head and pulling him close, their mouths melding together. The firm press of Travis's tongue against his own made Gage's dick throb.

He really did miss these moments.

For long seconds, their tongues explored, hands groping, fumbling as they stoked that fire into a conflagration. Finally, when it was obvious Travis couldn't take much more, Gage dropped to the tiled seat, gripping Travis's thick cock in his fist and guiding him closer.

Travis's blue-gray eyes glittered dangerously as he stared down at him, fingers twining into Gage's hair. Lightning spiraled through his nerve endings when Travis tightened his grip and pulled him forward. Circling his tongue around the engorged head, Gage teased Travis for as long as he was allowed. And when Travis growled and forced his cock past Gage's lips, he willingly drew him in, sliding his tongue around Travis's steely length.

"Fuck, yes," Travis hissed. "Love when you do that."

Gage knew plenty of tricks that Travis loved, and having his dick sucked while Gage fingered his ass was one way to send the man into hyperspace. Since his main objective was to make Travis come, he didn't hold back.

Travis widened his stance, giving Gage better access as he breached his tight hole with one finger.

"Fuck," Travis exhaled. "Don't stop."

Gage got the impression that Travis possibly needed more than he was willing to ask for, and he wondered briefly if this little water activity might take a different turn from what Gage had originally expected.

Not that he minded either way. Having his dick buried in Travis's tight ass or having Travis lodged to the hilt in his... Both were intensely satisfying for him.

"Suck me," Travis commanded. "Harder."

Travis kept a tight grip on Gage's hair, shoving his cock deep, retreating, then pushing home again. Over and over, Gage sucked, teased, tormented, never letting up as he drove Travis closer and closer to the edge.

Gage groaned, allowing the vibrations to shoot up Travis's shaft while he forced one finger into Travis's ass. He sought Travis's prostate, and when he found the spongy tissue, he focused his attention on driving Travis out of his mind.

"Oh, hell," Travis growled. "You want me to come?"

Gage lifted his gaze and met Travis's. Gage nodded.

"In your mouth?" Travis asked. "Or in your ass? Your choice."

Well, when he put it that way... Gage released Travis's dick from between his lips and removed his finger as he got to his feet.

Standing once again, Gage succumbed to the onslaught of Travis's mouth on his, allowing his hands to slide over the smooth skin of Travis's back. God, he loved this man. More and more every single day, but it was moments like this, when they became one—regardless of how they chose to express their feelings, slow and sweet or fast and dirty—that Gage found himself so caught up he wasn't sure how he'd ever lived without the two people who'd completed his world and given him everything he'd never thought he would have.

Travis pulled his mouth away, spinning Gage around.

"Against the wall," Travis instructed.

Gage stepped forward until his chest came into contact with the cool tile, elbows tucked into his sides, palms flat.

Travis positioned him the way he wanted, forcing Gage to put one foot on the bench, making him widen his stance.

The click of a bottle being uncapped sounded from behind him, and a moment later, the thick head of Travis's cock was breaching the tight ring of muscles. Gage sucked in a breath, forced himself to relax.

"Take all of me," Travis whispered, his mouth against Gage's shoulder.

He loved when Travis showed that softer dominant side. It wasn't easy to get the man to give up even a small measure of control, but the way he showed Gage and Kylie how much they meant to him was proof that the man was mushy beneath the rough edges.

"Aw, yes, Gage."

Travis pumped his hips forward, lodging himself deep inside Gage. Growling his approval, Gage tried to push back against the intrusion, but Travis maintained control, his fingers digging into Gage's hips, situating him just how he needed as he began ramming deep, over and over.

"Love you," Travis groaned, finding Gage's hands and linking their fingers before lifting them over Gage's head. "So fucking much."

And yes, instances like that, when Travis Walker, a man Gage had at one time wondered whether he had any feelings at all, blurted things like that, Gage couldn't control his own response.

Pressed to the wall, trapped between Travis's hard body and the slick tile, Gage allowed the sensations to take over. Travis impaled him, fucking him hard and fast, then alternating to slow and easy. It was an infuriating pace, difficult to keep up, but it was just what Gage needed to fan the flames, summoning his release from deep inside.

When Travis released his hands, Gage reached down, wrapping his hand around his cock, jerking himself as Travis fucked him relentlessly.

"Love you," Gage muttered. "Make me come, Trav. Fuck. Make me come."

It seemed that Travis focused all of his attention on doing just that, his fingers digging into Gage's hips again as he thrust harder, faster, deeper. Until nothing could be heard over the sound of their combined grunts and groans.

"Fuck, Trav!" Gage's release barreled upon him, taking him completely by surprise. "Coming!"

"So hot. Gonna make me … come … too," Travis murmured against his ear as he pressed his chest to Gage's back, his hips still pumping, cock still lodged deep. Travis grunted again, and Gage felt his cock pulse in his ass.

For a moment, they stood just like that, still locked together, the water cascading over them as they attempted to catch their breath.

"Good?" Travis asked.

"For a little while," Gage joked, putting his foot on the floor when Travis pulled out of him. "I'll be up for a replay in an hour."

"Don't tempt me," Travis grumbled, cupping Gage's face when he turned back around. "Or you'll find yourself with my dick inside you later today."

"At your parents' house?" Gage asked, smiling.

"I'm not shy," Travis said. "And there're plenty of places no one will find the three of us."

"The three of us?" Gage loved the sound of that.

"Yeah. While everyone dotes on Kate, I'll sneak you and Kylie off for a little after-dinner fun."

"Hmm. Sounds like the perfect Thanksgiving," Gage told him, meeting Travis's gaze. "But for some reason, I don't think you have it in you."

The corner of Travis's lips quirked, and Gage knew Travis was entertaining the notion.

And that meant today was going to be a Thanksgiving celebration that he'd remember forever.

CHAPTER 2

For Kylie Walker-Matthews, the morning flew by in a rush, as did much of the afternoon. After helping Lorrie cook alongside her sisters-in-law Zoey, V, Cheyenne, and Kennedy, as well as her own sister, Jessie, Kylie decided to slip upstairs for a shower. She'd bypassed one that morning, instead giving Gage and Travis a few minutes alone.

Although they never asked for it, Kylie knew their private time, just the two of them, was limited. She, however, got to spend quite a bit of time with each of them alone, though real life was getting in the way due to so much going on. Not that she was complaining. Everyone had to deal with the trials and tribulations of the real world at some point. Not to mention, they had a beautiful baby girl, family they got to see every week, stable jobs that allowed them to provide for one another. All in all, Kylie knew they were blessed.

But now, she got to steal a few minutes alone to take a shower in Ethan's old room, which had been turned into a guest room after Jared had moved into Kaleb's old house. After locking the bedroom door, Kylie rummaged through the bag she'd brought with her extra clothes, then laid them out on the bed. She grabbed her toiletry items, stripped, then hurried through her shower. Afterward, she wrapped the towel around herself, then used the spare hair dryer beneath the sink to dry her hair.

A sound in the bedroom startled her, and Kylie opened the door and peeked out.

Nothing.

Pushing the door open all the way, she saw where the noise had come from.

There, lying on the bed on his side, was one of her beautiful husbands.

"What're you doin'?" she asked Travis, noticing the mischievous gleam in his blue-gray eyes.

"Watchin' you get dressed."

"Is that so?" she taunted, taking a step closer to the bed. "Where's Gage?"

"Talkin' to Ethan and Beau."

"So you slipped away?"

Travis nodded. "I figured it'd be my only chance before dinner."

"They'll realize you're gone, you know." Allowing the towel to fall to the floor, Kylie watched Travis carefully.

The way his eyes widened and his nostrils flared with obvious approval sent a chill down her spine. She'd never had body image issues, but after giving birth to Kate, as with most mothers, her body wasn't the same as it used to be. So seeing the subtle yet definite approval made her body hum.

"You're not gettin' lucky right now," she told him as she reached for her panties and then slid them on. Her bra came next, then her shirt, and finally her jeans.

"You know, I like it much better when your clothes are comin' off," Travis grumbled, dropping to his back, his gaze never leaving her.

"Well, if you're lucky…"

A deep, rumbling growl came from Travis's chest, and Kylie laughed.

"Is everyone here yet?" she asked as she shoved her dirty clothes into the bag to take back home and wash later.

"Almost. Waitin' on Sawyer and Kaleb."

"Where'd they go?"

"To get more lights for the house."

"More? I'm not sure this house can handle any more lights."

"Oh, it's not for Mom and Dad's house. They're gettin' more lights for their houses."

Yep, they were definitely starting a new tradition. While the Walker family still strung the lights and put up the tree at Curtis and Lorrie's house on Thanksgiving night, the brothers were now battling it out over whose house could have the most elaborate decorations. Since they were all now married off, or close, anyway, they had their own houses and their own families. Which meant new traditions were forming. Only, when it came to the seven brothers, those traditions were quite competitive. At least this one, anyway.

"Let me guess," Kylie said, taking Travis's hand and pulling him up from the bed. Not that she did much in the way of getting him up, but he did get the hint and got to his feet. "You and Gage stocked up."

"Damn right we did," he said with a shit-eating grin.

Travis pulled her into his arms, linking his fingers behind her back as he stared down at her. "Don't think for a minute that I'm lettin' Braydon and Jessie win again."

Kylie didn't mind a little competition, and since her sister had won last year, she was fully behind Travis's need to go bigger this year. But she also knew that this could get way out of hand. And probably would, whether she wanted it to or not.

"Plus," Travis said, leaning down and kissing the tip of her nose, "Kate will love it."

He was right about that. Their little princess had just turned one, and Kylie knew that the lights would likely be the highlight of her holiday.

That and all the gifts Kylie suspected Kate's daddies would be getting her.

"Okay, fine," she agreed, taking his hand and opening the bedroom door so they could go back downstairs. "You just have to promise to keep it reasonable."

Travis chuckled. "Define reasonable."

The gleam in her husband's eye told her everything she needed to know. Over the top … yeah, that would probably be an understatement before all was said and done.

As usual, the feast at his parents' house was impressive. The number of people in attendance had doubled in the past few years because Travis's brothers had all paired off and many of his cousins were coming around more and more often. Not to mention the babies and the in-laws. And of course, the pets. It was almost to the point that the family gatherings had outgrown Lorrie and Curtis's house. Next year, they might have to rent a banquet hall just to get everyone together.

And with the sheer volume of people came a tremendous amount of noise. Conversations, laughter, babies crying, dogs barking. It was their new normal.

After helping his brothers clear the table, pack up the leftovers, and clean up in the kitchen, Travis took a seat on the couch closest to his father, who was holding Kate in his lap while watching Kennedy and Cheyenne sort ornaments. Behind them, Brendon and Jared were putting up the artificial tree.

"Lemme guess," Curtis said, glancing over at Travis, "the boys are all outside?"

Travis nodded. "They're gettin' the lights put up on the house."

"'Course they are. So they can head home and do their own."

"That's the plan," Travis told him with a smirk. In fact, for the past few weeks, he and his brothers had been talking about the holiday decorations, ordering lights and other accessories online, picking up some in the stores when the big retailers had started putting them out.

"You gonna let Bray and Jess outdo you again this year?" Curtis joked, smiling over at him.

"Not a chance," he said softly, not wanting the others to hear.

"Da!" Kate cooed when she noticed him. Her little chubby arms lifted, and Travis leaned over, taking his daughter from his father's lap.

He tossed her up in the air, then brought her down, burying his face in her sweet-smelling neck and blowing air against her skin, making her giggle.

"When're y'all gonna have another one?" Curtis asked.

"Pop, she just turned one," he said, as though that explained anything at all.

"Don't matter. She needs a brother or sister."

Well, if Travis had anything to say about it, she'd have several more. Eventually. He didn't care if it was nine months from now or two years. Whenever it happened, he was ready.

However, right now, these were the moments he lived for, the ones that seemed to be few and far between these days.

"How're things at AI?" his father asked, taking a cup of coffee from Zoey when she delivered it. "Thank you, darlin'."

"You want some?" Zoey asked Travis.

"I'm good. Thanks, though." Turning his attention back to his father while Kate ran her little fingers over the bristle on his face, he said, "AI's doin' good. Busy."

"That's what you wanted, right?"

He nodded. "It is." It definitely was, but he had to admit that when he'd decided to go all in, he hadn't actually thought he'd ever be married with a kid. Sometimes he felt as though he gave more to the resort than to Kylie, Gage, and Kate, and that was the last thing Travis wanted to happen.

"Well, boy," Curtis said, sipping his coffee, "just don't let it take all your time."

"I'm tryin'."

Someone turned on Christmas music, and everyone's eyes lifted, trying to find who the culprit was. Travis peered over his shoulder to see Zane grinning like a fool before darting out through the back door.

Crazy little shit. He always moaned and complained about the music, but this year he was the one to kick it off.

Figured.

Getting to his feet, Travis held Kate close to him. "I'm gonna take her outside to see the lights."

His father nodded. "I'm gonna stay right here and supervise."

"You do that."

"Hey!" Jared called out from his spot behind the tree. "Can Derrick and Mason go with you?"

"Absolutely," Travis said, smiling down at Jared's two-year-old son, Derrick, and Kaleb's almost-two-year-old boy, Mason. "Y'all wanna go see the lights?"

Both boys jumped to their feet, and when Derrick started jumping up and down, hollering, Mason was quick to follow.

"Come on, let's go." Travis urged the boys in front of him, and as he passed through the kitchen, he snagged Sawyer to help out.

Peering over, Travis noticed his mother was cooing over Reid, Zane, and V's five-month-old little boy, while Zoey held Kellan, her and Kaleb's four-month-old boy, in her arms nearby.

"What's up, little one?" Sawyer asked, squeezing Kate's cheeks when he joined them. She practically leapt into her uncle's arms, and Travis passed her over.

"How're the weddin' plans?" Travis asked as they followed the boys down the steps and around to the front of the house.

"Done."

Travis's head snapped over to his brother. "Seriously? How'd you manage that?"

"My girl's simple like that. Now the only thing left is the gettin' hitched part."

"Cold feet?"

"Hell no," Sawyer said, then glanced at Kate as though he hoped she didn't repeat what he'd said. "I just wish we coulda done it already." Sawyer kissed Kate's cheek. "I'm ready to start makin' babies."

Travis laughed.

Buster, Sawyer's cocker spaniel, came bounding over, sniffing around Mason and Derrick as the boys watched in awe as Kaleb, Braydon, Beau, and Ethan all attempted to string the lights up in one of the trees while Zane instructed from the ground.

"You gonna decorate this year?" Sawyer asked, bouncing Kate gently on his hip.

"A little," he told him. "I think Kate'll get a kick out of it."

Kate's little hands clapped together as she stared up at the house, where the lights were already hung and flashing. There was a huge smile on her face, which made his chest swell.

His thoughts drifted to his own house and the decorations he and Gage had bought already. If he knew his brothers, he was going to need to make another run to the store in the very near future, because he fully intended to win this year.

"For Kate, huh?" Sawyer's gruff chuckle told him he hadn't gotten anything past his brother.

"That's my story and I'm stickin' to it."

CHAPTER 3

"Is she asleep?" Gage asked Kylie when he joined her in the living room, referring to their daughter. It was late, so he figured he knew the answer already, but he asked anyway.

Kylie smiled up at him from her spot in front of the recently decorated tree. "Yep. I put her in her bed. She passed out while staring up at the lights."

God, Kylie was beautiful. He admired her from a few feet away, watching as she fingered one of the dangling ornaments, her eyes flashing with excitement. She stifled a yawn, then leaned back, stretching her legs out in front of her while propping herself up on her elbows.

"Long day," he said, moving to join her on the floor.

"Definitely. But it was nice."

It had been nice. They'd spent most of the day at Lorrie and Curtis's for Thanksgiving dinner, then they'd come home and decorated their own tree, the one Gage and Travis had snuck out to get yesterday so they'd have it for tonight.

While Kate had sat on the floor by her mother, Travis and Gage had strung the lights, then Kylie was in charge of the ornaments. According to her, if she let them do it, they'd all be crowded in one place. Women. Sometimes he wondered whether she realized they did some things on purpose, merely for attention from her. Just because.

"Where's Travis?" she asked, glancing over at him when he lowered himself onto the floor.

"Right here," Travis called out from behind them.

Gage glanced over his shoulder to see Travis flipping off the light switches with his elbow before coming toward them, three steaming ceramic mugs in his hands.

"Is that…?" Kylie's eyes lit up.

"Hot chocolate," Travis said with a smirk.

"Hopefully there's a touch of liquor in there," Gage grumbled good-naturedly. Or a lot of liquor. He wasn't a fan of hot chocolate, but he knew Kylie was.

"Just a little." Travis winked.

After passing them the mugs, Travis eased down onto the floor on the other side of Kylie, his back propped against the couch, the three of them staring up at the tree.

They remained quiet for a moment, the colorful lights flashing red, green, yellow, while most of the room was shrouded in darkness. Gage was at peace, enjoying the simple calmness of it all, until Travis turned, retrieved something from the cushion above him.

When he pulled it into his lap, Gage saw what it was.

An iPad. He smiled.

"Are we gonna watch porn?" Kylie huffed, a teasing smirk lighting up her face.

Best idea yet.

"That hadn't been the plan, but…" Travis glanced over at her.

"No? That's surprising," Gage said, feigning disappointment as he placed his mug of hot chocolate on the table that had been pushed out of the way to make room for the tree.

"Oh. My. God." Kylie barked out a laugh. "You have got to be kidding."

"What?" Travis's face was a mask of innocence.

Gage dropped his gaze to the iPad to see a video playing. More specifically, a video of people putting up holiday lights.

Gage chuckled. Yep, Travis had it bad. He was out to win the contest this year, and Gage didn't see him letting up until the final decision was made.

"Y'all aren't gonna let this one go, are you?" Kylie's head swiveled back and forth between them. "You're gonna spend the next few weeks putting up lights and decorations until it's impossible to see the house."

"That's the plan," Travis agreed, nodding his head at Gage.

Gage leaned over and pressed his lips to Kylie's ear. "That might be *his* plan," he whispered. "But mine involves something else."

"Yeah?" she rasped. "What's that?"

"You naked. Beneath me."

"I like the way you think," she said, turning her head so that their lips brushed.

Kylie shifted, reaching up and putting her arm around his neck, pulling him to her. Gage adjusted his position so that he was leaning over her, resting on one elbow. He slid his free hand beneath the T-shirt she'd put on. One of Travis's, if he wasn't mistaken.

When her lips parted against his, Gage groaned as he licked into her mouth, tasting her sweetness combined with the chocolate. He slid his hand higher until he found one bare breast. Cupping her and sliding his thumb back and forth across her nipple, he felt it pebble beneath his touch.

Kylie sighed into his mouth, her arm tightening around his neck.

"Fine," Travis grunted with a laugh. "The lights'll have to wait."

Gage felt Kylie smile against his lips. If the man could focus on anything other than the sexy woman laid out between them, then he had far more willpower than Gage did.

Forcing the soft cotton T-shirt up over her belly, then higher, Gage finally revealed her breasts to his hungry gaze.

"So pretty," he mumbled, grazing his lips over her jaw as he ventured lower.

Kylie released him as she reclined on the floor, peering up at both of them. Travis had stretched out on her other side, resting on his right elbow as he watched them. "Don't stop on my account."

His voice was rough with the obvious lust coursing through him. Gage knew how he felt. It'd been a while since they'd stopped long enough to enjoy a moment like this. Sure, their sex life was still going strong, but the spontaneity had died down some. Most of the time, they were in their bed before one or more of them got the urge.

But tonight, here in the living room in front of the tree, Gage was looking forward to what was to come.

KYLIE SENSED THAT GAGE WANTED TO TAKE things slow, so she decided to oblige him despite the fact her body was on fire, aching for their touch. Since that morning, when she'd heard them in the shower together, she'd been hot and bothered. Putting things off until tonight hadn't been easy, either, especially when she had found Travis in the bedroom waiting for her after she'd taken a shower.

But now she was glad she had waited, because having the two of them… It didn't get much better than this.

"Shirt off," Travis instructed as he cupped one of her breasts in his big, warm hand, his tongue darting out to lash across her nipple.

Thankfully, Gage assisted, pulling the shirt up over her head and discarding it somewhere behind him. His attention immediately returned to her, his mouth latching onto her other nipple, causing her to moan from the sheer ecstasy of it all.

As much as she wanted to take things slow, it wasn't easy when they were drowning her in pleasure, teasing, tormenting, driving her absolutely mad as they used their mouths on her breasts. She needed their hands, their fingers, their cocks. She needed all of them on all of her, or she was going to explode.

"Relax, baby," Gage crooned, gripping her wrist in his fist when she tried to free the button on his jeans. "Not yet."

She groaned her disappointment, which only made them both laugh.

"If I have to have my shirt off, y'all should, too," she said, thrusting her chest upward to meet their teasing mouths. "It's only fair."

Travis bit her nipple gently, making her cry out. But then his mouth disappeared, the cool air making it tighten more. To her relief, he didn't go far, but he did shed his shirt as she'd asked. Hoping he wouldn't stop her, she flattened her palm against his washboard stomach and grazed the warm skin of his torso.

She peered over at Gage when he knelt beside her. His shirt disappeared, and she did the same to him with her other hand, allowing her fingers to slide through the trail of soft hair that disappeared into his jeans.

"Better?" Gage asked.

"Much." She wasn't completely satisfied, because yes, they still had on their jeans, but anytime she got the opportunity to see them shirtless, she was a happy woman.

19

Granted, that strip tease didn't last long. Their mouths returned to her flesh, sending goose bumps over her arms as she was once again drowning in sensation.

"Mmm," Travis mumbled as his mouth trailed lower, over her abdomen, then lower still.

He bypassed her panty-covered mound and kissed the inside of her thigh, making her groan with disappointment. Again, he simply chuckled. They both had always enjoyed pushing her to her limits. There was no doubt that they knew exactly what they were doing.

The next thing she knew, Travis was pulling her panties down her legs, then tossing them aside. Her inner hussy was screaming, *hell yeah*. Instinct had her widening her legs, hoping he would get the hint.

"Almost," he told her, eyes glittering as he met her gaze. "But I've got another idea."

Holding her breath while she waited for him to explain, Kylie's hands balled into fists at her sides.

Travis reached for her, helping her to sit up while he lowered himself to the rug, on his back.

"Sit on my face," he said, the words more of a gruff command than a request.

Without hesitation, she crawled over him, then straddled his face, facing Gage, who was still watching them intently.

Travis's head tilted back, and he looked directly at Gage. "Jeans off."

It didn't take a genius to figure out what Travis's plan was, which was probably why Gage was up on his feet and shedding his jeans in record time. Then he was kneeling once again, his beautiful cock bobbing out in front of him, directly above Travis's face.

Kylie gripped Gage's shoulders as she reached deep down inside for her patience. She wanted to feel Travis's—

"Yes!" she hissed when his hands pulled her hips forward, his tongue sliding between her slick folds, right where she needed him.

He lavished her with attention for a few seconds, drawing ragged moans from her, but then his head tilted, and it was Gage's turn to groan his pleasure.

"Fuck, yes," Gage growled, but he jerked Kylie toward him, cupping the back of her head and slanting his lips over hers in a kiss so hot she briefly worried that they'd burn down the house.

For long minutes, Travis continued to pleasure them with his lips and tongue, fucking Kylie gently, then sucking Gage into his mouth. They were puppets in Travis's hands as he shifted them so that the angle worked for him, but Kylie didn't mind. With Gage's strong fingers kneading her breasts and Travis's wicked tongue lapping at her pussy, she was slowly coming undone.

"Please," she begged when it was clear Travis wasn't going to give her that gentle nudge she needed to send her over into oblivion. He seemed content with keeping her hovering on the precipice.

"Both of us?" Gage asked.

Kylie didn't need him to elaborate. She knew what his request was. Double penetration wasn't something they did often, but it was something she enjoyed. And right now, she didn't care what they wanted, just as long as one of them was inside her. And soon.

Nodding, she scooted back, sliding down Travis's body. She didn't stop until she was straddling his knees, and it was then that she freed the button and lowered the zipper on his jeans. Gage disappeared but returned almost instantly with a bottle of lube in his hand. Where he got it from, she had no idea. Nor did she really care.

After helping Travis remove his jeans, she straddled his hips once again, leaning down, her breasts crushed against his chest as she kissed him. Their tongues languidly dueled, her fingers tugging at the short strands of his hair.

"I love you," Travis whispered, never pulling his mouth from hers.

"I love you, too," she said with a smile. "And I'll love you more if you'd—" Her request was cut off when Travis shifted his hips, pushing the thick head of his cock past her entrance, sliding deep in one quick thrust. "Oh, God! Yes!"

Travis grabbed the back of her head, pulling her face down to his and crushing their mouths together while he rocked up into her, making her whimper from the sheer ecstasy that consumed her.

Gage didn't waste any time, either. When his lubed fingers breached her anus, she flinched but then relaxed against Travis.

"That's it, baby," Gage mumbled from behind her. "Let us make you feel good."

And feel good she would, just as soon as they were inside her. Kylie needed more than they were giving, but she didn't want to rush Gage.

What felt like hours was likely only mere minutes before Gage was pushing his cock inside her, stretching her with a blaze of heat inside her ass, but then the brief spark of pain dissipated, and pleasure ignited, hot and bright.

"More," she pleaded on a breathless moan, unable to move now that she was pinned between them, both of them filling her.

"Ride me, baby," Travis encouraged.

Kylie rocked back and forth while Travis and Gage each rested their hands on her hips. The sensation was exquisite. She was full, so incredibly full, but she never wanted it to end. It wasn't easy to keep a steady rhythm considering the angles, but she did her best for as long as Travis allowed her.

As was usually the case, Travis's patience ran out as his fingers dug into her hips, stilling her movements. "Our turn," he told her.

Relaxing on top of him, Kylie allowed them to take over. They started slow, a gentle rocking of their hips, but then Gage was fucking her hard, impaling her on Travis's thick cock while he filled her ass.

"Oh, God, yes!" she cried out, her body humming as her climax neared. Tingles ignited, intensified until she was a mass of sensation, heat blooming in her core. "Travis!" Her fingers clutched at his shoulders as she tried to push herself up, needing that extra push to send her over. "Gage! Harder, Gage!"

Her husbands gave her what she needed, fucking her so perfectly until her body filled with warmth, that tingle in her core turned into a blazing inferno that radiated through her limbs, sending her higher and higher until…

"Fuck!" she cried out as her orgasm crashed through her, her muscles locking.

"Goddamn," Travis grunted, his hands gripping her hips tightly. "Coming!"

Gage grunted from behind her, his body stilling, hips slamming against her ass as he came.

Thankfully, they didn't need her to do anything because at that point, Kylie's muscles were mush, her body sated and exhausted. So, she collapsed against Travis and closed her eyes, allowing them to figure out how to get her upstairs to their bed.

Two weeks later

"WHERE'S THE TRUCK?" TRAVIS CALLED DOWN FROM his spot on the roof.

"On its way," Gage hollered. "They got lost."

Of course they did. Travis was anxious for the material to be delivered so they could start working on the newest piece for their holiday display, a sixty-foot tower that would be erected in the center of the yard so they could hang roughly sixty-five thousand lights from it for the largest Christmas tree display in Coyote Ridge. He would've gone bigger if he'd had the chance, but since this was a last-minute suggestion, he'd had to settle for what he could get.

"Is Kylie still out shopping?" he asked Gage, glancing over at him as Travis backed down the ladder.

"For now. But we don't have much time."

"Think she'll be back before we get it set up?" Travis asked, noticing the huge flatbed truck turning down the road in front of their house.

Gage's eyes widened when he saw the massive steel pipes on the back of it. "I don't see how she won't," he muttered. "That's gonna take a while."

Travis grinned. Yeah. It would.

Then again, it had taken nearly a week for them to get the concrete work done in the yard so that they would have something to bolt it to. It hadn't been easy convincing Kylie that it was necessary for the display, but she'd finally tossed her hands up and told them they were on their own.

Okay, so maybe they were going a little overboard, but after hearing what his brothers were doing, Travis knew it was something he had to do.

The truck turned down the long dirt drive and parked near the house. He and Gage headed toward the driver as he climbed down from the truck, smiling.

"Christmas decorations?" the guy asked.

"Crazy, right?" Gage tossed back.

"A little. Y'all wanna give me a hand?"

Travis and Gage nodded, then followed him around to the back of the truck.

For the next few hours, they unloaded the material, and when the lift truck arrived that would allow them to get to the top of the sixty-foot pole, they got to work. Luckily they'd started early, because it was dark by the time they were finished. And they'd only managed to work so quickly because he'd called in a few favors and gotten his cousins over to help out.

"Y'all done yet?" Kylie asked when she stepped out onto the porch, Kate on her hip. "Dinner's ready."

Perfect timing. Travis was starving and he imagined everyone else was, too. They'd worked right through lunch.

Making his way to the porch, he smiled as Kate pointed toward him. "Da!"

"That's right, sugar bug. You like the tree?" Taking her from Kylie, he spun his daughter around as they stared up at the tree, currently lit in white. Before they were done, the tree would flash different colors, all tuned to music programmed on a laptop currently set up in his office.

"You've been at this for two weeks and that's all you've got?" Kylie teased.

Gage stepped up onto the porch, grabbed Kylie around the waist, and spun her around. "You ain't seen nothin' yet, darlin'."

Nope. She hadn't.

24

By the time they were finished, their house would be visible from space.

Or at least that was the plan.

"Come on, boys," Kylie said to Jared and CJ, who were tying off the last of the lights. "We've got enough for everyone."

Mumbled agreements came from both men as they hurried, then ambled toward them with a grin.

"You think it'll win?" Kylie asked them.

"It's good," Jared agreed. "I'll give you that much."

"Who's judgin' this thing, anyway?" CJ asked.

Travis opened the screen door and allowed the others to precede him inside, passing Kate over to Gage when she reached for him.

"The kids," Kylie told him. "And Curtis and Lorrie."

"What kids?" CJ grinned. "Maybe you can bribe them."

Laughter echoed in the house. If only it were that easy.

"I'm not sure you can bribe Mason, Derrick, and Kate. They're pretty picky," Jared said.

"The other displays look good so far," CJ told them when they had all taken their seats at the table. "The town's freaking out."

"It's all anyone can talk about," Kylie said. "Jessie and I went to the diner for lunch the other day, and people were stopping to ask what else we were doing."

"What'd you tell them?" Gage asked, passing the bowl of mashed potatoes to Travis.

"That they'd have to talk to y'all. I told 'em I wasn't privy to that information." Kylie set two jars of baby food in front of Kate.

"I bet that got 'em goin'." Jared chuckled.

"Someone's callin' it the Walker brothers' holiday free-for-all," Kylie noted.

CJ chuckled. "And to think, Braydon and Jessie won last year because they had an animated blow-up Santa on the roof."

Travis spooned peas onto his mashed potatoes. "Not this year."

"Oh, it's gonna get interesting," Jared offered. "I've seen some big trucks passing by the ranch."

"Going to Kaleb's?" Gage stopped with his fork in midair.

"Yep."

They were definitely going to have to check out the competition. Then again, Travis wasn't sure when they'd have time. They had a few more deliveries being made this week, and he was hoping they could get down to Austin to check out a store he'd heard about. They were still missing a few things that would tie it all together, and their deadline was coming up fast.

"We agreed to have it all in place by next Friday, the eighteenth," Gage said. "So they better work fast."

"Well, you know what you could do?" CJ questioned, grinning like a fool. "Tie 'em all up at the resort. Keep 'em busy with work and you've got it made."

Travis and Gage laughed. If only that were an option. And as much as he wanted to win, he still wanted it to be a fair fight.

After all, what was the point in winning otherwise?

"WHAT DO YOU THINK, KATE? TOO MUCH?" Gage asked his daughter as they sat out on the front porch after dinner. He'd wrapped her in a blanket to ward off the cool night air so they could watch as Travis fiddled on the laptop, trying to get the lights to do what he wanted them to do.

While Kate relaxed in his arms, lifting her little hand every now and again to point at something that caught her attention, Gage was content to sit there. It seemed they were making a conscious effort to spend more time together, though not one of them had brought up the subject. Interesting how a family just knew when things were starting to unravel a little, and they also knew when it was time to pull on the thread and bring it all back together again.

That was where they were. Not that they'd drifted apart, but they knew it was possible if they didn't put forth the effort.

"It's just right," Travis said, still staring at the screen. "And when we pick up the last few things, it'll be perfect."

Gage kept his eyes on Travis. He loved how enthusiastic Travis was about this. It was great to see him engrossed in something other than work. They spent so much time at the resort, it was nice to relax and enjoy what they worked so hard to accomplish.

"Did you see Brendon's display?" Gage asked Travis.

"No, but I heard about it," he said, glancing up at them briefly. "Ethan called."

Gage chuckled. "Funny that he's worried about it. I didn't think he'd get into the spirit of it all."

Ethan had pretended not to care, but Gage had heard him talking to Beau. Ethan had something planned; he just didn't know what.

"He's goin' all out this year. Told me he'd be givin' me a run for my money. He's pretty convinced he'll win."

"Good." Gage liked the competitive nature between the brothers. They were a close-knit family, and he knew, in the end, the winner would definitely rub it in, but not to the point it angered anyone. The only problem was that next year, it would likely get even more out of hand. And that was saying something, considering he was staring up at a sixty-foot LCD Christmas tree in his front yard.

When the lights started flashing blue and white, Kate bounced in his lap, pointing at the tree.

"You think your daddies are crazy, don't you, sugar?" Gage asked Kate, kissing her on the top of her head.

He could see it now … Kate at sixteen, insisting that this wasn't her house, and not acknowledging the millions of lights they'd likely have at that point. Or perhaps she'd get in the spirit and help out. It could go either way. By then, Gage could only hope there'd be a few more kiddos running around, adding their two cents, as well. By then, he figured there would be a whole new generation of Walkers to contend with.

Coyote Ridge wouldn't know what hit it.

CHAPTER 5

ON MONDAY AFTERNOON, KYLIE WAS SITTING AT Jessie's house, drinking coffee while her sister fawned over Kate. She was grateful for a brief reprieve from her routine since things had gotten entirely out of hand with Travis and Gage regarding the holiday decorations, but the moment she'd pulled up to Jessie's, she'd realized that whatever holiday spirit they'd been inflicted with was in the water.

The difference … the inside of Jessie and Braydon's house was about as overdone as the outside. At least at her house, Kylie had some semblance of order. This looked as though the holiday section at Wal-Mart had exploded and rained back down all over the place.

"What do you think?" Jessie asked, nodding toward the giant Christmas tree in the corner. At least it wasn't sagging beneath the weight of all those ornaments.

"It's beautiful. You went with different colors than last year."

Jessie nodded. "Thought we'd change it up a little. Not that Braydon even noticed." She laughed. "He's so busy working on the exterior stuff, I could've put the tree upside down and he probably would've said it looked great."

"I know the feeling," Kylie said with a chuckle. "Travis … oh my gosh. He's gone crazy. But I can't complain, because he's havin' fun and Kate loves it. I just wonder how long it'll take to get it all down once the holidays are over."

"Not to mention, where are they gonna store this stuff?" Jessie teased. "I told Braydon that when they're done, all seven of them should have to pool all their crap together, and next year, they could do a drawing. Whatever they end up with is what they have to work with."

"That's a brilliant idea," Kylie exclaimed. "I don't even wanna know how much all this stuff has cost." It wouldn't be too hard to check, but she really didn't want to know.

"And it's not just the lights." Jessie glanced up at her after showing Kate how to drop the ball into the basketball hoop on the toy Jessie had bought her. "The computer program, all the little things they use to hold up the decorations."

"The extension cords," Kylie added. "Oh, I know. It's extreme."

"I think Brendon's comin' over later to help Braydon with an idea."

"Well, don't let Travis hear that. He'll only double his efforts if he thinks the twins are gangin' up on him."

"Bah!" Kate squealed, her chubby fist pointing at the ball on the floor.

Jessie handed it to her.

"Well, I'm kinda anxious for it to be over," Kylie admitted. "At least the adding part. Once they're set, it'll be cool. And the kids'll love it."

"Yes, they will." Jessie watched Kate. "Won't you?" Her gaze swung back to Kylie. "Did you hear Brendon's gonna have a concession stand?"

Kylie nearly fell out of her chair. "Are you serious?" She sobered instantly. "Cheyenne's not gonna sing, right? If she does, that's so not cool. The whole town will love them."

If Kylie's famous future sister-in-law gave a live performance… Surely she wouldn't. The thought made her laugh, though, because at this point, there was no telling how far they were willing to take things. She could totally see Brendon coercing her into doing it so they could win.

"I heard Sawyer found a place that has retired mall displays."

"Holy crap. Seriously?" Okay, so now Kylie knew she was going to enjoy it. As much as she hoped Travis would win—because she knew soothing his wounded pride would take time if he didn't—she looked forward to all the creative ideas.

"Yep," Jessie confirmed. "And"—she lowered her voice— "don't tell anyone I told you, but Kaleb's got a train."

Kylie's eyes widened. "A real one?"

"Track and all." Jessie's grin lit up her entire face. "It's freaking cool."

"What's Braydon's coup de grâce going to be?" Kylie asked curiously.

"He won't tell me," Jessie huffed. "He knows I'll tell you, and he doesn't want the secret out."

"Well, that's probably for the best. That way Travis can't torture me for information, either." However, Travis's sensual form of torture was quite incredible.

"Good thing we've only got a few days left of this madness."

"For this year, anyway," Kylie agreed. "So, tell me this…"

Jessie looked up at her inquisitively.

Kylie loved to be nosey, especially when it came to her sister. "Next year … will there be a little Braydon or Jessie here to enjoy the holidays, too?"

"It's quite possible," Jessie said, her smile never wavering. "And I promise, you'll be the first to know. Well, aside from Braydon, of course."

"Of course."

What Kylie didn't tell Jessie was that, if her sister was being honest, then they might just be pregnant together.

If they were lucky.

Not that two pregnancies in the Walker family at one time were easy, but Zoey and V had proven it could be done. They were just lucky that they'd been almost a month apart in due dates. Once the babies were born, it had been pure, beautiful chaos.

So, adding two more to the mix … yeah, it was going to be an interesting ride.

TRAVIS PULLED UP TO KALEB'S HOUSE AROUND five thirty. He'd intended to come snooping after he'd heard a rumor that his brother had some sort of fancy train that he was going to use to give the kids rides on this year. Unfortunately, it was too dark to see much other than the house, so he settled for going up to the door.

"Hey," Zoey greeted with a confused expression on her face as she answered, wiping her hands on a towel. "What're you doin' here?"

When she took a step back and motioned him inside, Travis entered the house, took a look around, and noticed that it looked much like his own house. Toys scattered everywhere, television on, playing some cartoon show, a tree in the corner glittering from the lights. It was cozy and festive, and he suddenly missed his own house.

"Kaleb here?"

Zoey nodded. "He's finishing up the dishes. Want some coffee?"

"I'll never turn down coffee," he told his sister-in-law, following her into the kitchen.

There was a baby monitor sitting on the kitchen table, but there was no noise coming from it. "Kellan asleep?"

"Yep," Kaleb said with a smirk. "What brings you by?"

"Just wanted to chat," he lied.

Kaleb clearly caught on to his fib, though, because his grin turned wicked. "You came by to snoop around, didn't you?"

Zoey laughed, taking a box of baby wipes over to the high chair, where Mason was playing with what appeared to be mashed potatoes.

"I'm surprised you can keep him in that thing," Travis said, changing the subject as he nodded toward Mason. "Kate's already tryin' to get outta hers."

"It's not easy. He thinks he's a little man," Zoey said, tapping Mason on the nose and making him laugh. "But he's so rambunctious, if we didn't, we'd never get to eat."

"You hear about the train?" Kaleb asked, dragging the subject back around.

"I heard," Travis said. "The kids are gonna ride it?"

"If I can get it runnin' right, sure." Kaleb frowned. "They used to use it at a Christmas carnival a few years ago. Got some problems with the engine, though."

Travis knew that the train was likely going to put Kaleb at the head of the pack when it came to the contest, but he liked the idea of the kids getting a chance to ride it.

"It's too late tonight," Travis told his brother, "but why don't we get Ethan and Beau over here tomorrow. Have 'em look at it."

"That was gonna be my next step." Kaleb lifted the tray off the high chair when Zoey finished cleaning Mason up. "You wanna see Uncle Trav?"

Mason started squealing as Kaleb lifted him up and practically tossed him toward Travis. Catching the little boy in his arms, he tickled him in greeting. "What's up, little man? Where're your cowboy boots?"

"Oh, crap," Zoey said, spinning around.

That was when Travis realized he'd brought up a sore subject.

"The B-O-O-T-S are gone. No salvaging those bad boys."

Mason put his hands on Travis's face. "Boots."

Travis smiled. "Looks like Santa's got somethin' at the top of his list this year, huh?"

"Boots!" Mason hollered.

"Go get your horse," Kaleb told Mason.

Travis set the boy down on the ground and watched as Mason torpedoed out of the room with Kaleb fast on his heels.

"How's Kylie and Kate?" Zoey asked, wiping down the table before bringing two mugs of coffee over.

Travis took a seat. "They're good. Kate's keepin' her momma busy."

Zoey laughed. "I know the feelin'. And Gage? How's he doin'? I heard there were some issues this mornin'."

"Nothin' major," Travis told her, sipping his coffee. "We had a couple of journalists who tried to sneak in. It ain't easy keepin' that place a secret anymore."

"Oh, I know," Zoey told him. "And I've got the easy part with the hotel and all."

Zoey was spending more and more time at the resort these days after having taken off time when Kellan was born. She'd taken back over the task of managing the hotel, among other things. When they'd gone into business together, Travis hadn't really known what to expect from the woman who'd been a long-time neighbor to his parents, but it was obvious, when Zoey put her mind to something, she was like a dog with a bone. And the hotel ran like nothing he'd ever seen.

But she was right. Keeping the hotel running smoothly was a hell of a lot easier than managing the fetish side of things. With the clubs and the interaction areas … Travis and his brothers had their work cut out for them, even now, after being open for nearly two years.

"So, who'd you hear about the train from?" Zoey asked, her eyes glittering with mischief.

Travis smirked. "Ain't tellin'. But you can let your husband know he can't keep a secret for shit. He was sittin' on a gold mine with that train."

Kylie laughed. "I tried to tell him that. You know him, though. He's more interested in the kids gettin' to ride it than winnin' this thing."

"Well, we'll get it runnin'. And he'll still probably win," Travis said with a smile.

Mason chose that moment to run back into the room, trying to keep a small stick horse from tripping him up.

"Horse!" he yelled, running right into Travis's leg.

"Lemme see that thing," Travis told him. He peered down at the horse while Mason watched him carefully. "You know how to ride it?"

Mason nodded, then took the horse and ran back into the other room again.

"He's learnin'." Zoey chuckled. "But now Kaleb's talkin' about gettin' a real horse."

"Yeah? That'll keep him busy."

"There's not enough minutes in the day as it is," Zoey huffed.

Travis knew the feeling.

"Well, I better get back home," he told Zoey, getting to his feet. "Kate's goin' to bed early these days, and I wanna spend some time with her before she goes down."

"Thanks for offerin' to help with the train," she told him, holding her coffee cup between her hands.

"My pleasure," he told her.

On his way back through the living room, Travis saw Kaleb coming down the stairs, Kellan cuddled in his arms. Travis stopped for a minute, admiring the little boy and, not for the first time in the last few months, wishing for another one of his own. He'd never thought he'd be a dad, but now that he was, Travis found that the most important thing in the world to him was his family.

"Leavin' so soon?" Kaleb asked, keeping his voice low.

"Yep. Gotta get home before Kate goes to bed."

"Give her a kiss for me," Kaleb told him, walking Travis to the front door.

"I'll talk to Ethan in the mornin'," Travis told Kaleb. "Then we'll all get by here tomorrow before it gets dark. Get that thing workin'."

"Thanks, man." Kaleb looked sincerely grateful for the help.

"Not a problem. See ya tomorrow."

With that, Travis headed out to his truck, suddenly anxious to get home to his husband, wife, and daughter. He wasn't sure what it was, but these days, the longer he was away from home, the more he wished he had more time to spend with them.

CHAPTER 6

GAGE WAS THE LAST TO ARRIVE AT Kaleb's the following night. He'd been stuck back at the resort handling an employee issue with one of the nightly security guards. Gage had heard a rumor that the guy had needed some time off to be with his kids on Christmas, and Gage had wanted to ensure he got what he needed. He could still remember the guy's wide, startled eyes when Gage told him how he'd already reworked the schedule so he could spend Christmas with his boys.

It was the little things that made the holidays so worthwhile.

"There's the man of the hour!" Sawyer called out when Gage approached the group huddled around the front end of a rather impressive miniature locomotive. Ethan was on the ground, half under the train, while Beau was leaning in, talking to him from above the motor.

"You bring the beer?" Zane hollered.

"Didn't know I was s'posed to," he said, taking them all in.

Kaleb, Zane, Travis, Ethan, Braydon, Sawyer, and Brendon. And of course, Beau. Yep, they were all there.

"Wanna beer?" Travis asked when Gage came to stand beside him.

Nodding, he smiled over at his husband. Although they saw one another damn near all day at Alluring Indulgence, he found that times like this, when they weren't burdened by the job, were what he looked forward to most. If Kylie and Kate were there with them, he would've been complete. However, he was grateful for this, too.

"Sure," he answered.

Travis sauntered off but then returned a moment later. "Kylie took Kate over to Cheyenne's with the others."

"Oh, hell." Gage smirked behind the lip of his beer bottle. "It's always a gamble when the women get together."

"You're tellin' me," Brendon offered, moving closer to the two of them. "Last week, after Chey spent an evening with your wife, she was talkin' about teachin' me to cook."

Travis laughed.

"Y'all are settin' the bar way too high," Braydon noted, stepping closer.

"Don't get your feathers all ruffled," Travis said with a rumbling chuckle. "It doesn't happen as often as you think."

"No?" Brendon asked, clearly curious.

"No. We've just gotten good at making takeout look like we made it."

"Where'd you learn that trick?" Sawyer inquired.

Gage laughed, then glanced over at Travis.

"Pop," Travis admitted.

"Holy shit," Brendon barked. "How'd he manage to hide that?"

"Doubt he did," Gage said. "Do you really think your mom would fall for that?"

"No," Travis stated. "But I can see her goin' along with it so she could get him to cook dinner every now and again."

"True," Brendon agreed.

"How's the train comin' along?" Gage asked, tipping his bottle toward Ethan and Beau.

"They're almost done," Kaleb told him, moving into the huddle. "And if they can get the engine to turn over, then we'll be set."

"Keep your fingers crossed," Travis said.

"Are you doubtin' my abilities?" Ethan yelled from beneath the train.

"Not at all," Travis called back. "But you have had a coupla beers."

"One!" Ethan shouted. "I've had *one* beer, Mom."

Gage had to admit that the interactions between the brothers still made him laugh. They ranged in age from twenty-six to thirty-seven at this point, and they still acted as though they were all twelve. But he'd been around long enough to know that the dynamic within the Walker family was rare. They supported one another when it counted, and that was something Gage admired in them. Lorrie and Curtis had raised their boys with a firm hand, but they'd given them what they needed to succeed, and that was what mattered most.

Gage was honored to be a member of that family.

"Beau," Travis called out. "We're dependin' on you here."

Beau's head lifted and he grinned in response. He had streaks of grease along his cheek, and Gage had to wonder if that was from tonight or if they'd come right from work. If he had to guess, it was the latter. These days, Walker Demolition was getting busy. They'd even hired Reese Tavoularis, the brother of a friend of Brendon and Braydon, recently.

"Where's Zoey?" Gage asked Kaleb.

Nodding toward the guest house, Kaleb said, "She took the boys to hang with her dad for a bit."

"How's he doin'?" Gage knew that Carl Stranford was getting up there in age, but he was still getting around, for the most part. Last week, Gage had heard Kaleb tell someone that Carl had finally caved and agreed to wear the hearing aids they'd bought for him. Most of the time, anyway.

"Ornery as hell," Kaleb answered with a snort.

"So, still goin' strong?" Travis inquired.

"Yeah. So far so good."

"What about V? Where's she tonight?" Gage asked Zane.

"Oh, she's with the girls. Probably plottin' a way to get me to buy the house down the street from Cheyenne."

"Y'all do need a bigger place," Sawyer told him. "You don't have any bedrooms."

Brendon bumped shoulders with Zane. "On top of that, that place is a steal."

Zane looked sheepish for a moment. "Don't I know it."

"So? What's the holdup?" Travis asked.

"No hold up. But it's supposed to be a surprise."

"You did not!" Sawyer hollered, jerking around to face Zane fully, his beer sloshing out of the bottle. "You bought your ol' lady a house for Christmas? What are you thinkin'?"

Gage couldn't help it, he laughed. He knew precisely where Sawyer was headed with that one.

"What's wrong with that?" Zane asked, the epitome of innocence.

"Bro, if you buy her a house, the others'll want one."

A roar of laughter erupted from the group, and Zane's face turned bright red.

"Let's see if this bad boy starts!" Beau yelled, hopping down to the ground with an audible thud.

They converged on the train, Travis giving Ethan a hand when he rolled out from beneath it. Beau leaned in, his brow furrowed. A twist of his hand and...

The engine roared to life.

Cheers erupted, splitting the otherwise silent night.

"Hot damn!" Kaleb shouted.

"You know he's gonna win this one, right?" Gage asked Travis, nudging his arm lightly.

"It's possible," Travis replied. "But it'll be worth it."

True. Watching the kids' faces light up when they got to ride on that train would definitely be worth it.

And if Kaleb did win, then Gage and Kylie would get the opportunity to console Travis.

Another win, as far as he was concerned.

KYLIE WALKED IN THE DOOR ONLY A few minutes before Travis and Gage appeared. She was getting Kate ready for bed when both men sauntered into the kitchen, grinning like fools.

"Did you get it fixed?" Kylie asked, hopeful.

"Ethan and Beau did," Gage answered.

"Da!" Kate squealed when Gage approached, lifting her arms for him to pick her up.

"Hey, precious," he said, pulling her into his arms and kissing her forehead. "She ready for bed?"

"She's been fightin' it." For the past hour, Kylie had been doing whatever it took to keep Kate awake so her daddies could spend a few minutes with her. It hadn't been easy, and truth was, Kylie was exhausted.

"Mind if I read to her tonight?" Gage asked, leaning down and kissing her gently on the lips.

"Be my guest. Where's Travis?"

Gage nodded his head toward the living room. "On the phone."

Kylie followed Gage, and sure enough, Travis was standing in the living room, his cell phone pressed to his ear. When he caught sight of Kate, he grinned.

"Perfect, man. I'll see you tomorrow then." A slight pause, followed by, "Cool. Talk to you later."

"Da!" Kate blurted, waving her arm, though Kylie could tell it was taking every ounce of her willpower to stay awake. She was stubborn, just like her fathers.

"Hey, sugar bug," Travis said to Kate. "You goin' to bed?"

"Gage is gonna read to her," Kylie told him.

"Need me to help?" Travis asked Gage.

"Nope. We've got this, don't we?" Gage grinned at Kate, bouncing her in his arms.

Travis kissed Kate again. "I'll see you in the mornin' then. I'm gonna go in late to the office, so I'll be here when she gets up."

Gage's eyes narrowed, and Kylie knew what that look meant. Thinking back to the phone call, she put two and two together. If she had to guess, he'd gone and figured out something else to put their holiday decorations over the top, and it would be delivered tomorrow.

"I'll be back down in a bit," Gage said, leaning Kate toward Kylie so she could kiss her good night.

When the two of them were up the stairs, Kylie turned her attention to Travis. "What did you do?"

The sexy, lopsided grin he shot her way sent a ribbon of heat curling through her belly. The man was good at seduction.

And changing the subject.

"Come here," he said huskily. "I missed you today."

"Did you now?" Yep, definitely good at changing the subject.

"Know what I wanna do?" he asked, his voice a low rumble against her ear.

"I can imagine," she said.

"Think so?" Travis stood to his full height, then stared down at her.

She didn't answer because he took her hand and tugged her toward the couch. She let out a squeal when he tossed her down and settled himself on top of her, making her laugh.

"This what you were thinking?" he asked mischievously.

"Something like that," she said, loving the smile on his face.

"Good. Now kiss me."

Travis didn't lean down to her; he made it so she had to lift her head to meet his lips. When she pressed hers to his, she felt his smile. The man was incorrigible, but that was something she loved about him.

"Mmm," he grumbled against her lips. "Have I mentioned how good you taste?"

"Not lately, no." Kylie wrapped her arms around his neck and twined her fingers in the silky-smooth hair at the nape of his neck. He needed a haircut.

When his hand snaked beneath her sweater, Kylie shifted to give him more room. His warm hand traveled over her stomach, then over her breast, cupping her firmly.

"You've got too many clothes on," he muttered.

"With two hundred pounds of alpha male on top of me, I won't be able to do anything about that," she said with a giggle.

"No? Well, let me help you out."

In a flash, Travis was up on one knee, his hands gripping the bottom of her sweater and quickly helping her out of it. He then got to his feet and worked her leggings and panties down her hips, leaving her clad in only her bra.

"That's gotta go, too," he said, his eyes full of heat as they raked over her naked body.

Reaching one hand beneath her, Kylie unhooked her bra, then yanked it down her arms and tossed it to the floor with the rest of her clothes.

"Better," Travis growled.

"But now you've got on too many clothes," she told him.

"I can fix that," he said, almost as though it were a dare.

"What're you waitin' for?" she teased.

Nothing, apparently, because within a minute, Travis had stripped down to bare skin and was hovering over her once again, his knee pressed between her legs, the heavy length of his cock resting on her belly.

"I love this part," Travis whispered.

"Which part is that?" she asked, keeping her voice low as she wound her arms around him again, pulling him closer, enjoying the skin-to-skin contact.

"The part..." Travis shifted. "Where I get..." He shifted again, the thick head of his cock sliding through her slick folds. "To be inside you."

"Travis!" The word escaped on a breathless moan as he aligned their bodies and thrust into her.

He growled again, his elbows sliding up next to her sides, bracketing her beneath him. His hips retreated, then slammed forward again, stealing the air from her lungs thanks to the surge of pleasure that assaulted her.

"Like that?" he whispered.

"Love it. So much. Don't stop," she pleaded.

Nearly crushed beneath him, Kylie dug her fingernails into his broad shoulders as he rolled his hips, causing a chain reaction of glorious sensation as he lit up the sensitive nerve endings deep inside her.

"Tight," he groaned. "Fuck, baby. So good."

Minutes passed as he continued to make love to her in a way only Travis knew how. He didn't rush, but never slowed, either, his hips working as he impaled her over and over, rolling, circling, hitting all the right spots. It was the perfect end to an incredible day. The only way it could've possibly been better was if Gage were there, but she couldn't deny the one-on-one time with Travis was fantastic, too.

"You gonna come for me?" he asked, the bristle of his cheek sliding against hers. "I wanna feel your pussy grip my dick, Kylie. Come for me, baby."

When he focused all of his energy on her, Kylie knew she had no chance of surviving it. She gave herself over to the sensation, spurred on by his rough groans of pleasure. When he shifted again, his hand sliding between their bodies, she knew he was going to send her spiraling into the abyss when he—

"Oh, God! Travis!" Rolling her hips, Kylie tried to increase the friction of him inside her, along with the fantastic pressure of his thumb on her clit.

"That's it," he said, peering down at her as he lifted his head. "Come for me."

Kylie closed her eyes, immersed in the overwhelming sensations. He drove his hips forward, back, forward, back until that warm glow deep in her core turned into a blaze of heat and energy, surging outward. Her body tensed, her back bowed, and she ground her teeth together as she cried out from the orgasm that ripped through her.

"So fucking pretty," Travis growled, then slammed into her again and again. "Ah, yeah. Fuck. Gonna come, Ky. Gonna come inside you."

"Please," she begged, digging her nails into his back as she urged him.

"Fuck." Travis's hips stilled, and she could feel him pulsing inside her.

They remained just like that for a few moments, staring at one another in the dimly lit living room.

"If we're lucky," he whispered, leaning down and brushing his mouth against hers, "then we'll be pregnant again before the year's out."

A smile formed on her mouth and her heart swelled. She hoped that was the case, as well. Another baby with the two men she loved most in the world.

Kylie couldn't think of a better Christmas present than that.

CHAPTER

7

Two days later,
Thursday

"WHAT'RE YOU DOIN' OUT HERE?" KYLIE ASKED when she appeared on the front porch next to his chair.

Gage smiled up at her. "Just watchin' the lights."

"Can I sit with you?"

"Of course." Taking in the long skirt and loose-fitting sweater she wore, Gage's body hardened instantly at the thought of her sitting on his lap. Since he was in the wide, cushioned wicker chair, there wasn't much room for her otherwise. Though she could sit on him easily, beside him wasn't really an option.

Grabbing her hips, he started to pull her down, but Kylie clearly had other plans. Turning to face him, she placed one knee beside his hip, raising her skirt out of the way. He held on to her while she straddled his lap, facing her.

"What're you up to?" he asked, keeping his voice low.

"Nothing," she said sweetly, her tone belying her actions as she ground against his dick. The only things separating them were his sweatpants and whatever she had on beneath her skirt. His cock came to life, thickening from the thought of her riding him right here on the porch.

"Where's Travis?" he asked.

"Putting Kate to bed."

Gage smiled, sliding his hands beneath the flimsy material of her skirt until he found her smooth, warm thighs. He ventured higher, gliding his fingertips along soft skin, stopping when his fingertips grazed the apex of her thighs.

He groaned. "You're missin' your panties."

"I must've forgotten to put them on," she said teasingly.

Taking advantage of that, Gage used his thumbs to separate her folds, teasing her gently as she hummed her pleasure.

Kylie leaned forward, resting her elbows on his shoulders, her hands sliding into his hair as she stared back at him. The woman was breathtaking, probably more so now than ever before. It seemed she got prettier with every passing day. Sometimes he thought he fell in love with both of them more and more with every minute he got to spend with them. He wasn't sure that was even possible, but his heart didn't seem to know that.

"I love you," Kylie whispered, leaning in and pressing her lips to his.

"Love you, too, baby." Pulling his hands out from beneath her skirt, Gage cupped her head, holding her as their lips melded together, tongue sliding against tongue.

He was lost in the kiss, content to simply sit there and make out with her, but it didn't take long before Kylie was attempting to work his dick out of his sweatpants.

Pulling back from her, he chuckled. "Lookin' for somethin'?"

"Yes," she said with a smirk. "I want you inside me. Right now."

There was no way in hell he could say no to that.

Lifting his hips, he managed to shove his sweatpants down while Kylie crawled closer. With a little adjustment, he guided his dick to the entrance of her body. With her help, he seated himself fully inside her with a strangled grunt, the pleasure locking up all of his muscles briefly.

Their eyes remained locked together as Kylie began rocking her hips, taking him deep inside her body. He tried to keep quiet, but it wasn't easy. They didn't have any neighbors, so he wasn't worried too much about anyone hearing them, but they were outside. There were a few cars that would travel down the road in front of their house from time to time. Not that he thought they could see them, because the porch light was off and the lights from the tree in the yard would offer a buffer, but still.

"Gage," she said breathlessly.

"Tell me, baby," he encouraged. "Tell me what you need."

"More of this," she said. "Just like this."

Gripping her hips, he guided her, forward, back, again and again, his dick sliding through her slickness, the smooth walls of her pussy stroking against him. The pleasure was intoxicating.

Content to keep at it for as long as she would allow him, Gage simply watched her.

A moment later, the screen door squeaked. Gage glanced over as Kylie stilled on his lap.

"Don't stop on my account," Travis said softly. "I just came out to get a better view."

Gage grinned, then pulled Kylie's mouth down to his while she resumed her pace, riding him slowly.

Travis perched on the railing nearby, and Gage could feel his eyes on them. It was hot to know that Travis was watching them. Kylie must've thought so, too, because she began to move faster, her hips jerking forward and back as she attempted to take him deeper.

"Hold that thought," Gage told her, stilling her hips with his hands.

Bracing her ass, he shifted so that he could get to his feet, holding her against him, his cock still lodged deep, sweatpants around his thighs. Setting her on the wide railing beside Travis, Gage lifted her legs, taking control as he began fucking her slow and deep.

"Move the skirt outta the way," Travis instructed, placing his arm around her.

Kylie used one hand to pull up the skirt, offering them both a view of Gage's glistening cock sliding in and out of her pussy.

"Damn, that's pretty," Travis said roughly.

Gage felt the tingle in his spine, a sure warning that his release wasn't far off. He didn't want to stop, but it felt too good.

"Harder," Kylie pleaded. "Faster."

Adjusting his hold on her legs, he pulled her toward him so that Travis had to hold her in place to keep her from falling off the wooden rail. He began fucking her hard and fast, just as she'd asked. He felt another electrical pulse inside him and knew he'd have to send her over soon.

"Come for me, Kylie," he ground out, never stopping.

Kylie cried out as he slammed into her, over and over. Just when he thought he was going to come before she ever got to that point, her body tensed, her muscles locking down on his dick. She milked his release from him, along with a rough growl.

It took a minute for the lusty fog to clear from his brain, but when it did, he found Kylie smiling up at him.

"That was perfect," she said.

"I'd have to agree," Travis said with a chuckle. "But next time, let me know beforehand so I can catch the whole show."

"Sure," Gage said, still trying to catch his breath. "Because when a hot chick wants to ride your dick, the first thing you think about is making sure you have an audience."

Travis's laugh echoed in the cool night air. "Hey, can't blame me for tryin'."

AFTER TAKING A SHOWER, TRAVIS CRAWLED INTO bed beside Kylie, sliding his arm over her and finding Gage on the other side. He was tired, and for the first time in a long time, his brain wasn't overloaded with thoughts of work, what needed to be done tomorrow, or what chores needed to get done. He was content with the quiet that had settled in his head for now.

"You ready for the judging tomorrow?" Kylie whispered, turning to face him.

"Yep," he said. Not because he was worried about winning, although there was that. But more so because he was looking forward to spending more time with Kate and Kylie and Gage. They'd all agreed to take the day off, including his brothers and their wives.

"So, is this a new tradition we're starting?" Kylie asked.

"Maybe." He'd like to think so. For all of his life, his mother and father had immersed them in tradition, strengthening the foundation of their family, and Travis knew that was important. He wanted that to continue with each of their families. It would be so easy for all of them to go their own ways, to become so involved in their day-to-day that they didn't have time for things such as a holiday free-for-all.

Travis hoped, with the help of his brothers, they could keep the traditions going for the next generation of Walkers.

"Well, I hope you win," Kylie whispered.

"*We*," he corrected.

"Yes, *we*," she said with a chuckle. "Because we all know I had any say in the madness."

"You didn't stop him," Gage mumbled sleepily, shifting so that he was facing them, his chest to Kylie's back. "It's the same thing."

"True," Kylie agreed. "Regardless, Kate and I are proud of you. We'll vote for you, no matter what."

Travis grinned. "Wait till she rides on the train. She might not be as on board with a sixty-foot Christmas tree at that point."

Hell, Travis wished *he* could ride that train.

Not that he intended to tell anyone that.

Ever.

CHAPTER 8

JUDGING DAY HAD FINALLY ARRIVED, AND TRAVIS could feel the excitement in the air.

They'd arrived at his parents' house a little after nine for breakfast. His mother had surprised them all by making homemade donuts, something she hadn't done in ... hell, probably not since he was in high school. When they'd been kids, it had been the most thrilling breakfast she could've possibly come up with, and it didn't seem that much had changed.

And now, after having two, Travis was seated at the table with his father and Kate, waiting for the others to arrive.

Zane, V, and Reid were the next to arrive, followed closely by Brendon and Cheyenne. After Zane had rummaged through the different options—sprinkles, no sprinkles, glazed, cake, chocolate, the list went on and on—his brothers and their better halves settled in the dining room with Kylie and Gage.

Everyone seemed to be making their way through the door, looking tired until they smelled the donuts. But Travis had to admit, one of his brothers was more excited than the others. The minute Sawyer walked in the back door, Kennedy at his side, Travis watched his brother's face light up, his nose sniffing the air. His eyes widened, and he let out a whoop so loud it had startled Buster.

"Donuts! You have got to be kidding me," Sawyer exclaimed. "Holy—"

"Watch it," Curtis growled with a grin, picking up his coffee mug.

"You made all these?" Sawyer asked, kissing Lorrie on the cheek as he passed her.

"Your father helped," she replied, and all eyes turned to Curtis.

"Seriously?" Travis wasn't sure he believed it.

"I've got more skills than you know, boy," Curtis retorted with a grin.

"Of course you do." But donut making? He never would've guessed.

Kate smacked her hands on the table, giggling when Buster put his front paws on Travis's leg, obviously trying to get her attention. That or he was hoping for her to drop some of her Cheerios so he could snatch them.

Kaleb came through the door, ducking low because Mason was propped on his shoulders, his fingers clutching Kaleb's hair. Zoey stepped in behind him, Kellan cuddled in her arms. Once again, Travis watched until the moment Kaleb realized there were donuts.

"Okay, Mom wins," Kaleb announced. "The holiday free-for-all award goes to her."

"Pop helped," Sawyer mentioned around a mouthful of donut.

Kaleb's eyes widened and laughter erupted.

Before long, the rest of them trickled in. Ethan and Beau, Braydon and Jessie, Jared and Derrick, along with Travis's cousins Chelsea, Reilly, Donovan, Stone, Jaxson, and CJ. Even the twins, Kaden and Keegan, Jared's brothers, had graced them with their presence.

Definitely a free-for-all.

Not that it would've been a new tradition if Travis's in-laws, Kylie's father and stepmother, hadn't shown up. Joe and Melissa were greeted as though they'd been part of the family forever.

Travis finally lost count after a while, taking Kate out of the main path into the house to join Gage and Kylie in the dining room with the others.

"What's the plan today?" Jessie asked, reaching up to take Kate from him.

"I'm betting Mom plans to feed us all day," Braydon said.

Travis had heard Kylie mentioning the smorgasbord of different snack foods that Lorrie had stockpiled in the refrigerator, so he'd take that bet. And dinner… He knew his mother wouldn't be able to not cook for them all. It was something she loved to do, and Travis definitely wasn't complaining.

"Well, I know the boys are gonna grumble, but we've got some games," Cheyenne informed them, looking somewhat shy as she spoke.

And as she'd predicted, every man in the room grumbled. Travis did not particularly care for games. He could get into the spirit just like the next guy, but he had his limits.

"Like what?" Jessie asked, clearly excited.

"Well…" Cheyenne looked at Kennedy.

Kennedy grinned. "We're gonna fill stockings with candy."

"How's that a game?" Brendon asked, downing an energy drink.

"You only get to use a spoon to do it. And the first team to fill their stocking wins."

Travis grumbled again.

"Sounds easy enough," Zane told the women.

"Yeah?" V laughed.

"You wouldn't say that if you knew we had fifty stockings to fill," Cheyenne told him, a smile on her face.

"Fifty? Why fifty?" Braydon groused.

"After they're filled, your mom and dad are gonna take them to the church," Kennedy told them.

Well, in that case, Travis could probably get on board with the idea. Maybe.

"Then there's a scavenger hunt," Kylie said with a beaming smile.

Travis narrowed his eyes at her. Clearly she'd been part of this, and she hadn't bothered to tell him.

"*What?*" she asked innocently. "You've got your secrets and I've got mine."

God, he loved her.

Unable to help himself, he smiled.

"And then…?" Zane probed.

"And then, after dinner, we'll start the judging."

Travis met his brother's gaze. That's what they were really waiting for.

"Well, we better get a move on. We don't have all day," Sawyer said with a wink.

KYLIE STILL COULDN'T BELIEVE THEY'D SPENT THE last two hours filling stockings with candy. Not that it was the actual task that surprised her, but that it took them that long to do it. Then again, the game had been hilarious. First, they'd split the group into teams, separating the spouses from one another. Then, each team had to figure out how to fill the stocking with just a spoon. Kylie would be the first to admit that it sounded a lot easier than it was.

Watching Sawyer and Zane get completely frustrated had been the best part. They'd kept everyone rolling on the floor in peals of laughter while they tried every which way to get the candy into the stocking, failing over and over again.

Thankfully, they'd brought that game to a close, helping Curtis pile the stockings into the backseat of his truck so he and Lorrie—along with Kylie's parents, who'd volunteered to go along for the ride—could take them down to the church while everyone else set out on the scavenger hunt. Travis's cousins, Reilly and Donovan, had agreed to hang back at the house and watch the kids. With them out, that had left twenty-one people since Greyson, as well as Beth, another of Travis's cousins, had arrived at the last minute. To make it easy, they'd broken into teams of three.

Of course, she'd insisted that she be paired with her husbands.

Then they had:

Zoey, Kaleb, and Stone.

Kennedy, Sawyer, and Greyson.

Cheyenne, Brendon, and CJ.

Ethan, Beau, and Jaxson.

Braydon, Jessie, and Jared.

V, Zane, and Chelsea.

Keegan, Kaden, and Beth.

The excitement was buzzing in the air while everyone waited outside, ready to hop in their vehicles to get moving.

"Who has the lists?" Kaleb asked, causing everyone to look around.

The sound of an SUV pulling up could barely be heard over the drone of conversation.

"Who's that?" she asked, directing her question to Travis.

"No idea," he replied with a shrug of his wide shoulders.

The Escalade came to a stop in the empty space off to the side of the driveway. The windows were tinted, so she couldn't see who was inside.

Three doors opened and out came...

Kylie smiled when she saw Reese Tavoularis, along with Reese's brother, Z, and Z's husband, RT.

"Well, I'll be damned!" Brendon hollered, making his way over to his high school friend. "What the hell're you doin' here?"

"I heard y'all needed some help," Z said with a giant grin. He held up a stack of papers, waving them teasingly at the group.

"Oh, hell," Braydon grumbled. "Please tell me y'all did not get to pick the ideas for this hunt."

"We did," Z confirmed.

RT grabbed a few sheets of paper from Z and glanced down at them, distributing them obviously in some sort of order. And when he got to the last one, his gaze traveled the group until it landed on Travis.

"Shit," Travis groaned when RT's smile widened. "You might not wanna be on my team."

Kylie couldn't hold back the laugh that bubbled up. She knew RT was looking to get back at Travis for the teasing he'd done in the past. Back when RT had been denying his feelings for Z. It only seemed fair that RT would get him back; she just hadn't expected this.

"This, my friend," RT said to Travis, "is for you."

Travis took the page but didn't bother to look at it. Kylie tried to take a peek, but he hid it before she could. Then Gage was behind her, wrapping her in his arms. She felt the vibration from his chest when he greeted RT. "Good to see you, man."

"You might not think that if you're paired off with this one," RT said, his eyes dancing with mischief.

"Let's get this show on the road so we can be back here for dinner," Zane hollered loud enough to be heard over everyone.

"Hold up!" Brendon called out. Turning his attention to RT and Z, he added, "Since the three of you are here, and someone obviously knew about this whole setup"—his eyes cut to his wife suspiciously—"then it's only fair that y'all have to participate as well."

Holding a few more papers in his hands, Reese peered down at them.

"Nope," Braydon said, snatching the papers away, "you don't get to pick what you do." Braydon skimmed the papers, then smiled before handing one back to Z. "Good luck with that."

"Before you go," Cheyenne said, "everyone has four hours to complete this. Be back here no later than five thirty or you forfeit. The team with the most items on their list wins. Good luck!"

Kylie had barely gotten her feet moving when Gage was urging her toward his truck, Travis leading the way, still clutching the paper in his hand.

"What's on that list?" she asked as she climbed into the backseat.

"You don't wanna know," Travis murmured when Gage hopped in and started the truck.

Dust swirled around them as the cars, trucks, and SUVs fled the driveway, all in a hurry to get the items on their list.

Kylie simply wanted to see what was in store for them.

Clearly Travis wasn't in a hurry to show her.

SINCE IT WAS CLEAR TRAVIS WASN'T INTERESTED in sharing their scavenger hunt items, Gage stole the paper from him, then handed it back to Kylie as he drove down the road that would lead them into town.

"Read it off," he instructed.

There was a silent pause, followed by several chuckles before Kylie let out a booming laugh. She tried to talk, but it took her a minute to calm down.

"Okay, we've got fifteen things."

Fifteen? That shouldn't be too hard.

"Just wait," Travis mumbled.

"It's broken into three different lists: items, pictures, videos."

Gage glanced over at Travis to see him shaking his head.

Kylie continued, "The items are a restaurant napkin, a receipt for sixty cents' worth of gas, a buy one, get one free coupon, a name tag with a name that starts with the letter R, and a disposable toilet seat cover."

"Oh, hell," Gage said, chuckling.

"In the list for pictures, we need one of all three of us sitting with an unknown family at a restaurant, one of a team member hugging a stranger, one of a team member putting gas in a stranger's car, a member of the group handcuffed to a police officer, and the last one is a picture with someone who is at least eighty-five years old."

Gage took the turn to take them to the center of town, not sure where they planned to start. "And the videos?" he asked.

Kylie giggled. "Travis singing "Mary Had a Little Lamb" with a kid."

"Travis? It says that?" Gage asked, darting his eyes to Travis again.

"It says that," he confirmed.

"Okay, go on," Gage said, pulling the truck into the only gas station in town. When a car pulled in behind them, stopping in front of a gas pump, he smiled. "Hold that thought. You better get your phone out, though."

Jumping out of the truck, Gage strolled over to the car, trying not to look like a complete psychopath as he approached the young woman.

"Do you mind if I put gas in your car for you?" he asked.

Her eyes widened in confusion.

"We're doin' a scavenger hunt, and I need to get a picture putting gas into a stranger's car."

The woman's eyes traveled the parking lot briefly, and Gage turned to point at his truck. "My husband and wife are in there. I swear, I'm not gonna do anything weird."

"Husband *and* wife?" she asked, her eyes growing to the size of saucers.

"Long story," he said, smiling to himself. The woman was approached by a stranger in a gas station parking lot, and *that* was the one thing she questioned. Figured.

"Okay," she finally said, swiping her credit card and then stepping back out of the way.

It took five minutes to fill the tank, but then he thanked the woman and walked back to the truck. Taking out his own credit card, he swiped it, then gently squeezed the pump, aiming for sixty cents' worth. He had to do it twice before he got the correct number, and he doubted he got but a drop of gas.

"Two down," Kylie chirped when he hopped in, holding her phone out for him to see.

After handing her the gas receipt, Gage put the truck in drive, heading back to the road. "What were the other videos?"

Kylie's sweet chuckle filled the air. "Gage getting a drink out of a water fountain with Travis on his back."

Travis groaned. Gage laughed. He had to give RT and Z credit, these were pretty creative.

"In Mama's Diner, Travis has to put on a tiara and wave to the people there, saying 'I am the queen of England.'"

Gage thought he might wreck his truck when he was overwhelmed by laughter.

"Fuck off," Travis groused.

"Hey, it's gonna be funny."

"Gonna be?" Travis asked, his head snapping toward him. "You actually think I'm gonna do that?"

"Yes," Kylie said matter-of-factly. "We're gonna win this thing."

"What else?" Gage inquired, pulling the truck into Mama's Diner. He figured he might as well get that one out of the way. And they could get the restaurant napkin at the same time.

"The last two," Kylie said as Gage opened her door for her. "A video of one of us buying cookies with pennies only, and then one of us carrying a stranger's groceries to their car."

Gage closed the door, then watched as Travis grudgingly came around to meet them.

"Y'all are really gonna make me do this, aren't you?" he asked, watching them both intently.

"Yes," Kylie said, leaning up on tiptoe and kissing him on the cheek. She lowered her voice, but Gage could still hear her. "And if we win, then Gage and I will make it up to you tonight."

Travis's eyebrows lifted. "How so?"

"Whatever you want," she said with a sweet smile.

That earned a grin from Travis, and Gage knew without a doubt that they were about to win this thing. And probably with an hour to spare.

TRAVIS WANTED TO KILL RT AND Z, but mostly RT. He still couldn't believe the things they'd managed to get him to do over the course of the day. And yes, because of Kylie's promise for later tonight, he'd eagerly performed every single task, including putting on a tiara—which they'd had to pick up at the small independent toy store in town—and telling everyone inside Mama's Diner that he was the queen of England.

He wasn't sure he would ever live that one down.

But now, as he perched on the arm of the couch in his parents' living room, listening to all the crazy things the others had done today in order to complete their list, he didn't feel quite so bad.

"Do you know how hard it is to get the front page of the Coyote Ridge Gazette?" Ethan asked. "No one reads the paper, and we weren't allowed to buy it."

"How'd you get it?" V asked.

"We went door to door," Beau said with a grin.

"At least you didn't have to convince a stranger to let you taste their food," Kaden said.

Beth chimed in, "What was funnier is that when we did find a woman who was willing, she insisted that both Kaden and Keegan do it at the same time, since they're twins. And then she took her own picture."

"You didn't tell them the best part," Keegan said with a smirk.

Beth's cheeks turned pink. "She told them the only way she'd allow it was if they took their shirts off."

"I'm sure that'll be up on the Internet before long," Zane said. "You'll have your own fan club."

"That would've been great..." Keegan said. "When I was twenty."

"How old are you now?" Zane asked their cousin.

"Thirty-two and counting," he answered with a frown.

"And still not married," Sawyer teased. "What a shame."

"Hey, if I recall correctly, y'all won't be married until tomorrow night," Kaden countered.

"Tomorrow, y'all. That was the key word there. Seriously." V stated. "How can the two of you be so calm? I was a wreck for a week before my wedding, and you're just sittin' here like it's just another day."

Kennedy smiled up at Sawyer. "Oh, it's not just another day, but I think we're ready for it to happen."

"That way we can start makin' babies," Sawyer said teasingly.

"Nope. No way," Ethan called out. "Do not want to hear that shit."

The group laughed, and Travis sighed. This was a good day. Maybe he wasn't into the whole game thing, but he had to admit, spending the day acting like a fool with Kylie and Gage... He couldn't remember ever having quite as much fun.

"Did you get it?" Z asked, his attention turning to Cheyenne and Brendon.

"Which one?" Brendon asked.

"Singing with a police officer," Z said.

"We did," Cheyenne said with a grin. "But that one was easy."

"How'd you do it?" Jessie asked.

"I went into the police station, asked who wanted front row seats to her next concert, and the three guys inside all lined up."

"They did not," Jared said in disbelief.

"They did," Brendon said, beaming with pride as he held out his cell phone, which was playing the video of Cheyenne singing the national anthem with all three of the deputies at the sheriff's office.

"Well, I'll be damned."

"Okay, so we've tallied everything up," Donovan announced when he stepped into the room. He'd volunteered to check off all the items on the lists to see who'd done the most.

"And?" Braydon asked.

"We've actually got a tie," Donovan noted. "But each of those teams is missing one item. So, if you've got the videos for me to see, then I'll be able to announce the winners."

"Who?" Beau questioned, his eyes lighting up.

"Ethan, Beau, and Jaxson," Donovan told him, looking their way. "I have yet to see the video of the two of you skipping through the toy store, carrying Barbies while screaming, 'Oh my goodness, it's really a Barbie.'"

Travis laughed, imagining Beau and Ethan doing just that.

"Who're they tied with?" Kaleb inquired.

"Travis, Kylie, and Gage," Donovan answered. "I need the video of Travis singing "Mary Had a Little Lamb" with a kid."

Out of the corner of his eye, Travis saw Gage flipping through the videos on his phone, grinning like a fool as he did. He grunted, remembering that whole incident.

"We've got ours," Jaxson said, holding up his phone.

Everyone leaned in to watch as, sure enough, Ethan and Beau went skipping through a store, each carrying at least three Barbies in each arm, yelling at the top of their lungs. The video continued, showing the store manager kindly asking them to leave.

Laughter erupted as everyone watched.

"What happens if there's another tie?" Kylie inquired, looking directly at Donovan.

"Then the one with the best video wins," he said. "We'll vote."

"It's gonna be hard to top that one," Zane said.

Travis didn't look up; he continued to stare at his hands, praying that he wasn't blushing, because he'd never live that one down.

"I've got ours," Gage called out, holding up his phone as the video started to play.

The room went eerily silent as all eyes went to that small screen.

"Where are y'all at?" Zoey asked.

"The daycare in town," Kylie told her.

Travis gritted his teeth together.

"Oh. My. God!" Sawyer exclaimed. "Is that…?"

Rumbles of laughter exploded, and Travis knew exactly which part they were watching.

Someone bumped his shoulder, and Travis looked up to see RT grinning like a fool. "You…" He was laughing so hard he couldn't speak. "You put on a…" More cackling. "A dress!"

Travis shook his head in disbelief. He had put on a dress. In fact, the daycare had the whole getup, and he'd managed to fit in it enough to get the gist of it. Then, with the daycare center's help, they'd gathered all the kids together, and he'd sung "Mary Had a Little Lamb." At the top of his lungs.

"Trav wins!" Ethan exclaimed. "No doubt about it! Can't beat that one."

"Send me that video," Kaleb hollered to Gage.

"Don't you dare," Travis snarled.

Gage grinned up at him, eyes twinkling. "Don't worry, that one's just for us."

Sliding his gaze over to Kylie, Travis waited until she looked his way. Her eyes flickered with recognition, and he knew she remembered the promise she'd made him earlier.

They'd won.

And he fully intended to collect tonight.

CHAPTER 10

AFTER DINNER, EVERYONE WAS GIVEN AN HOUR to go home and get their lights on and ready for the judging. The place had cleared out within seconds, but Kylie had stayed back with Kate to help Lorrie clean up since Travis and Gage were more than capable of handling their stuff on their own. Jared had hung back with Mason and Derrick since the boys would ultimately be the official judges for the evening.

"Are you ready for this?" Curtis asked, sitting at the small kitchen table, drinking coffee.

"I'm not sure any of us are ready for this," she teased.

"I've seen 'em all," Jared noted. "It's gonna be interesting."

She knew what her house looked like, knew that when the lights were on outside, she didn't need to turn any on inside because of how bright they were. But, Kylie had to admit, it was rather impressive. She was more anxious to see everyone else's, but only because she wanted to see her daughter's reaction to it all.

"How do y'all plan to do this?" Kylie asked, regarding Curtis and Jared briefly.

"Figured we'd just pile in the truck and start at Brendon's and end with Kaleb's," Curtis replied.

That made sense considering they could snake their way through town, out to her house, then back this way.

"Do you know if Mason has seen the train yet?" she asked.

"I don't think so," Lorrie answered, wiping the counter. "Kaleb wanted it to be a surprise."

Kylie wasn't sure how he'd managed to hide that thing, but she understood why. And that was another reason she was grateful they'd end at Kaleb's. The kids were going to be over the moon once they got a chance to ride the train.

She had just finished putting the last dish into the cabinet when Curtis's cell phone chimed with a text. He hadn't even had a chance to read it before another one came in. Then another and another.

Apparently everyone was set up and ready to go.

As Kylie was pulling Kate's coat on, the screen door squeaked, announcing an arrival. She looked up in time to see Gage and Travis, their faces relaxing when they saw her. She loved when they did that. It was as though they hated being away from her and were only content when she was with them. She felt the same way about them.

Smiling, she lifted Kate and turned her to face her daddies. "Look who's here."

"Da!" Kate squealed, pointing toward them.

Travis took her from Kylie while Gage helped Jared wrangle Mason and Derrick.

"We'll take Kate and Kylie with us," Travis told his father. "And follow y'all."

It took a few minutes for everyone to get situated in the vehicles, and by the time they were pulling out of Lorrie and Curtis's driveway, there was a line of trucks waiting to follow them. She counted them off as they passed. Kaleb, Zane, Ethan, Braydon, and Sawyer. They were all ready to go to Brendon and Cheyenne's house to start this thing.

"You warm back there?" Travis asked, peering at her in the rearview mirror.

"Yep, we're good."

A few minutes later, they pulled in front of Brendon's, the line of trucks dispersing to park along the sides of the road. Apparently there were other onlookers out tonight, checking out the lights, because the street was busy.

Gage unbuckled Kate from her car seat, lifting her into his arms while Travis opened her door and helped her out. When he took her hand, she linked her fingers with his as the four of them headed up to the house.

Turning at the sound of her daughter's excited rambling, Kylie saw Kate's eyes widen as she took it all in.

"Wow," Gage muttered.

"Very cool," Travis chimed in.

Kylie took in the sight before her. Brendon and Cheyenne had gone all out. And by all out, she meant they'd turned Cheyenne's front yard into a winter wonderland. It was true, in Texas, snow didn't fall much, but here, standing in front of this house, it was hard to believe that.

They had what appeared to be a commercial-grade snow machine that was blanketing the area with white. They'd created a path with ropes and candy cane poles that sectioned off various holiday scenes.

"Is that a polar bear?" Gage asked, his tone wistful.

Kylie smiled to herself because she could tell he was impressed.

"Come on," Travis said, tugging her arm as others began descending upon the yard.

It took about ten minutes to wander through, to see each scene, all while snow fell from above them. Kate seemed so entranced by the white powder falling on her head she'd hardly paid any attention to the life-sized holiday decorations.

"What do you think?" Gage asked Kate.

She giggled sweetly and pointed.

Kylie looked over to see Mason and Derrick running around in circles, whooping and hollering as they paid attention to the snow. Based on the amount of energy they were expending, she knew they were going to sleep well tonight.

The next house on the list was theirs, and after a ten-minute drive, everyone once again piled out of the trucks and made their way in front of her house. Travis retrieved the laptop he'd brought with him, hit a few keys, and then…

Kylie's jaw dropped. The scene before her was amazing. And to think her husbands had created this extraordinary display. Music blared from speakers she couldn't see while the lights danced along with it. Letters appeared, then disappeared, spelling out words in the song. They had stars flashing brightly, running in patterns from the house down to the trees near the road.

"What do you think?" Gage asked her, wrapping her in his arms and pulling her back against him.

"I love it," she whispered. It was the most beautiful thing she'd ever seen. Sure, she'd watched it as they'd pieced it together over the past few weeks, but they hadn't let her see the final result, because they'd wanted it to be a surprise.

She was pleasantly surprised.

The song lasted for about three minutes, and then everything went dark. Kylie was about to turn away, but Gage held her in place. Waiting, she searched the darkness, trying to anticipate what would come next.

And then she saw it, a huge Santa Claus, equipped with sleigh and reindeer, appeared, spotlights showing it as it rose from the back of the house before stopping on the ridge of the roof. Her eyes were fixed on the scene when the Santa started waving back at them.

"Ho-ho-ho," came the voice from the speakers, followed by a jolly laugh. "Merry Christmas, Kylie and Kate."

Cheers from the others erupted as another song started, more lights flashing. Tears formed in her eyes as she swallowed past the knot that formed in her throat. Travis and Gage had done this for her and Kate. That gesture alone made her feel like the luckiest woman in the world.

"Love you," Gage whispered against her ear.

Emotion made it impossible to speak, but she spun around and hugged him tightly, burying her face in his chest. Travis came to stand beside them, his arm going around behind Gage's back, one hand rubbing her arm as the four of them stood there for a moment.

And though the contest was between the brothers, Kylie couldn't help but think that she was the one who'd won tonight.

BY THE TIME THEY ENDED UP AT Kaleb's for the final house of the night, Gage was reeling from all the remarkable scenes he'd seen.

Zane had created a toy shop out in front of his house, equipped with giant bears and remote control cars, even dancing dolls. Braydon would definitely get credit for the most lights, there was no doubt about that. Gage didn't think there was an inch of his house visible after the light show had begun. Sawyer's theme was animal-related, and Buster had even donned a reindeer outfit for the occasion. As for Ethan and Beau ... they would get the award for most creative. And it had been obvious that they'd had Mason and Derrick in mind when they created theirs. It was all about trucks, including the kid-sized monster truck track they'd designed to wind through the various scenes.

Needless to say, it hadn't been easy pulling the boys away from that one.

And now, they were all gearing up for what they expected to be the highlight of the night.

After pulling into the driveway, everyone climbed out, looking around in awe. The trees were wrapped in lights, as was the house. But other than that, there wasn't much to it.

But then, Kaleb disappeared behind the house, and a few minutes later, lights started flashing along the ground, a chasing pattern that started from the house and kept going. It took a minute to realize that they were lighting up the train track that snaked across the yard, around the house, over near the old barn, and back.

Gage was holding Kate in his arms when the whistle on the train sounded. She jumped, momentarily startled by the noise, but then a spotlight came on, highlighting the train, and more lights flashed, giving everyone the first view of the red and green locomotive with the giant wreath attached to the front, followed by one railcar and the caboose.

It was every boy's dream right there in front of them, and Mason and Derrick proved it when they started to jump up and down, yelling. Derrick was tugging Jared's hand, urging him toward the train, while Mason was hopping up and down in front of Zoey.

"You wanna ride on the train?" Travis asked Kate from behind them.

Her eyes were wide, but she didn't answer. With Travis and Kylie right behind them, they followed the others, making their way over so the kids could get on. Kate's grip tightened around his neck as they got closer, and when the whistle blew again, she jumped into his arms.

"It's a train, sugar," he told her. "I've got you."

At first, Kate wanted nothing to do with it, but finally, Kylie offered to ride with them. At that point, Gage knew the kids had definitely picked the winner. And quite frankly, though impressed by it all, Gage would have to agree.

After an hour of riding the train around in circles, everyone had had a chance to climb on, including all the brothers, which had resulted in a ton of pictures that would likely be looked at for years to come.

"Yep, Kaleb's definitely the winner tonight," Travis said, coming to stand beside him and linking their hands together.

"Looks that way," Gage agreed. Although deep down, he couldn't help but think they'd all won something tonight. The chance to spend the holidays together.

And he felt completely blessed to be a part of it.

CHAPTER 11

TRAVIS CARRIED KATE IN FROM THE TRUCK, then got her ready for bed while she slept soundly. It was almost midnight, and he'd been stunned that his daughter had made it through all the events of the evening. If they were lucky, she would sleep through the night, and they would, too.

Only Travis had no intention of going to sleep anytime in the near future.

Closing Kate's door after turning on the video monitor, he noticed the rest of the house was dark. He could hear Kylie's and Gage's voices drifting down the hall from their bedroom, so he made his way in there.

"We thought you'd never get here," Gage said, sitting on the edge of the bed, Kylie kneeling behind him and massaging his shoulders.

"Yeah?" He watched the two of them, noticing the way they eyed him from time to time. "Were you waitin' for somethin'?"

"Instruction," Kylie said with a sexy smirk.

"For what?" He knew exactly what they were waiting for—as was he—but he enjoyed playing the game with them. It kept things interesting.

"For whatever you want," she said.

"Whatever I want," he repeated.

"Yep, that was the deal."

"So what did you have in mind?" Gage asked as he pulled his shirt off, giving Travis a glimpse of his amazing upper body.

What he wanted to do was run his mouth over every single inch of them both until they were begging him to make them come.

But tonight he wanted to do something a little different.

"Oh no," Kylie said with a chuckle, falling back on the bed and regarding him closely. "I know that look."

"What look is that?"

"The one that says this is gonna be a good night," she teased.

"It's already been a good night." It had been a spectacular night, actually.

Yes, Kaleb had definitely won the free-for-all, but as far as Travis was concerned, they all had, as well. Spending time together was what was important, and even though they were a competitive bunch, deep down, it had all been done for the love of family.

"It has," Kylie conceded. "A very good night."

"That's about to get a whole lot better," he told her as he approached the bed, stopping when his knees hit the mattress.

"So what is it that you want tonight?" Gage asked, getting to his feet and coming to stand behind him.

Travis leaned back against Gage when he wrapped his arms around him.

"I want..." Travis sucked in a breath when Gage sucked on the sensitive skin of his neck. "I want you and Kylie to do whatever you want to me."

He noticed the slow smile that formed on Kylie's mouth. "Really?"

"Yes," he whispered, tilting his head to give Gage better access to his mouth. "As long as I don't have to wear a fucking dress."

That earned a chuckle from both of them.

"Oh, I can promise you won't be wearing a dress," Gage mumbled against his skin. "In fact, you won't be wearing anything at all."

He definitely liked the sound of that.

Travis wasn't eager to move because Gage's mouth felt way too good on his neck, so it was good that Kylie took the lead, crawling to the end of the bed and kneeling in front of him. He watched her, loving the way her eyes raked over him slowly while her hands reached for his belt buckle. Without breaking eye contact, she worked his jeans open while Gage managed to lift his shirt up and over his head.

When Gage's warm lips traveled down his spine, goose bumps broke out over his skin. They knew the exact spots that would make him crazy.

Travis hissed in a breath when Kylie's cool finger wrapped around his cock, stroking him until he was fully erect. She smiled sweetly back at him before bending down and kissing the swollen head. He watched her, not moving a muscle, enjoying the way she teased him.

"Boots," Gage said as he knelt behind Travis.

Travis quickly toed off his boots, and then Gage was yanking his jeans down his legs. Travis kicked them off his feet, then allowed Gage to remove his socks.

When he was standing stark naked between them, his body temperature soared a few hundred degrees. Fully immersed in the sensations, he closed his eyes as their hands and mouths trailed over him, teasing, tormenting, making him crazy. And when his legs threatened to buckle beneath him, he was grateful Gage was there to catch him.

"On the bed," Kylie instructed, backing up and giving him room to join her.

Travis crawled onto the bed and turned over onto his back, placing his hands behind his head. He enjoyed the show when Kylie helped to strip Gage before he did the same to her. Travis still couldn't get over how incredibly beautiful they were. He could've laid there and stared at them all night long, just like this.

But they obviously had other plans for him. When they were both naked, they joined him on the bed, Kylie kneeling between his legs as she took his shaft in her small hands, stroking him slowly as she met his gaze. Gage kneeled beside him, his mouth lowering until…

"Fuck," Travis groaned when Gage's lips wrapped around the sensitive head of his cock.

Kylie continued to stroke him while Gage laved him with his tongue.

"You like that?" Kylie asked.

"Love it," he mumbled. "So fucking much."

More than she would ever realize.

"Good." She smiled, her teeth flashing in the dim light from the lamps by the bed. "'Cause we're just getting started."

He really liked the sound of that.

However, when a good ten minutes had passed, Travis was ready to buck off the bed; his body was strung so tight he could hardly breathe. They'd assaulted him with pleasure, using only their hands and their mouths. It was too much but not nearly enough. And it wasn't fucking easy not ordering them what to do. It was the way he was programed and they knew it. Only he'd placed himself in their hands tonight, and he didn't want to change that.

So, for now, he'd have to rein in his patience.

A feat that wasn't nearly as easy as it sounded.

ALTHOUGH GAGE LOVED THE SEXY, DOMINANT SIDE of Travis, he couldn't complain about this, either. For Travis to put himself in their hands… It said a lot about his love for them. Not that they'd ever hurt him, but Gage knew how hard it was for Travis to relinquish control of anything. But he was doing a fairly good job.

Wrapping his lips around Travis's dick, Gage leaned down and took him as far as he could. He'd had to slow down, not wanting to push Travis over the edge just yet. After all, he did have some other ideas on what he wanted to do to Travis tonight. And that included fucking his ass until Travis was begging for more.

But first, he wanted to play.

After a few minutes of sucking him steadily, Gage released Travis's cock from his mouth, then slid off the bed and retrieved a couple of things from the dresser drawer. He didn't bother trying to hide them, either.

Travis growled when he saw the items, as Gage expected he would.

Joining them once again, Kylie took the lubricant and the prostate massager from Gage, preparing it for use. With the vibrating cock ring in hand, Gage worked it over Travis's softening cock, then began working Travis's dick again, watching his face as the pleasure registered.

"Damn," Travis growled when Gage hit the button to turn on the vibration.

"Good?"

"Mmmhmm," Travis groaned, his eyes locked on the sight between his legs.

Gage continued to jack him off while Kylie got the prostate massager in position, slowly working it into Travis's ass.

Travis bent his knee, widening his legs, giving Kylie more room to play. More moans escaped him as he writhed on the bed, completely at the mercy of the pleasure. They continued to tease him until sweat beaded on Travis's forehead and his breaths rasped in and out of his lungs.

"More," Travis pleaded. "Need more."

"Gettin' there, baby," Kylie crooned to him.

She worked the slim, vibrating wand in Travis's ass, just as they'd showed her, hitting that perfect spot and making Travis's stomach muscles flex from the sensations. Travis's dick swelled and pulsed in his hand, pre-cum leaking. Leaning down, Kylie sucked the thick, swollen head into her mouth, humming as she did. Gage knew Travis would be overwhelmed by all the vibrations, but Gage was impressed because Travis held his own, never moving his hands from behind his head.

While he continued to stroke the steely length of Travis's shaft, Gage took his own dick in hand, working himself to the same rhythm. He was eager to feel Travis's body clasped around him, milking his dick until neither of them could take any more.

"Don't," Travis bit out through clenched teeth. "Don't … make me come yet."

Gage stopped stroking him, and Kylie released him from her mouth.

"What do you want?" Kylie asked after pulling the wand out and tossing it aside.

She crawled over Travis, straddling his hips.

True to form, Travis's patience had clearly run out. He flipped Kylie over, then drove himself deep while Gage watched. Reaching for the lube, he coated his cock thoroughly, barely holding back. While they'd worked Travis into a frenzy, they'd both been affected just as much.

And now Gage was gearing up for the ride.

KYLIE'S BACK BOWED AS TRAVIS FILLED HER with one swift jerk of his hips. She grabbed his shoulders, her nails digging into the skin covering the thick, hard muscles that flexed beneath her touch.

"Fuck yes," Travis hissed through clenched teeth. "Feet on my shoulders."

Kylie smiled up at him as he held himself still above her. She worked her legs up between his arms and rested her feet on his shoulders. Bent in half, Kylie took slow, deep breaths as Travis shifted over her, making the position more comfortable.

His gaze locked with hers as he said, "Better?"

She nodded.

The mattress dipped, and she could see Gage moving behind Travis, who remained completely still above her, lodged to the hilt inside her. She wanted to move, wanted to encourage him to fuck her, but she knew he wouldn't until he was ready, so she relaxed.

"Ahh, yeah," Gage groaned. "So fucking tight."

Travis ground his hips, and Kylie felt the clit stimulator from the cock ring he wore vibrating against her. Another adjustment and she was crying out as the vibration hit its intended target.

"Fuck me," Travis growled, glancing over his shoulder at Gage. "Hard."

Kylie could tell he was hanging on by a thread, and she knew exactly how he felt. Teasing Travis and Gage was something she enjoyed immensely, though they didn't allow her the pleasure often. Nope, her husbands were very attentive, and they generally turned their focus on her. So tonight had been a pleasant surprise.

Travis's hips began to move, Gage's forceful thrusts pushing Travis deeper inside her while Kylie rocked her hips. She loved the way Travis felt inside her, but for some reason, when they were like this, it was always better.

Once again, Travis stilled and Gage picked up the pace. Kylie cupped Travis's face in her hands while Gage fucked his ass ruthlessly. She wanted to kiss him, but the position wouldn't allow it, so she rocked her hips, driving herself closer to orgasm with every press of the vibration against her clit.

It wouldn't take much to send her over, but she knew Travis was going to hold back until Gage came. He always did.

"Tight," Gage groaned. "So tight."

His hips were slamming against Travis's ass, and Kylie's body was absorbing the impact. It was a sweet assault, but she needed more, and she didn't want to wait. Releasing Travis's face, she planted her palms flat on the mattress, trying to move against him, but he held her in place with his body above hers.

"Not yet, baby," he said, his eyes glazed with desire. She knew he was close, knew he was working to hold back.

"Gonna come, Trav," Gage roared.

"Come," Travis pleaded.

A few more jerky thrusts and the bodies above her stilled, but that only lasted a heartbeat. Then Gage fell to the mattress beside them, his hand cupping her breast as Travis shifted onto his knees and began fucking her hard and fast.

She locked her eyes with his, watching for that moment when he hit the point of no return. Gage's hand traveled lower, and she felt his rough fingers on her clit, and that was her tipping point. Unable to hold back any longer, she closed her eyes as the pleasure built to a crescendo, then slammed through her at the same time Travis drove deep, his dick pulsing as he came.

It took several minutes before she could catch her breath, and by the time she did, both men had retreated to the bathroom. She heard the shower turn on at the same time Gage returned with a washcloth. As usual, she blushed as he cleaned her so gently, his lips finding hers.

"Love you," he whispered.

"Love you, too," she told him.

She must have drifted off to sleep because she briefly came to when Travis and Gage joined her in the bed. Travis spooned behind her, wrapping her in his strong arms, his warm breath fanning her neck.

"Love you, baby," he said softly.

"Love you, too," she replied, dozing again.

"Love you, Gage," Travis said, his voice a little louder.

"Love you," Gage responded.

Kylie managed to keep from drifting off, but just barely. "So, are y'all done with the surprises yet?"

"As far as the decorations go?" Gage asked.

"Mmmhmm," she mumbled.

"Yes," Travis assured her.

"But as for other surprises…" Gage placed his arm over her.

"What other surprises?" she slurred.

"You'll just have to wait and see, baby," Travis murmured against her ear. "It's not Christmas yet."

With that, she allowed herself to succumb to sleep, drifting off with the knowledge that these two men would forever be the best surprises she could ever get, and as she placed her hand over her stomach, she smiled to herself, because little did they know, but she had a surprise in store for them, as well.

 # Gift Dilemma

Ryan Trexler and Zachariah Tavoularis

from *Never Say Never*

SITTING IN HIS OFFICE, STARING AT HIS computer screen, Ryan Trexler wanted to pull his hair out.

One week.

One freaking week until Christmas and he still hadn't bought Z a gift. No matter how hard he tried, he didn't know what to get him. And it was driving him fucking crazy.

Why wasn't there a Google search that would tell him the best present to buy the man he loved? Hell, he could practically Google anything else he wanted, but not this. Oh, sure, he'd found article after article of suggestions—most of them involving jewelry—but nothing that even came close to what Ryan was hoping to find. Anyone who knew Z knew he didn't wear jewelry. Well, nothing more than his wedding band, anyway.

"Ugh," Ryan grumbled, closing his laptop lid, stopping short of slamming the damn thing shut.

A knock on his office door had him looking up in time to see Z waltzing in. Why the man even bothered to knock was beyond him. If Ryan really wanted to keep Z out, he would have to lock the door.

Not that he wanted to.

"Hey," Z greeted, his face softening the instant he met Ryan's gaze.

God, he loved this man. More and more every single day.

"Hey," Ryan replied, some of the tension from the day easing out of his shoulders from the mere sight of Z. "You ready to go?"

Z nodded, then came around and perched on the edge of Ryan's desk. "Whenever you are."

"I'm done here," Ryan admitted. He hadn't actually been working for the past hour, but Z didn't need to know that.

"Wanna grab some dinner?"

Ryan leaned back in his chair and studied Z, noticing the way his eyelids were at half-mast, his lips curved up slightly. He looked like he was ready to slam Ryan up against the wall and fuck his brains out. Wouldn't have been the first time they'd had sex in Ryan's office.

And didn't that just sound like heaven right this moment. It would at least give Ryan a minute or two not to worry about the most important thing that would happen to him all year.

Christmas.

This was his first Christmas with Z as a married couple. He was obligated to buy him a gift, but not just any gift. An amazing gift. A phenomenal gift. Something that would blow Z's mind and make him think about RT for the entire next year.

"Dinner's good," Ryan said with a sigh. "What were you thinkin'?"

"You," Z replied softly, that devilish smirk transforming his face.

"Maybe if you're good," Ryan told him, getting to his feet.

"I'm always good," Z countered. "At least that's the impression I get when you're screaming my name and begging for more."

Ryan blushed. It was something he found he often did when around Z. The man knew just what to do to embarrass him, even if they were the only two people in the room.

Even if what he said was true.

"Come on," Ryan grumbled. "Let's get food, then go home and go to bed."

"Hopefully not to sleep," Z noted, following Ryan as he headed toward the door. "'Cause I'm not the least bit tired right now."

Of course he wasn't. Z had the stamina of a damn long-distance runner. On crack.

Not that Ryan wasn't able to keep up. He didn't have a problem, but he still enjoyed giving Z a hard time about it.

An hour and a half later, after having dinner at Denny's, a place Ryan had recently learned was one of Z's favorites—the man had a penchant for breakfast any and all times of the day—they headed home.

For the time being, they were living in Ryan's house on the Kogan/Trexler compound until they found a house they both liked. They'd since sold Z's portion of the warehouse that he and Trace had shared to Trace and Marissa. Ryan's sister and brother-in-law had been more than happy to take it off their hands, telling Ryan they had plans to renovate for the growing family they planned to have.

Turned out that buying a house wasn't high on Ryan's or Z's priority list at the moment. Work was taking up a majority of their time as they worked through the changes Ryan had implemented, creating the new positions as well as dealing with a relatively new acquisition that had come to light in recent weeks. They were still working on the logistics, but it appeared as though the staff at Sniper 1 Security was about to grow, as was their business. Which, for Ryan, was definitely a good thing.

So, for now, Z had moved his things in with Ryan, and they were living comfortably in the two bedrooms they had. The second bedroom had been modified somewhat so that Z could have some office space of his own, which Ryan found out *after* they'd moved things around was for a treadmill. Not a desk. A freaking treadmill. According to Z, he did his best work away from the house, unless, of course, they were talking about sex, then Z insisted he did his best work wherever they were at that moment.

Ryan couldn't argue with him there.

Once inside, Ryan made his way to the kitchen after tossing his jacket on the back of the couch and looking over his shoulder to see Z pick it up, place it on a hanger, and then put it in the coat closet. Granted, it hadn't been a coat closet until Z had moved in. Ryan simply wasn't that organized.

Or, rather, he hadn't been until Z had come along and restructured his life. He had to admit, it was kind of nice.

"I'm gonna take a shower," Z told him, stopping in the living room.

"'Kay."

"I expect you to be in the bed, naked, when I get out."

Ryan smiled. "Is that an order?"

"Damn straight it is." With that, Z headed down the hall toward their bedroom.

As he stood there in the kitchen, Ryan's smile grew. Yeah, for the past few months, his life had certainly changed in so many ways. And thanks to Z, he didn't have a single complaint.

Z MADE QUICK WORK OF SHOWERING, SHAVING, and brushing his teeth. After flipping off the lights, he came out of the bathroom to find RT in bed, propped up against the headboard with his iPad in hand.

"Unless you're watchin' porn, that thing's gotta go," he told him, keeping his eyes locked on RT's as his husband peered over. The way RT's intense ice-blue gaze roamed over Z's naked body made his dick stir to life.

To his surprise, RT instantly tucked the iPad away in the nightstand, then turned his full attention to Z.

"Damn," Z mumbled with a grin. "I thought for sure that was porn."

"What do I need porn for?" RT asked.

"Everyone needs porn," he countered.

"Not when they've got you waltzing around naked and proud."

Z struck a pose and RT laughed, as he'd hoped he would.

"Get over here," RT commanded, patting the bed.

Z slid in beneath the blankets, meeting RT in the middle of their oversized king bed. They were both big men, so Z had insisted that they get a new bed—one much sturdier than the one RT had previously—when he'd moved in so they'd have plenty of room to roll around ... er ... to sleep.

Curling up against RT, Z sighed. "You're warm."

"Want me to warm you up?"

"Damn skippy." He laughed when RT slid beneath the blankets.

That laughter died instantly when RT's warm hand curled around his dick, stroking him slowly, firmly.

"Oh, yeah," Z moaned. "Wrap your lips around me."

RT's exquisite mouth slid over the sensitive head of Z's dick, and he sucked in a breath. Damn, that felt good. For a few minutes, he relished the feel of RT's mouth on him. It didn't take long before he was, in fact, warmed up. Once his skin heated, he shoved the blankets down, revealing RT lying between his legs, fisting Z's cock while sucking him at the same time.

"You look so good when you do that," Z told RT, sliding his fingers into RT's silky blond hair. "But I can't let you have all the fun."

Z managed to turn the tables, so to speak, flipping RT onto his back so that Z was straddling his head and leaning over RT's hips, staring down at the huge cock waiting for him. He focused on driving RT mad, slowly sucking him between his lips, using his tongue to follow the vein down to RT's balls before sucking them into his mouth and growling.

"Fuck," RT hissed, bucking his hips.

Z smiled to himself.

Long minutes passed while he entertained himself by feasting on RT. Stroking him with his hand, laving him with his tongue, sucking him with his mouth. Z could've gone on all night, just to hear RT moan. It was a beautiful sound.

RT obviously had other plans, because he managed to buck Z off of him, making him laugh as he fell to the bed, looking up to see RT staring back at him. Z watched as RT retrieved the tube of lubricant that they kept tucked into the nightstand drawer.

"You ready for this?" RT teased.

Z didn't answer, simply spread his arms, grabbed hold of two of the posts on the end of the bed, and planted his feet flat on the mattress, legs spread.

"I'll take that as a yes."

Z smiled back at RT as he moved over him, his lubed fingers sliding between Z's ass cheeks, teasing his asshole.

RT played with him for long minutes while he pressed kisses over Z's chest, his neck, his jaw. When RT lowered his mouth to Z's, he opened for him, meeting his tongue. Tentatively at first, playing along as RT continued to toy with his ass, sliding one finger inside, then two, then three.

His skin was on fire, heating even more when RT relaxed against him, their mouths still fused while RT finger-fucked him until he was delirious with pleasure.

"You ready to feel me?"

"Mm-hmm," he moaned against RT's mouth. "So ready."

"Don't move," RT ordered, repositioning himself so that he was kneeling between Z's legs.

Holding his head up, he continued to watch as RT guided his glistening dick toward Z's ass, his hand stroking Z's cock gently, teasingly.

Z's hands tightened around the posts when the thick head of RT's cock breached his anus, slowly pushing deeper, drawing a groan from Z's chest.

"Hurt?"

"Fuck no." It felt so damn good Z was nearly blinded by the pleasure that coursed through him. "Need more."

RT's grin was radiant as he met Z's gaze, driving his hips forward, burying himself deeper and deeper until Z was sure that he was filling him.

RT reached behind him and grabbed his pillow, then shoved it beneath Z's hips.

Their gazes were locked on one another as RT began to retreat slowly, pulling out completely, then forcing himself back in. He repeated the sensual torture until the muscles in Z's stomach hurt from flexing so much.

"More," Z begged. "Harder."

"I love watching you like this. At my mercy."

Z would forever be at RT's mercy and not just here in the privacy of their bedroom. He loved this man, would spend the rest of his life loving him.

RT's hips punched forward, and Z cried out from the pleasure that detonated, making his eyes cross.

"Hold on, baby," RT crooned, his hands sliding beneath Z's knees to lift his legs.

Again, Z tightened his grip on the posts, still watching RT.

Several more painfully slow thrusts had Z breathing heavy, desperate for more friction. And then...

"Ah, God, yes," Z hissed when RT began impaling him, driving into him. Still deep, still slow, but the pace was faster than it had been.

Z couldn't take his eyes off RT, loving the way his face contorted as he watched the place where their bodies were joined. Once, twice, three times RT would thrust into him, and the pace would quicken. Faster, harder, deeper. Over and over until the room was ablaze from the heat that generated between their bodies.

RT's face contorted, his eyes lifting to meet Z's, and Z knew he was close. The teasing was always fun, but it would only last so long before the overwhelming pleasure won out.

Unable to resist, Z released one of the posts, then reached between his legs and fisted his dick, stroking in time with the pounding RT was giving him.

"Beautiful," RT mumbled, his eyes drifting down to watch Z jack himself off. "Come for me, Z."

Z dropped his head to the mattress, sucking in air as he continued to stroke his cock, his balls drawing up close to his body as RT continued to fuck him, alternating between mind-numbingly shallow strokes that teased him and long, deep ones that made Z see stars.

An electrical hum started at the base of his spine, growing stronger by the second until his body was pulsing with electricity. He grunted and groaned, clenching his teeth, desperate to hold off until RT was ready, but it quickly became too much. With a muted roar, Z let go.

"Ah, yeah," RT groaned, his hips pummeling him several more times before he stilled, his dick pulsing in Z's ass.

When RT fell forward on top of him, Z wrapped his arms around him, holding him tight.

"Love you," he whispered against RT's ear.

"Love you more."

Z's smile widened until he thought his face would crack.

CHAPTER 2

THE FOLLOWING EVENING, RYAN WALKED INTO THE house, his nose instantly sniffing the air when the scent of… God, he didn't know what the smell was, but it was amazing. Tossing his coat onto the back of the couch, he made a beeline for the kitchen.

"What are you making?" he asked Z, who was moving around the kitchen with the ease of a man much, much smaller than his six-foot-seven-inch frame should allow.

"Dinner," he said, turning and shooting a blinding smile at Ryan.

"What is it?" Ryan moved around the island, trying to peek into the oven to see for himself.

"Nuh-uh," Z admonished, grabbing Ryan's face and planting a kiss on his lips before gripping his shoulders and spinning him back around. "It'll be ready soon enough. Go sit down and I'll get you something to drink."

Ryan grumbled good-naturedly as he headed to their bedroom and grabbed his iPad. He hadn't had time all day to do any searching for what to get Z for Christmas, so while he waited for dinner, he figured he'd check out a few things.

When he came back through the living room, he noticed the Christmas tree lights were on, flashing brightly. There were several presents beneath the tree, most of the gifts for their friends and family, but he noticed one that hadn't been there before.

"What's this?" he asked, moving closer.

"Don't touch that!" Z called from the kitchen.

Ryan glanced over his shoulder, but Z wasn't there to see him, so he reached down.

"Don't you dare!"

Ryan jumped when Z's voice sounded from right behind him. How the hell did a man that big move that fast? And that quietly? With a heavy sigh, Ryan stood upright. "Who's it for?"

"Not tellin' you." Z's smile lit up his entire face.

"What is it?"

"Not tellin' you that, either."

Which meant the present was for Ryan. There were a couple of other ones he'd noticed beneath the tree, as well. And every time he had attempted to pick them up to rattle the box to see if he could get some idea, Z would always stop him. Hell, one time, Z had called at the exact moment Ryan had been about to grab one. It was as though he'd known what Ryan was up to.

He instantly looked up into the corners, checking for cameras. He wouldn't put it past Z to wire the place just so he could keep an eye on him. The thought made him smile, but he quickly remembered that Z had reprimanded him.

Pasting a frown on his face, Ryan took his iPad back to the kitchen and slid into his chair, facing Z.

"You workin'?" Z asked, nodding toward the iPad.

"You could say that." Working to find the best damn Christmas present of all time.

"Somethin' wrong? New case? Or is this about the merger?"

Ryan shook his head.

"Did you stay at the office all day today?"

For weeks now, Ryan and Z had managed to take Saturday or Sunday off, sometimes both. Today, although it was Saturday, Ryan had needed to get some things cleared off his desk, so he'd opted to go in for a few hours. It was easier without all the distractions.

"I'm not meeting with Alex McDermott until after the holidays. He's given me his requirements for the acquisition. I just need to talk to Conner about them." He looked up at Z. "And no, I didn't stay in the office all day, either."

And he hadn't. Although their jobs usually required a bit of danger and risk, Ryan hadn't spent the day dealing with security issues. Instead, he'd done the riskiest, most dangerous thing of all. He'd gone to the mall.

On the weekend before Christmas.

It hadn't taken long for him to realize his mistake. People were freaking crazy when it came to finding last-minute gifts, so he'd checked out a couple of places and then hightailed it out of the danger zone.

"You go by and see your parents?" Z asked.

"Yeah."

"How're they doin'?"

"Good. Mom's goin' overboard about Christmas dinner, but that's not unusual. Luckily Lilah's there to keep her calm." Lilah was the saving grace in the Trexler kitchen. She'd been working for Ryan's parents for more than thirty years, and thankfully she was still willing to help plan a holiday meal that was big enough to feed a small army.

"Did you remind them I'm makin' pies?" Z asked, peering over at Ryan from his spot at the stove.

"I did. What kind are you making?"

"Pumpkin, cherry, and I'm lookin' for my recipe for Jack Daniel's pecan pie. My dad used to make them when we were kids. Can't find it anywhere."

"Can't you just pull one up on the Internet?" Ryan asked.

Z's *get real* face gave him his answer.

It was true, Ryan wasn't much of a cook. And he definitely wasn't a baker. He didn't know the first thing about the kitchen, other than how to heat a TV dinner in the microwave. Until Z had moved in, that had been all that he ate, anyway. Since then, though … Z didn't even allow Ryan to buy TV dinners anymore.

Not that he could complain, because Z was keeping him fed and fed well. In fact, Ryan had gained at least five pounds since they'd gotten married. According to Z, he'd been too skinny. Now, Ryan was having to pay extra attention to keep from overdoing it.

"Have you asked your mom?" Ryan questioned as he typed *Jack Daniel's pecan pie recipes* into his iPad.

"Yeah. She said she'd look for it. I need it by Wednesday, though, if I expect to get enough pies made."

Speaking of Wednesday… "We've got a lunch date with Buddy tomorrow and dinner on Saturday after Christmas."

"Yep," Z confirmed. "And don't forget the company Christmas party on Monday afternoon."

How could he forget that? His cousin Kira, along with Sniper 1's loyal receptionist, Jayden, had decided to do a white elephant exchange at the office on Monday as their official Christmas party. Kira and Jayden had said that they couldn't buy alcohol to trade because that was too easy, which was true, because that had always been Ryan's choice. People would fight over the cheapest liquor at one of these things.

Luckily, Z was the king of buying gifts, and he'd gone out last week and found one for each of them.

Which was good, because it left Ryan with time to figure out what to get Z. Too bad he still had no idea, and they were T minus six days and counting.

AFTER PLACING THE FOOD ON THE TABLE, along with two plates and silverware, Z joined RT, watching as RT turned off his iPad and pushed it to the side.

"This smells fabulous," RT noted, dishing pot roast onto his plate. Little did RT know, but that was one of the easiest meals Z made, especially considering he let it cook in the Crock-Pot all day. The only thing Z had to do was make rice, which took all of five minutes.

Dishing food on his own plate, Z continued to steal glimpses of RT. He could tell that something was bothering him. And he was pretty sure he knew what it was. After all, he was trained to read people, and RT ... well, for Z, RT was like an open book. Granted, it hadn't always been that way, but since they'd finally given in to the overwhelming lust they'd both battled for years and taken that plunge, Z didn't have a hard time figuring out what RT was thinking.

But if it was what Z thought it was—RT looking for the perfect gift for him for Christmas—Z wasn't sure he should even bring it up.

Hell, he'd been leaving hints about it for the past week, but apparently RT was too caught up in his own thoughts to notice.

First, Z had suggested they get a new coffee maker. Possibly one of those fancy Keurig deals or even that Starbucks thing that made lattes. After all, RT drank as much, if not more, coffee than Z.

Nothing.

Then, last weekend when Z had been making a cake to take to the nursing home, he'd mentioned that he could use a new mixer. He'd even broken off into a conversation about the cool standing mixers he'd seen in an ad.

Nothing.

And *then*, Z had gone so far as to take an ad from Bed Bath & Beyond and circle a number of things, including a Pyrex storage container set, a stainless steel Crock-Pot, measuring cups, oven mitts. Hell, he'd even put a star beside that cool Magic Bullet thing out now.

Still nothing.

Aside from writing a list and putting it on the bathroom mirror for RT to notice, Z wasn't sure how to get his attention. Truth was, he didn't really want a gift—he already had the greatest gift he could ever have, and that was RT's love—but he knew RT was getting worked up over the fact he wanted to buy something for Z.

So what if Z loved to spend time in the kitchen? It wasn't like he could depend on RT to cook for them. Not because RT wouldn't do it. He would if Z asked. More because RT *couldn't* do it. The man was not meant to be in a kitchen. Not unless the house was being demolished and the fastest way to do that was to burn it to the ground.

"Have you heard from your sister?" RT asked, pulling Z back to the moment.

Z frowned, shaking his head as he chewed. He'd been hoping he would get the chance to see his brother and sister for Christmas, but it looked as though that wasn't going to happen. Z was going to have lunch with his mother next Sunday, a couple of days after Christmas, with RT, but it didn't look as though Jensyn and Reese were going to make it to Dallas this year.

Hopefully, if they were lucky, Z would get to spend some time with them in January if the crazy shit at the office didn't explode in their faces by then. There was a big merger underway, and Z knew that it was taking a lot of RT's time.

"What about Reese? Work going good for him?"

Z looked up at RT and nodded. "Talked to him yesterday. They're busy right now."

Reese had taken a job with Walker Demolition—the company owned by some of Z's friends from high school. The last time he'd talked to Reese, his brother had mentioned that they had quite a bit of overtime lately. Apparently, it wasn't necessarily a bad thing to be in the construction business during the winter in Texas. Considering the mild temperatures, it was probably better than working in the summer.

The last time Z had seen Reese, though, had been on Thanksgiving, when RT had suggested they head down to Coyote Ridge for the weekend. Z had been ecstatic to get to spend more than a few hours with his kid brother.

"Well, maybe we can get down there for New Year's," RT mentioned, finishing off what was on his plate.

Z drank his tea and watched RT over the rim of his cup, nodding. "That would be fantastic."

As would figuring out what was bothering RT and how Z could make it better.

CHAPTER 3

Ryan waited for Z to join him as they walked toward the nursing home where Z's father lived. When they stepped inside the doors, the woman at the receptionist desk greeted them both by name and smiled when Z placed a small gift bag on her desk.

"Merry Christmas, doll," Z told her with that mischievous grin he was famous for.

"Merry Christmas," she said, her cheeks turning the same bright red as the bag.

They didn't stay for her to open the gift because Z was obviously a man on a mission. Ryan fell into step with Z when he headed toward the doors that led to the section where Z's comatose father had been for the past four, going on five, years.

Z made his rounds, handing out gifts to all of the nurses who were there, leaving several more for those who worked different shifts. Ryan found it endearing that Z was so thoughtful when it came to the people in his life. Although he probably didn't know some of the staff at the nursing home, he'd made sure to get something for every person there. That was one of the many reasons people loved Z. Not because he brought gifts but because he saw everyone as someone important.

When Z had handed out all of his gifts, he took the cake that Ryan had carried in and set it down on the nurse's station counter before taking Ryan's hand and leading him down the hall toward Thomas Tavoularis's room.

"Hey, Dad," Z announced when they walked into the room, the same as he always did. "We came to check on you."

Ryan smiled, looking around the room to see if anything had changed since they'd last been there. He noticed a few more Christmas cards had been pinned to the bulletin board on the wall. Although Thomas would likely never see them since the odds of him waking up from the coma were minimal, Z still held out hope, which meant Ryan did, as well.

"Ah, my boys are here. I thought I heard a ruckus in the hallway."

Ryan turned around to see Buddy Stallone, one of the residents of the nursing home and a good friend of Z's, slowly making his way into the room. Today he was using a walker to help him around.

"Hey, Buddy," Ryan greeted, shaking Buddy's hand. "You're lookin' good."

Buddy grinned from ear to ear. "You like it?" Buddy glanced down at his Christmas sweater. "It's tacky sweater day."

Ryan laughed, stepping out of the way when Z made his way over to them.

Z shook Buddy's hand as well.

"I came by to see your ol' man this mornin'," Buddy told Z. "I added some of his cards to the wall. And put a new ornament on the tree."

Ryan glanced over at the small Christmas tree sitting on the dresser beside Thomas's bed. The lights were on, twinkling away.

"I noticed that," Z said. "You make it?"

"I did. Those crazy ladies keep askin' me to go to the arts and crafts room."

Ryan fought the urge to laugh when Buddy blushed.

"I hope you're not flirtin' with them," Z teased. "They'll never give you a minute's peace if you do."

"Don't I know it," Buddy said with a gravelly chuckle.

"You hungry yet?" Z asked Buddy after turning his attention back from the tree.

"Whenever you boys are."

"You know Z," Ryan said, "he's always hungry."

Buddy smiled at them both, a knowing look in his eyes. Z had told Ryan the stories about how Buddy had always wanted to hear about Z's adventures. But there had been one in particular that Buddy had fixated on, and it was the last one he and Z had been on together, when they'd been hired to keep an eye on a painting down near the coast.

According to Buddy, he was a sucker for a good romance.

Every time Z mentioned that story, Ryan blushed as well. Although he didn't exactly consider it a romance, he could see it from Buddy's perspective. It had been the point in Ryan's life that had sent his world into a tailspin, the moment when he realized just what he'd been missing in his life.

Love.

And Z.

Which were, now that he thought about it, one and the same. At least for him.

"Food's waitin'," Buddy said as he turned and headed for the door.

Ryan accepted Z's hand when he held it out to him, and they followed Buddy to the cafeteria.

"HEY," Z SAID TO BUDDY WHEN THE three of them were sitting at a table in the cafeteria, chowing down on chicken and mashed potatoes. "You should tell RT about the gift you bought your wife when y'all were first married."

Buddy's face lit up like the Christmas tree in the corner of the cafeteria. Z knew how much Buddy loved talking about his deceased wife; he'd been honored to hear the stories multiple times during the time they'd known each other. And this one was one of his favorites.

Buddy smiled at RT, then launched right into his story. "Meg and I were married in 1952. We share a birthday, so we were both twenty-two at the time. Piss-poor but living on love, so it didn't really matter until it came time for a holiday or anniversary. I was always hoping to buy her the biggest, flashiest gift I could find. I'd been looking for three weeks for something to get her. I found plenty, but everything I wanted to get her cost more than I had to spend, so I started a list with all my ideas and kept it taped behind the dresser in our bedroom, hoping she wouldn't find it.

"I'd underestimated my wife, because a week before Christmas, she found the list. I'd come home to find her sitting on the bed, staring at the list with tears in her eyes. I immediately panicked and asked her what was wrong."

Buddy's eyes seemed to glaze over, and Z knew he was reliving that day.

"Meggie? What's wrong, honey?"

Buddy took a deep breath and stepped into their bedroom, his eyes glued to the piece of paper in her hand. He pulled open the top drawer and grabbed a handkerchief, holding it out for her. Meg took it from him but didn't look up at his face, which concerned him.

He knew exactly what that paper was. What he didn't understand was why she was crying. He had the list memorized, so he ran through it several times while he stared down at his beautiful bride sitting on the edge of the mattress, her hair pulled back from her face, tears dripping from her chin.

She sniffled, then pressed the handkerchief to her nose before lifting her dark brown eyes to meet his. For the first time since he'd stepped into the room, Buddy took a breath. She didn't look angry, but still, it didn't explain why she was sad.

"I found this behind the dresser," she said softly. "I wasn't snooping, I promise. I dropped something and reached behind it to get it and found this." She held the paper up in front of her. "What is it?"

Buddy walked over and sat on the mattress beside her, knowing he had to explain. "It's a list of gifts I want to buy you."

Meg's dark eyes rested on his face, a soft smile on her lips, and Buddy relaxed a little. "We don't have the money for these things."

Buddy nodded. He knew that, but it didn't change the fact that he wanted to get them for her. If he had the money, he would've bought everything on the list and then some.

Meg touched his face with her soft fingers, and Buddy met her gaze. "Could you tell me why you picked them?"

Buddy frowned, confused.

"It's the thought that counts, Buddy," Meg explained. "And these gifts... They are very thoughtful. Maybe you could explain what made you want to get them for me."

Buddy's heart fell. Was Meg making fun of him? She'd never been the type of girl to pick on anyone, but he felt as though she was.

Her hand cupped his cheek. "Buddy Stallone, don't you start overthinking this."

She knew him so well.

Meg gave a watery chuckle, then tugged at his arm. "Come on. Climb up here and tell me why you wanted to get me these things."

He watched as Meg moved up against the headboard of their bed, propping up pillows for him to lean against. After kicking off his shoes and unbuttoning the cuffs on his shirt, he walked around to the other side of the bed and climbed in with her. As he rested his back against the headboard, Meg curled up next to him, her head on his shoulder as she handed him the paper.

"Tell me why you wanted to get this," she said, pointing to the first item on the list.

Buddy grinned. "I thought you'd want a television so you could watch I Love Lucy," he told her. He knew that show was her absolute favorite. Since her parents had a television and they'd yet to get one of their own, they usually went over there so she could watch.

"I do love that show," she admitted softly. "She's so fun. But you know I like to read more."

True. His beautiful bride did love to read. Some days, she spent more time at the library than she did at home.

"And this one?" she said, pointing to the next item.

He glanced at her sideways. "Wouldn't you want a dishwasher? It's supposed to make washing dishes easier."

"But washing dishes is already easy," she told him, tapping his lower lip the way she always did when she was telling him he was being silly. "I do love how you want me to be happy."

"That's the only thing I want," he whispered against her hair.

Meg lifted her gaze to meet his. "Well, then you're in luck. 'Cause you already make me happy."

Buddy's heart swelled in his chest. Since the day he'd met her three years ago, Meg had become his entire world. He loved her with every piece of himself, and it was true, her happiness was all that mattered. And that was one of the reasons he longed to buy her nice things... He wanted to put a beautiful smile on her face.

"And this one?"

"Those were the heels you were looking at in the window at that little boutique downtown. I saw the way your eyes lit up when you saw them."

"You remember that?" Meg's eyes were wide as she turned to look at him again. *"That was … that was more than six months ago."*

"I remember everything from that day," he explained. *"You had your hair curled, and your lips were pink from that new lipstick you'd finally bought after months of me telling you to get it. You were wearing that pretty yellow sundress and those little brown sandals. You had tried on a pair of sunglasses in one of the shops, but I told you they covered up too much of your pretty face, which made you laugh at me."* It was true, Buddy didn't forget anything when it came to Meg.

More tears formed, and her eyes glistened, making his heart hurt again.

But when she smiled, he forgot everything.

"The greatest gift you could give me, Buddy Stallone, is the love you show me already. The fact that you remembered that … that's the greatest gift ever. I wish we had pictures from that day."

And that was the moment Buddy knew exactly what he would buy his beautiful bride for Christmas.

"You bought her a camera?" RT asked, looking back and forth between Buddy and Z.

Z smiled.

"Am I right?"

"Sort of," Z admitted, grinning at Buddy.

"That year, I bought my beautiful Meg memories."

RT frowned, obviously confused.

"Yes," Buddy said with a laugh. "I bought her a camera. And I bought her a picture book. But I made a promise to myself that I would take many pictures with her, of her. And I did. For years and years, we collected pictures of all the things that made us both happy. And we filled up many albums with those images."

RT grabbed his tea glass while Z watched him, trying to figure out what was going through his beautiful brain. The man worked so hard, was so good at what he did, but sometimes, he overlooked the little things. Z knew RT was trying to find the perfect gift, but just like Meg, Z already had the greatest gift in the world. The fact that RT would worry so much over trying to make Z happy … well, that made Z happier than any gift he could possibly come up with.

"So, did you find that recipe you were looking for?" Buddy asked, pulling Z's attention back to him.

"Not yet, no. But I'm not gonna give up yet."

On Monday afternoon, Ryan was finishing up an email when Z walked into his office after knocking briefly. He looked up and smiled, unable to help himself, because Z was grinning from ear to ear, his dark eyes dancing.

"You ready?" Z asked.

"For?" Ryan leaned back in his chair.

"The white elephant exchange."

Oh, right. Shit. He'd forgotten all about it, actually.

"It's a good thing you've got me," Z told him as though reading Ryan's mind.

"It is," Ryan confirmed, and it had nothing to do with the fact Z kept him on track, either. He was simply lucky to have Z period. "Let me finish this email?"

"Sure. But you've got two minutes. Then I'm sending the others in to get you."

Ryan leaned forward and began typing instantly. He did not need Trace or Kira or Jayden coming in to give him a hard time.

"I've got the gifts, so you can just come join us."

Ryan nodded, typing away.

Five minutes later, he was in the main bullpen, where the others had gathered. Everyone was there. His sister, Marissa, and her husband, Trace. Trace's parents, Casper and Emily. The rest of the Kogan clan: Conner and Conner's daughter, Shelby, Hunter, and their sister, Courtney. Ryan didn't see Courtney's husband, but he wasn't necessarily surprised. The mob boss was probably busy … doing whatever it was he did.

Of course, Ryan's parents, Elizabeth and Bryce, were there. Ryan's uncle TJ and TJ's wife, Stephanie. Ryan's brothers Colby, Clay, and Austin, along with Ryan's cousins Tanner, Kira, Evan, and Dominic.

It wouldn't be complete without the others who worked for them. The S1S receptionist, Jayden, who had masterminded the entire thing with Kira's help. As well as Emma, Decker, Claire, Lilly, Ian, John, Craig, Shane, and a handful of others from support.

Everyone seemed to be having a good time already. There were finger foods, drinks, some holiday music in the background, and a whole lot of laughter and conversation. As he moved closer, someone placed a red Santa hat on his head, and Ryan fought the urge to roll his eyes. He'd never been accused of being jolly, but he could play along. These people were his family, the most important ones in his life.

Z approached, carrying two clear cups of punch, and handed one to Ryan. With a thank you and a smile, Ryan took it from him, then took a sip.

"I hope like hell no one's drivin' home after this," he muttered after his nostrils burned from the alcohol.

"There's not enough to go far, and they'll be here for a few hours yet. I'll keep an eye on 'em, though."

That was Z, always thoughtful.

Another reason Ryan wanted to buy him the perfect gift this year. Although he still wasn't any closer to finding one. Even after he'd heard Buddy's story yesterday. He knew the last thing Z needed was a camera. Granted, he was also aware that wasn't the moral of the story. He wasn't that dense, but still, he had yet to come up with an idea even as remotely romantic as the story Buddy had shared.

But he was working on it.

"Hey," Ryan's mother said when she came to stand beside Ryan and Z.

Ryan leaned in for a hug, as did Z when it was his turn.

"Did you find that recipe yet?" Liz asked Z.

"Not yet," he said.

Ryan could hear a little more frustration in his husband's tone. Everyone seemed to be asking about that recipe, which was why Ryan had started doing a little digging of his own. He knew Z didn't want one off the Internet, so that was out. There were a million different versions of it, from what he'd seen when he'd started his research, but Ryan understood the sentimentality of it being his father's recipe. Which was why he'd mentioned it to Buddy before leaving the nursing home yesterday. Asked him to keep an eye out, even to check what few personal effects Thomas had there at the home with him.

He'd also called Z's mother, Cindy. She knew of the recipe, but she'd had no luck in finding it. After that quick call, Ryan had also reached out to Z's brother, Reese, to see if he could take a look around his house. Reese was currently living in the family home in Coyote Ridge, where Z had grown up. Ryan figured if it was anywhere, it would be there.

Still, he hadn't heard anything from Reese yet.

"Who's ready to get this party started?" Jayden asked, donning her bright green LED Christmas tree glasses that flashed.

A chorus of cheers erupted, and everyone found seats, most of them sitting on top of the desks littering the bullpen. They'd all been rearranged so that they circled a table in the middle, which held a pile of wrapped gifts.

"All right, so y'all know the rules were simple this year," Jayden explained. "Gifts needed to be roughly ten dollars and no alcohol." When some people grumbled, Jayden grinned. "Alcohol is too easy and not nearly as fun. Anyway. When y'all came in, you were given a number. Who has number one?"

Decker Bromwell raised his hand, holding up a small slip of paper.

"Congrats," Jayden said cheerfully. "You get to pick first."

Ryan sat on the table beside Z, watching as Deck went to the table and began picking up presents, shaking them as he grinned. When he seemed content with his pick, he returned to his spot.

Everyone's attention was focused on him as he unwrapped the long, thin box.

Some people laughed as Deck frowned when he held up the white sweatshirt. When he turned it around so everyone could see, laughter erupted throughout the room. Ryan's eyes widened when he saw what had been ironed on the sweatshirt.

"Please tell me you did not bring that," he muttered to Z.

"Not me," Z confirmed, chuckling.

Ryan prayed he wasn't blushing as Deck held up the sweatshirt proudly. There, on the front, was a huge picture of Ryan's face. Someone had taken a candid shot of him somewhere, and he had to admit, it wasn't his best face. But to each his own.

"I'm gonna wear this proudly," Deck announced.

"Not if I get a chance to steal it," Z told him, making everyone laugh.

"Who's got number two?" Jayden inquired.

Conner's fourteen-year-old daughter, Shelby, raised her hand, then moved to the front and shyly grabbed the first present she could reach before retreating to her chair beside her father. Everyone watched as she opened the gift.

"What is it?" Marissa asked.

Conner grumbled.

"Beer Pong Head Game," Shelby told them.

Ryan looked at the picture, which showed a guy wearing an inflatable hat that held six Solo cups on the top.

"Someone better steal that from my daughter," Conner growled, looking around.

Ryan laughed.

For the next half hour, he sat there, watching as people opened more gifts, some stealing the presents that had already been opened, forcing the original person to go back and select another. Poor Shelby continued to get the alcohol-themed gifts, including a light-up cocktail shaker, bourbon marshmallows, a sour-puss beer Koozie, and a flask set with its own removable shot glass. Finally, after Conner had squirmed a half dozen times, Shelby ended up picking a set of temporary knuckle tattoos. Although her father wasn't all that happy, he warned anyone that if they stole them from her, he'd hunt them down.

When it was Z's turn, he did as he'd promised and stole the sweatshirt with Ryan's face on it from Trace, who had stolen it from Deck. With it safely in Z's possession—a gift could only be taken twice—he seemed to be a happy man.

Not that Ryan enjoyed looking over to see Z wearing that damn thing, but he guessed it could've been worse.

And then it was Ryan's turn.

He considered all the gifts he'd seen thus far, including a retro game controller phone case, an emoji pillow, a variety of bacon gifts, and a ruler that read: size matters. None of which appealed to him, so he figured he would take his chances.

The instant he had it open, he knew he would get hell for it.

"What is it?" Casper asked.

Ryan shook his head as he lifted it out of the package. He'd unwrapped a bright pink cupcake shower cap, complete with a cherry on top.

Z clapped, then grabbed the cap, removed the Santa hat Ryan had been wearing, and thrust it over Ryan's head.

More clapping ensued, and Ryan hoped his face wasn't as red as the cherry.

Z WAS PRETTY SURE THE HIGHLIGHT OF his day was watching RT turn beet red when Z had placed that shower cap on his head. Surprisingly, no one had stolen it from him, either, which made it all the better.

The game had lasted approximately three hours, and then RT had made a speech, thanking everyone for all their hard work, and ended by ordering pizza for everyone and convincing them to stick around. The man didn't realize how much this group loved him. Although most of the people employed by Sniper 1 Security were family, there were a lot who weren't, but they were loyal just the same. And it was the thoughtfulness of the Kogans and Trexlers that made it that way. They treated every member of the team as though they were.

"So does this mean I don't get to make you dinner tonight?" Z asked RT as they sat at the break room table, eating pizza.

"I thought you had some pies to make."

"I do," he confirmed. "But that doesn't mean I can't cook for you."

RT's eyes softened and Z's heart fluttered. He knew that RT didn't realize how he looked at him, but Z noticed. And every damn time was like the first.

"Okay, y'all knock that shit off," Trace stated firmly, elbowing Z. "They make rooms for that."

"You're one to talk," Z retorted, glancing over at his best friend. Trace grinned.

"Have y'all started renovating the warehouse yet?" Hunter asked Trace.

Trace turned to Marissa, then to look at his brother. "We have."

"Yeah?" Hunter took a bite of pizza.

"What're y'all turning it into?" Courtney asked.

Z noticed Courtney's face light up as she stared back at her brother and her best friend. It was then that Z knew what was going on, and he waited patiently for the news.

Thankfully, he didn't have to wait long.

"We're putting in a staircase that leads down to the first floor, and we're remodeling to add a master bedroom."

Z knew that his old loft apartment was far too big to just be a master bedroom. "And...?"

"And an office," Trace said nonchalantly. "That way Marissa will have a place to work."

Z looked at Marissa. Her cheeks were pink and her eyes a little glassy as she stared back at her husband. Yep, there was definitely more to this story.

"And...?" Z repeated.

The room was quiet for a moment as all eyes turned to Trace.

And just as Z had expected, a shit-eating grin split across his best friend's face as he placed his arm around his wife's shoulders. "And a nursery."

The silence was replaced by earsplitting excitement, which caused others to rush into the room, looking around to see what was going on.

"They're havin' a baby," Courtney announced. "I'm gonna be an aunt."

"Congrats, bro," Z offered, clapping Trace on the back with one hand and shaking his hand with the other.

"Thanks."

Z turned to look at RT, noticing he was smiling over at his sister. "You're gonna be an uncle," Z told him.

"I know. And so are you."

Z's eyes widened as that sank in. Launching to his feet, he glanced around the room, momentarily stunned as that news sank in. "I'm gonna… Holy shit… I'm gonna be an uncle."

Laughter erupted as all eyes turned to him.

"Holy shit," he muttered again, lowering himself into his chair.

RT leaned over and chuckled, pressing his lips close to Z's ear. "Congrats. Maybe tonight we can celebrate the good news."

Z's gaze snapped over to RT. "You're damn right we will," he said softly, hoping no one else heard but not really caring if they did or not.

Two hours later, as the party was thinning out, after Z and RT had helped Jayden and Kira clean everything up, Z managed to corner RT just outside the conference room. Without saying a word, he grabbed RT's hand and led him across the hall.

"What're you doin'?" RT asked, watching Z carefully when they stepped into RT's office and Z closed the door behind him.

"Nothin'," Z said, pretending he had no idea what RT was talking about. "What are *you* doin'?"

RT smirked. "Z."

It was amazing how RT could drawl that one letter out into several syllables. And every time he did, Z's dick stood at attention.

Since RT knew him so well, Z knew it would benefit no one for him to stall any longer, so he simply pushed RT up against the door and kissed him. Hard.

When RT kissed him back, fisting his shirt and jerking him closer, Z knew he had RT right where he wanted him. Only, they weren't in the exact location Z wanted him, so he took a step back, grabbed RT's hand again, and led him around his desk and into the chair.

RT dropped down into the leather, his eyes never leaving Z.

"What are you doing?" RT repeated.

"I'm giving you an early Christmas present," Z told him, kneeling between RT's legs.

RT didn't stop him when he worked open his jeans, but he did help him to work them down RT's legs. And when RT's cock sprang free, Z knew by how thick it was that RT was definitely on board with this plan.

Only Z didn't intend to give anything. Not unless RT was willing to take it. Because he knew RT enjoyed that shit more than anything. It could've been the fact that Z was bigger and stronger, but Z had figured out early on that RT loved to be in control.

"What are you waiting for?" RT rasped.

Z didn't say a word, simply glanced down at RT's long, thick cock, his mouth watering to taste it.

RT gripped his dick, stroking slowly, and Z noticed the instant RT realized what Z was offering. While Z continued to kneel, RT got to his feet and perched on the edge of the desk. A tingle shot down Z's spine when RT reached for him, tugging him by his hair, urging him forward.

Z did as RT wanted, crawling closer until he was right where RT wanted him.

"Open your mouth, Z."

Z didn't move.

RT chuckled, the sound sending electrical pulses of pleasure straight to Z's dick.

"You want it that way, huh?"

No, you do, Z thought, fighting a grin.

RT roughly tilted Z's head back, then placed his thumb on Z's chin, forcing his mouth open.

"Don't move," RT growled before sliding the swollen head across Z's lips.

Z fought the urge to moan, loving every second of this.

Sometimes he had to encourage RT, but once RT realized what Z was willing to give him, the man didn't need any encouragement.

"Suck me," RT commanded, sliding his dick into Z's mouth.

Z wrapped his lips around him, gently teasing him with his tongue. He was definitely not going to make this easy for RT. Where was the fun in that?

As he continued to watch RT, Z sucked and licked, never giving RT what he obviously needed. But soon, that didn't matter, because Z was no longer in control. RT grabbed Z's head and forced his cock deep into Z's mouth.

"Suck. Me."

Yes, sir. Z gave RT just what he needed, allowing RT to use his mouth, to fuck his face, to drive his cock deep into Z's throat while he tried not to gag and choke. It was heaven and hell all mixed into one, and Z loved every second of it because it was what RT wanted, what he needed.

And Z was always trying to find ways to please him, to show him just what he meant to him.

"Ah, Z," RT groaned. "So good, baby. Love your mouth."

Z hummed his approval, and RT gripped his hair tighter.

"You want me to come in your mouth?" RT asked roughly.

Nodding, Z continued to take all that RT would give him. Z's cock was rock hard, but he didn't touch himself, didn't want to. This was about RT.

"Fuck, baby. I'm gonna come. You sure that's what you want?"

Z hummed again, then focused on working RT's dick with his mouth and tongue, loving the way RT still held his head, fucking his mouth like he owned him.

Then again, he did. Mind, body, and soul.

RT groaned, his hips stilling as he slammed into Z's throat one last time, his dick pulsing. Z fought to swallow, grateful when RT pulled out slightly, allowing him more air.

"I know what you did there," RT said, smiling as he tucked his cock back into his jeans, then zipped himself up.

Z got to his feet, grinning down at RT. "Do you?"

"Definitely." RT's arms wrapped around Z, pulling him close until they were touching from knee to chest.

"Did you like it?" Z asked.

RT cupped his face, then pressed his lips softly to Z's.

"I fucking loved it, Z. Love everything you give me."

And that was exactly the way Z had intended it.

CHAPTER
5

Tuesday evening

RYAN WAS SWEATING.

Not only because it was hot in the kitchen, but also because he was nervous. He'd left work early, making up an excuse that he had something he needed to do. Granted, it hadn't been a lie. He had needed to make a run to the grocery store to pick up a few things.

But now, as he stared at all the ingredients sitting out on the counter, he was nervous. What if he fucked this up?

That morning, Reese had called him, all excited that he'd found a copy of the recipe that Z had been looking for. After confirming that Reese hadn't told anyone, including Z, Ryan had told him to snap a picture and send it his way. A few minutes after that, the recipe had arrived, and he'd thought of nothing except buying those ingredients and getting home to make that pie for Z.

It was a surprise. One he didn't want to fuck up, but there was no doubt about it, he sucked in the kitchen.

Sure, the recipe seemed simple enough. He'd bought sugar, eggs, chocolate chips, Karo syrup, pecans, butter, vanilla, and pie crusts. Then he'd made a quick stop at the liquor store and picked up two bottles of Jack, figuring he'd use part of one for the recipe and he'd drink the other just so he could make it through this.

He hadn't had a drop of liquor at this point, but he was beginning to think it might be a good idea.

Figuring nothing would get accomplished unless he simply did it, Ryan pushed up his sleeves and got to work.

An hour and a half later, Ryan pulled the finished pie out of the oven, looking it over. He didn't know what it was supposed to look like, but it didn't look bad. Maybe lopsided, but not as though he'd ruined it.

"Honey, I'm home," Z called from the front door and Ryan jumped.

Setting the glass dish on a towel on the counter, he was still staring at it when Z walked into the kitchen a few seconds later.

"What is that smell?"

Ryan looked up at Z.

"It smells … good. Like…"

Z's eyes went to the dish on the counter, and Ryan held his breath, waiting to see what he would say.

"Is that…?" Z's eyes lifted to meet his.

Ryan nodded.

Z took a few steps closer, eyes on the pecan pie the entire time. Ryan watched as Z retrieved the iPad, which was on, the picture of the recipe on the screen.

"You…"

Ryan didn't breathe, didn't move, praying that Z wasn't angry, that he hadn't gone and ruined Christmas by making the pie instead of waiting for Z to do it. What if that was what Z wanted? What if Z wanted to be the one to make the pie? It was his father's recipe, after all.

Oh, shit.

What had he done?

Ryan hadn't realized he was staring down at the pie until Z stepped in front of him, cutting off his view.

Z's big hands came up and cupped his face, forcing him to look up at him.

"You made this for me?"

Ryan locked his gaze with Z's, noticed the dark brown orbs were glassy. Tears? Good or bad? A million questions ran through his head, but he couldn't seem to make his voice work.

"That is the best Christmas present anyone has or will ever give me, Ryan," Z said softly.

His heart shuddered momentarily. The best Christmas gift? That wasn't his gift to Z. No, he had wanted…

"I love you," Z whispered, leaning in and pressing his lips to Ryan's.

Ryan clutched Z's shirt. "You're not mad?"

Z's dark eyebrows shot downward. "Why would I be mad?"

Ryan shrugged.

"Tell me you love me, Ryan," Z commanded.

"I love you," Ryan told him softly. "So much."

Z pressed a quick kiss to Ryan's lips, then released him, turning so that he could look down at the pie again.

"I have to admit, it looks good," Z said. "I'm impressed, Ryan Trexler. If I were a bettin' man, I wouldn't have put odds on you spending an afternoon in the kitchen."

Ryan laughed, then elbowed Z gently. "Thanks."

"But it looks like you forgot one thing."

Oh, shit. Ryan stared down at the recipe on the iPad, mentally ticking off everything on the list. Hell, most of it was still on the counter, a huge mess that Ryan would have to clean up now that it was finished. From what he could tell, he hadn't missed a single ingredient.

Looking back at Z, Ryan raised his eyebrows in question, waiting.

Z's smile was blinding, and it sent a ribbon of heat curling through him, although he still didn't know what he'd missed.

Rather than ask, Ryan watched as Z made his way to the refrigerator. The door obscured his view of what Z was looking for, and when Z turned back to him, whatever he'd gotten was hidden behind his back.

"What did I miss?" he finally forced out, desperate to know, hating that he could've possibly screwed this up.

Z came around to stand behind Ryan, his chest to Ryan's back, his arms sliding around him. Ryan stared down at the counter as a bottle of chocolate syrup appeared in front of him. Cradled in between Z's massive arms, Ryan watched as Z popped the cap off, then tilted the bottle of chocolate syrup over the top of the pie.

"My dad always added just a little chocolate syrup after it was done," Z said, his voice low and rough against Ryan's ear.

"It's not in the recipe," Ryan told him, watching the way Z squeezed the bottle, adding only a little to the top of the pie.

"My dad always told me that you can use someone else's recipe, but you should always add a little something of your own to make it yours."

Great. Ryan wouldn't have thought to do anything like that. What could he possibly add?

"Turn around," Z whispered, a firm but soft command right against Ryan's ear.

Ryan managed to turn around to face Z, trapped between Z's big body and the counter. When he looked up into Z's eyes, he noticed a blaze of heat in the dark brown depths. He was so enthralled he didn't even notice what Z was doing until he placed his finger on Ryan's lip.

"Suck," Z ordered.

Ryan instantly wrapped his lips around Z's finger, sucking it into his mouth and licking the chocolate sauce from the tip.

Z's eyes flared again as he pulled his finger from Ryan's mouth.

"Unbutton your jeans," Z told him.

Ryan did as instructed, slowly unbuttoning his jeans while keeping his eyes locked on Z's face.

"Push 'em down."

Again, Ryan didn't argue, forcing his jeans down.

"Boxers, too."

Ryan forced his boxers down, freeing his now rock-hard cock to the cool air of the kitchen.

Right before him, Z lowered himself to his knees as they continued to stare back at one another. Z never broke eye contact, even when he took Ryan's cock in his hand, drawing a hiss from him. Ryan tried to maintain some semblance of control, but it shattered when Z drizzled chocolate syrup over the head of Ryan's dick.

He dropped his eyes, watching as Z's tongue darted out to lick the chocolate from him.

"Fuck," he mumbled, reaching instinctively to clutch Z's head.

"Mmm." Z proceeded to clean Ryan's dick with his lips and tongue before adding more chocolate.

By the time Z set the bottle down on the counter and drew Ryan into his mouth completely, Ryan was shaking from arousal. Another hiss escaped him as the warmth of Z's mouth replaced the cold from the chocolate.

Eyes focused and intent, Ryan watched as Z sucked him. Slow and easy, not rushing, not trying to send Ryan into orbit just yet. It was exquisite torture.

And he loved every second of it.

Z SUCKED AND LICKED, DRAWING MOANS FROM RT as he stood in the kitchen, completely at Z's mercy. The man continued to surprise him with everything he did.

Z still had a hard time grasping the fact that RT had somehow found that recipe and made the pecan pie for him. In all the time Z had known him and certainly since they'd gotten together, RT had never cooked anything. Well, nothing more than heating something in the microwave.

But this…

It made him love RT all the more.

Stroking RT's cock, Z sat back on his haunches, looking up at him. "I think you need a shower."

RT's smile was slow and seductive, creeping across his face as his eyes glittered with heat. "Won't argue with you there."

Z got to his feet, then took RT's hand, leading him back to their bedroom and right for the shower. He wanted to feel RT lodged deep inside him, and in order for that to happen, he had to make sure he got all the chocolate off. Though he was fairly certain he'd already done that, he still had a few ideas that would move things along.

RT took care of turning on the water while Z shed his clothes with lightning speed. Instead of getting into the shower, he moved toward RT and helped him out of his clothes, keeping their mouths fused while he did, lingering a little longer than necessary because he couldn't seem to get enough of this man.

At some point, RT must've taken the reins, because he led Z into the shower, closing the door behind them, their tongues still languidly sliding against one another, hands caressing smooth, warm skin covering hard muscle.

When RT leaned his head back and closed his eyes to let the water rain down on him, Z reached for the soap and proceeded to clean RT. Every. Single. Inch. He didn't stop until RT was moaning and arching into his hand as he jacked him slowly, using his free hand to glide the soap over his skin.

Z stood up straight, eye level with RT once again. "Need to feel you."

More heat glittered in RT's ice-blue gaze, and Z knew he was nearing the breaking point.

"Turn around," RT commanded, the words terse, rough with arousal.

Doing as he was told, Z turned around and faced the wall, planting his palms flat against the smooth tile. He sucked in a breath when RT's lips glided across his shoulder, his hands caressing Z's hips. When Z tried to push his hips back to meet RT, those strong hands stilled him, then disappeared entirely.

For the next few minutes, RT returned the favor, tormenting Z with his soapy hands, gliding them over his entire body, from his neck all the way down to his toes and then back up.

Z was mindless, numb from the overwhelming sensation, an endless stream of moans and groans as he rested his head against his arm, closing his eyes and enjoying every touch. He must've been drifting, pulled back to the moment when the head of RT's cock slid between his ass cheeks.

Giving him better access, Z spread his legs, leaning forward, offering himself up to this man he loved more than life itself.

"Ahh, yes," RT muttered as he breached Z's hole, pushing in slowly.

Z forced himself to relax, helped immensely by the way RT's hands continued to glide up and down his back, caressing him sweetly as he slowly penetrated him.

"So good, Z," RT said. "Love you."

Everything about the moment was perfect. Then again, everything about every moment he spent with RT was. Z loved him more than he would ever be able to express, and times like this, when it was just the two of them... Nothing could be better.

RT's hands slid upward, fingers curling over Z's shoulders as he pushed in to the hilt.

"Like that?"

Z nodded, eyes still closed as the sensations tore through him. "So much."

For endless minutes, they remained like that, RT pressing kisses across his back, the warm water raining down on them while RT gently rocked his hips, deep and slow.

"Need more," Z pleaded, loving the way RT's cock filled him, every so often hitting that perfect spot deep inside that sent electrical currents of pleasure pulsing through him.

"Hard?" RT asked, punctuating the question by thrusting forward.

"Oh, fuck, yes," Z muttered, bracing his hands on the wall.

RT withdrew slowly.

"Deep?"

Z growled when RT drove in deep.

"Fast?" RT bit out.

"Mmm-hmm." Z braced himself. "Aw, fuck. God, yes."

RT slammed into him. Harder, deeper, faster.

Z was nothing but sensation. He felt the hard bite of RT's fingertips against his skin, the glorious thickness of RT's cock tunneling in and out of him, stroking every nerve ending. Reaching down with one hand, Z gripped his cock hard, stroking in time with every wonderfully brutal thrust.

"Z." The sound of skin slapping skin echoed in the small space. "Fuck, Z. So good."

RT leaned forward, pressing one hand against Z's, which was still planted firmly on the wall. Z shifted, linking their fingers as RT continued to impale him over and over while Z stroked himself, his balls tightening as his orgasm neared.

"Gonna … come … Z. Fuck, baby."

Z was right there with him, his breath rushing in and out of his lungs as he succumbed to the pleasure, his cock pulsing in his hand.

A roar split the air, and Z wasn't sure if it was him or RT or both of them. His release slammed into him, driving the air from his lungs, muscles contracting as he came at the same time RT stopped pumping his hips, jerking against Z's ass as he filled him.

Z grabbed RT's arm as it came around his chest, holding him tight as RT leaned against him, both of them working to catch their breath. Z finally managed to force himself to stand upright, turning to face RT. Cupping his face, Z stared into the most beautiful face.

"I love you," he whispered, leaning in and kissing RT's mouth.

"Love you, too." RT cleared his throat and pulled back, looking at Z. "So does that count?"

"As…?" Z tried to process the question.

"As adding our own touch."

Z grinned, pulling RT closer and kissing him again. "It does. Definitely."

God, he loved this man.

CHAPTER
6

THE FOLLOWING AFTERNOON, RYAN WAS SITTING ON the couch, flipping through channels, while Z was working in the kitchen. He could hear the sounds of pots and pans, mixers, and yes, sometimes a few expletives, but he remained where he was, not wanting to interrupt.

Though Ryan's pecan pie had turned out good—they'd had some last night before they'd gone to bed—Z said he had to make several more to feed all the people who would be at Ryan's parents' house for Christmas dinner tomorrow night. Turned out that several more meant three of each, so Ryan had done his best to stay out of the way.

Now, as he stared at the gifts beneath the tree, he had the sudden urge to interrupt Z. To take his hand, lead him to the couch, sit him down, and give him the gift he'd bought.

He'd spent weeks trying to come up with the best idea for a gift, and he'd never figured it out. Not until he'd talked to Buddy, listened to the story that had changed Ryan's perspective on everything. He'd never been much on gift giving. For his family, it was easy. Buy them a gift card to their favorite place and let them figure out what they want. Not that Z had allowed him to do that this year, but it hadn't failed him before.

With Z, it wasn't that easy. He couldn't simply buy a gift card or run out to the closest store and grab just anything off the shelf. He wanted it to be special, something that Z would remember for years to come.

And that was when the idea had hit him.

Z walked into the room, pulling Ryan out of his thoughts when he flopped onto the couch beside him.

"Finally. The last of the pies are in the oven."

Ryan smiled. "You sure you'll have enough?"

Z turned his head slowly, glaring back at Ryan and making him laugh.

"Kidding. You'll have more than enough, I promise."

"I hope so." Z closed his eyes for a minute, and Ryan took the opportunity to watch him.

He did that from time to time. He loved watching Z. Whether Z was at work, at the gym, at the grocery store, in the shower, beneath Ryan while he slowly buried himself deep inside of Z, or even when he was asleep, one of Ryan's favorite pastimes was to watch him. He was beyond beautiful in every way. Inside and out.

"So when're you gonna open my present?" Z asked, opening one eye and peering over at Ryan.

"When you open mine."

Ryan could practically feel the warmth of Z's gaze as it raked over his face, Z seemingly studying him. Before he could ask what Z was thinking, the giant man was up off the couch and running to the tree. He dug out something from the back and returned to the couch, placing the brightly wrapped gift in front of him.

"Mine first," Z said with the enthusiasm of a kid on Christmas morning.

"Fine," he huffed, grinning as he lifted the huge box.

It was heavy. Heavier than he would've expected.

Glancing over at Z momentarily, Ryan peeled the paper back, revealing a plain brown cardboard box that had been taped shut. Within seconds, Ryan had the tape off and the box open. His heart was pounding as he lifted the helmet out of the box, staring wide-eyed at it.

"You didn't," he whispered, taking in the intricate air-brushing detail.

"I did," Z confirmed. "Myself."

Ryan's eyes widened, his gaze slamming into Z's face. "You did this?"

Z nodded, his cheeks turning pink with embarrassment. "I had some help, and it took me a while to get the airbrush thing down, but after weeks of practice…"

Ryan knew that Z was artistic. It was something he'd learned about him after they'd gotten married. There was so much depth to the man, Ryan figured they could spend a lifetime together, and Z would still be surprising him with all that he was capable of.

The helmet matched Ryan's bike, but it was the airbrushing that stole his breath. Ghost flames and skulls covered every inch. It was incredible. Not over the top, but Z would know that wasn't what Ryan wanted.

As Ryan lifted it to get a better look, something fell out.

It was a card.

Glancing at Z again, he retrieved the envelope, opened it, and read the card. It was cheesy, making him laugh, and the smile that lit up Z's face told Ryan that Z had gotten the reaction he'd wanted.

"What's this?" Ryan asked, taking another smaller envelope out of the card.

"Open it."

Ryan did. It was a sheet of paper. He unfolded it and scanned the page, smiling as excitement bloomed inside him. "You got me a year of racing?"

"Us," Z clarified.

They'd been talking about racing their bikes on a professional track because it was something they longed to do, but with so much going on, it was always one of those things they never got around to.

"This way, I've already paid, so we have to take the time."

Ryan didn't know what to say.

"Can I open mine now?" Z asked, making Ryan laugh.

Ryan reached over to the side table and retrieved the gift he'd placed there earlier. He handed it to Z and held his breath.

Z watched RT closely, noticing the shuttered look. It would be just like RT to be worried that Z wouldn't like the gift. It didn't matter what it was—hell, it could be a lopsided hand-knit scarf for all he cared—he would love it.

After tearing off the paper—being as messy as he possibly could—Z glanced down at the plain white box. He shook it, smiling at RT. It was heavy. Heavier than he'd thought it would be.

Definitely not a coffee maker. Box was too small.

Nor was it a mixer.

Could be silverware.

"Open it," RT grumbled, his hands clasped tightly in his lap as though he was trying to refrain from grabbing the box back from him.

Z grinned, lifted the lid off the box, and peered down at…

A photo album.

But not just any photo album.

This one had a silver cover, with the words *Zachariah Tavoularis and Ryan Trexler* on the front, along with a photo of them from their wedding.

Z looked up at RT to see him staring back, eyes hooded as though he was waiting for the fallout.

"It's beautiful," Z told him.

"Open it," RT instructed.

Z lifted the front cover and…

A sob tore from his throat when he saw the picture of his family—him, his mother, father, sister, brother. Z remembered the picture. He'd been a senior in high school, and they'd all gotten together to take a picture at Thanksgiving.

As he flipped through the pages, he saw many more pictures of him and his father, him and Reese, him and his mother and Jensyn. There were cards that Z had given his father on Father's Day, images Z had drawn his father as a child. There were a few recipes that had been snapshot and added to the book, as well as the one for the pecan pie that RT had gotten from Z's brother.

"Where…?" Z couldn't get the question out; he was too choked up.

"Keep going," RT said, moving closer and gripping Z's hand.

Z flipped the pages, smiling when he saw more pictures of him and Trace at Trace's wedding. Some candid shots of him alone, some of his bike, some of him with Buddy, some with all of the Trexlers and the Kogans.

"I sent out an email to people in the office," RT explained, "asking them to send me any photos they had of you. This is what I got back. I also talked to your mom and Reese and Jensyn. They gathered all that they could, and Buddy found a few things in your dad's room."

Z reached over and hugged RT, burying his face in RT's neck, trying to hide the emotion that gripped him.

"I wanted to get you something that you'd remember for a long time. And when Buddy told me the story, I decided I'd get you something that you could remember forever. I hadn't meant to fill it up completely, but that's what happened, so…"

RT was cupping Z's neck gently, holding him close, and Z managed to pull himself together.

Looking up, he met RT's eyes.

"There's something else in the box," RT told him.

Z placed the photo album on the table, then lifted a sheet of tissue paper, revealing another box beneath it. He opened the end and pulled out a picture frame with the words *Tavoularis-Trexler*.

RT leaned over and hit a button on the side, bringing the screen to life. There were more pictures that played on the screen.

"I figured we'd need something that would hold more than that. This way, we can upload them directly."

Z laughed. It was that or cry.

RT had been so worried about what to get him, and somehow he'd figured out the most precious thing he could get.

"I love you, Z," RT said, curling his finger beneath Z's chin. "And I want to make more memories with you."

Z leaned forward, pressing his forehead to RT's. "I love you, too. Thank you."

"So, did I do okay?" RT asked.

Z pulled back and grinned. "You did great. I only have one question…"

RT frowned.

"How do you expect to top this next Christmas?"

RT's eyes narrowed, which made Z chuckle.

"Kidding. You've got all year to think about it, so I'm not at all worried."

RT did not look at all happy about that.

CHAPTER 7

"SMELLS FANTASTIC, MOM," RYAN TOLD HIS MOTHER, hugging her when he and Z arrived at their house shortly after five on Christmas Day.

"Thanks, honey," Emily said, hugging him back. "Where's Z?"

"He's talkin' to Trace." Ryan spared a look into the dining room. "Where's Dad?"

Emily turned to face him, grinning. "He went to pick up Buddy from the nursing home."

Ryan nodded. He was so glad that he'd been able to get Buddy a pass so he could spend Christmas Day with them. Ryan and Z would take him back to the nursing home, but Ryan had wanted it to be a surprise, so he'd worked with his parents to help out.

"They're on the way back. Should be here any minute."

As though they'd heard her, the door to the garage opened, and Bryce stuck his head in. "Is the coast clear?"

Ryan laughed. "Bring him in, Dad."

Bryce nodded, then disappeared.

"Hey, Mrs. T," Z called from behind him, and Ryan turned instantly, forcing Z back into the other room, Ryan's mother laughing from behind them.

"I … uh … need your help," Ryan lied.

"With?" Z asked, looking around.

Ryan had nothing.

Thankfully, Z being Z, he made it dirty, which gave Ryan a brief opportunity to distract him. Or perhaps the other way around.

Z leaned in close to Ryan's ear. "I can lend a hand. Just say the word."

A bolt of heat soared through him, and Ryan had to remember where they were. It would not be cool to be caught making out with Z at his parents' house. People were streaming in now, which meant they would definitely be noticed if Ryan gave in.

So, instead, he placed his palms on Z's thick chest and forced him back a step. "Maybe later."

Z's eyes lit up and Ryan realized he shouldn't have said that. Z was the eternal optimist. He saw the positive in everything. Which wasn't necessarily a bad thing.

"Promise?" Z asked, placing his hands over Ryan's, still planted on Z's chest.

Ryan stared back at Z.

"Don't think I won't sneak you off and ravage you, Ryan Trexler. It's what I do best. And when you say stuff like that…"

"I know." Ryan chuckled. "You hear sex."

"That, I def—"

Before Z could finish the sentence, a voice called from the kitchen.

"Where're my boys?"

Z instantly stopped, eyes locking with Ryan's. "Is that…?"

Ryan smiled. "Yes, it is. Now go say hello."

Z didn't move and neither did Ryan. They stood there, locked in one another's gazes for a moment. Ryan waited to hear what Z would say, hoped he was as happy as Buddy was to be there.

"Ryan Trexler." Z lowered his voice to barely a whisper. "I'm not sure how you do it, but you make me love you more and more every single day."

Ryan's heart swelled in his chest. That had been exactly what he'd been hoping for.

"There they are," Buddy called, making his way into the hallway where Ryan and Z stood.

"Buddy." Ryan held out his hand to the older man. "So glad you could make it."

Buddy looked at Ryan. "So, did you pull it off?"

"Looks like it," he said, staring at Z, who seemed at a loss for words.

"Thanks for having me," Buddy told Ryan. "Such an honor to be here."

"Christmas wouldn't be the same without you," Ryan told him. And it was the truth. Buddy was family, plain and simple.

"Yeah," Z confirmed. "What he said."

"Food's ready!" Colby called from the dining room.

"Come on," Ryan urged Z. "Let's go grab a seat."

Z nodded, placing one huge hand gently on Buddy's back, following close behind and taking Ryan's hand in his and pulling him. Before they made it to the dining room, Z stopped abruptly, spinning around to face Ryan.

Looking up at him, he tried to hide his surprise.

"Don't think you're gonna get out of this," Z mumbled softly.

"Out of what?"

Z leaned closer. "I've always wondered what it would be like to have sex with you in your childhood bedroom."

Ryan laughed. "Z, my parents bought this place long after I moved out."

Z considered that for a moment, then added, "We'll pretend," right before he spun on his heel and disappeared.

Ryan covered his laugh with a cough, ignoring the looks that his brothers sent his way.

AFTER DINNER—OF WHICH Z ATE MORE than his fair share—everyone retired to the living room. Emily and Bryce had brought in more seating so that there would be enough. There were a lot of people there, no doubt about it, but they'd had plenty of food left over, which meant Lilah would likely be packing leftovers in to-go containers. Z fully intended to grab some before they left.

And now, as everyone sat in the living room and chatted about dinner, the gifts they'd received, the gifts they'd given, the reactions from the people they loved when they'd opened their presents, Z settled in and watched.

Although he wished his mother and father and his brother and sister were there, this was nice. The Trexlers and the Kogans had become a huge part of his life over the years, having welcomed him into the fold when he'd first come on board over a decade ago.

Not that he'd ever thought he'd have the pleasure of being able to call Emily and Bryce his in-laws. He'd been best friends with Trace for years, been in love (albeit secretly) with RT for quite a while, as well, but still, this was better than he'd expected.

Z looked up when Casper cleared his throat.

"I know y'all are waiting patiently to find out what we're doin'," Casper explained. "And this year, Shelby was the one who got to pick the game."

At that moment, Trace carried in an easel and a giant drawing pad, placing them at the front of the room.

"We're gonna split up into two teams," Shelby explained, grabbing the pen from Trace. "And I've already picked the teams." Turning toward the paper, she began writing the names as she called them out. "RT, Z, Trace, Marissa, Dominic, Conner, Buddy, Lilah, Elizabeth, Casper, Frank, Evan, and Hunter. The other team: Me, Emily, Bryce, Austin, Clay, Kira, Stephanie, TJ, Colby, Tanner, Courtney, and Max."

"What're we playin'?" Austin inquired while Shelby continued to write all the names out, looking around as though it wasn't obvious.

"Christmas carol charades," Shelby announced proudly, capping the pen and placing it on the table. She then grabbed a bucket and proceeded to carry it around, holding it out for people from each team to pick from.

When she came over to him, Z smiled. "You know my team's gonna win this, right? Then you'll have to crown me the king of Christmas."

Shelby laughed, her light gray eyes twinkling. "It's on," she challenged.

Turning to face Conner, Z asked, "You up for this, Daddy-o?"

Conner smiled and Shelby laughed at her father. "I'm not sure my dad even knows a Christmas carol."

Conner growled, grinning at his daughter. "You'd be surprised what I know, kiddo."

Shelby moved on to the other team, allowing them to pick three slips of paper from the bucket. When she was finished, she returned to the side of the room where her group had gathered and Z turned to his.

"Who's gonna go first for us?" he asked, looking at his team.

"We've nominated you for that," RT told him.

Of course they had.

"Smart people. I like it." Z got to his feet and took one of the slips of paper that they'd placed on the end table near them. He studied it closely.

"Okay, Z, your team goes first," Shelby called out. "Remember, no words allowed. And you have two minutes."

Ah, so that would add a bit of a challenge.

Z turned to face his team, then looked at the slip of paper in his hand before crumpling it and shoving it in his pocket.

Standing at the front of the room, Z held out six fingers.

"Six words," someone shouted.

Z held up one finger, then touched his ear.

"Sounds like. First word sounds like," Marissa squealed cheerfully, as though she'd solved the puzzle already.

Z smiled and pointed to his eye.

"I."

He nodded, then pretended to saw something.

"Saw."

He nodded, then pretended to rock a baby.

"Rocking."

"Uh ... cradle."

Z shook his head, repeated the motion.

"Arms."

Z frowned. Were they even thinking about Christmas carols?

When they didn't guess, he cut his hand as though to change. Then he pretended to kiss the air.

"Kiss!" Marissa yelled.

Z nodded.

"I saw kisses," Frank called out.

Z shook his head.

"I saw ... rock ... kiss..." Lilah was working it out.

Z pretended to grab his belly.

"I saw rock and belly," RT said.

Z frowned at his husband. Really?

Z repeated all of the movements in order.

"I ... saw ... rocking ... kissing ... belly."

Conner jumped to his feet. "I Saw Mommy Kissing Santa Claus."

Z clapped his hands. "Yes!"

A chorus of cheers erupted from their side of the room.

Z turned to Shelby and mimicked placing a crown on his head. She laughed at him, as he'd hoped.

RT pulled Z down onto the couch beside him. "I'm not sure I'll get that image outta my head."

Z leaned in and lowered his voice so no one else could hear. "Well, I've got another image I'll gladly put there. It involves my mouth and your—"

RT slammed his hand over Z's mouth, his eyes wide.

Z smirked behind his hand.

"Our turn," Kira announced, standing up and moving to the front of the room.

Z sat back and watched.

Kira held up seven fingers.

"Seven words," her team called out.

Kira nodded, then looked around the room. She ran over to Marissa, placed her hands on Marissa's belly, then ran back and pointed at Elizabeth and Emily.

"Grandma!" someone called out.

Kira laughed, nodded, then moved back to the front of the room.

"Grandma Got Run Over by a Reindeer!"

Well, that was totally not fair.

And now, it was on.

CHAPTER 8

ONCE THE GAME WAS FINISHED AND THE rest of the family was in the kitchen breaking into the desserts, Ryan found himself being led up the stairs by Z.

"Where're we goin'?" he asked Z, not really needing an answer. He already knew.

"We lost," Z said, brooding. "I need to go pout for a little while."

Yes, they'd lost, and Z had had to crown Shelby the queen of Christmas, but he'd done it with a smile. Then, he'd pouted. Or pretended to for Ryan's sake.

Ryan allowed Z to pull him down the hall and into the guest bedroom at the far end.

When they stepped inside, he pretended not to know why they were there, but when Z locked the door behind them, it was pretty obvious.

"This isn't my childhood bedroom," he told Z, laughing when Z pushed him down onto the queen-sized bed.

Z tumbled on top of him, holding himself up. "Close your eyes, we'll pretend."

Unable to resist taunting him, Ryan closed his eyes.

"Ah, yeah," Z mumbled softly. "I like you just like that."

Ryan opened his eyes.

"Nuh-uh. Close them."

Ryan closed his eyes once more.

"This is a fantasy I've had for a long time," Z whispered, his breath fanning over Ryan's mouth. "What it would've been like to sneak into your bedroom, to find you asleep on your bed."

Okay, so this role-playing thing was working for him. Ryan's cock swelled behind his zipper.

"Just like a teenager," Z mumbled, grinding his hips against Ryan's. "Hard and ready for me, huh?"

"Always," Ryan admitted.

Z pressed his lips to Ryan's, the kiss soft and sweet at first, but that didn't last long. The next thing Ryan knew, Z was trailing down his body, his big fingers working open the button and zipper on Ryan's jeans before he yanked them down.

Ryan instantly opened his eyes, watching as Z leaned forward and kissed the head of Ryan's dick, causing him to suck in a breath.

With a glimmer in his dark brown eyes, Z smiled, then took Ryan's cock in his mouth and sucked. Hard.

"Fuck," Ryan hissed.

Z pulled back. "Remember, your entire family is downstairs. You wouldn't want them to hear you, would you?"

Ryan clamped his teeth shut, grunting when Z took him in his mouth once more. The pleasure assaulted him. Warm, soft. Z's lips suctioned around his dick, his tongue circling the head before he hollowed his cheeks and sucked, taking Ryan all the way to his throat.

This was definitely not a good idea. Not because Ryan didn't enjoy Z tormenting him, but it was true, his entire family was downstairs, and more than likely someone would realize they were gone. It wouldn't take much to figure out what they were doing, either.

Obviously Z knew that, because he stopped sucking and crawled back over Ryan, kissing him gently.

"Turn over, baby," Z urged. "This is my fantasy, remember? So that means I get to take your ass right here in your old bedroom."

"It's not—"

Z shook his head as he placed his hand over Ryan's mouth, effectively shutting him up.

"My fantasy. Now turn over."

The deep rumble of Z's command had Ryan's dick twitching. He managed to roll over onto his stomach while Z worked his jeans down his legs.

"Feet on the floor."

Ryan scooted down, allowing his feet to drop to the floor, his jeans now around his ankles. He felt entirely too exposed, but his cock was throbbing, desperate for what Z would give him.

Then Z was leaning over him, a lubed finger sinking into Ryan's ass, slowly, gently.

"Mm. Gonna love feeling you wrapped around my dick," Z muttered softly.

Yeah, Ryan had a feeling he was going to love it, too.

If Z would get on with it.

Ryan bucked his hips back, trying to take Z's finger deeper. Z's rough chuckle told him he knew what he was doing. Another finger joined the first, and Ryan was grateful that Z had thought ahead for this.

"Ready for me, baby?" Z rumbled against Ryan's ear.

"Fuck yes," he groaned, gripping the comforter in his hands as he bent over the bed.

Z shifted off of him, then grabbed Ryan's hip. Ryan heard the sound of Z's zipper, then the blunt head of Z's cock pushed against his ass, and Ryan fought the urge to groan, biting his lip instead while Z worked inside him, filling him.

Ryan knew they had to be a sight. With their jeans around their ankles, their movements were limited, but Z was lying atop Ryan, his cock pumping deep inside him while Ryan tried to move, tried to increase the friction, to give Z a better angle, but to no avail. Not only was Z bigger, weighing nearly fifty pounds more than Ryan, the position kept him incapacitated, forced to take just what Z wanted him to have.

"You like me filling you?" Z asked, his voice so low it was hard for Ryan to hear him.

Ryan nodded.

"I would've snuck in your room every damn night for this," Z said, nipping Ryan's ear. "I would've waited until you turned off your lights to go to sleep, then I would've crawled up into your bed."

Z pushed his hips forward, retreating slowly. It was a devastatingly slow grind, but it was working for Ryan. As was Z's outline of events.

"I would've slipped beneath the blankets," Z groaned against Ryan's ear. "Spread your cheeks and fucked you with my tongue, eating your ass until you were begging for more."

Ryan hissed, his dick pulsing. "Gonna make me come, Z."

"That's the plan, baby."

Ryan turned his head toward Z. "Then fuck me. Hard."

"That what you want?" Z asked, his voice rough, as though he was holding back.

"Yeah. Fuck me hard. Make me feel it."

Z's weight lifted off him, and Ryan was jerked back when Z grabbed his hips. He bit back a groan when Z slammed into him, impaling him on his cock, making him whimper as the pleasure pummeled him.

And just as he'd asked, Z pounded him, fucking him hard, fast, deep. So fucking deep.

It took everything in him to keep from groaning, to keep from begging, but he managed, biting his lip until he tasted blood while Z fucked him so perfectly.

"Ryan… Baby … gonna come."

When Ryan felt Z's dick pulse in his ass, he let himself go, coming without ever touching himself while Z filled his ass.

And that was probably the best Christmas present Ryan could ever ask for.

Z WASN'T SURE HOW HE WAS GOING to be able to walk after that. Although he'd been the one to come up with the idea, the real thing had been far more intense than he'd thought it would be. And yeah, he hadn't been lying when he'd said he'd fantasized about sneaking into RT's bedroom, fucking him like that.

It had been phenomenal, only now he wanted more, and he knew he couldn't indulge, because yes, there was family downstairs, and they would likely be looking for them soon.

A knock sounded on the door, and Z jumped back, stumbling and falling on his ass because his jeans were still around his ankles.

"Yeah?" RT called out, glaring down at Z as he fumbled to pull up his jeans.

"What the hell are y'all doin' in there?"

Trace.

Z smiled up at RT.

"Be down in a minute," Z called out, not caring if his best friend realized Z and RT were in there together. Knowing Trace, he had been planning to sneak Marissa up there, anyway. Although unlike RT, Marissa's old bedroom was still intact, so they could've used it. Which meant Trace was just trying to fuck with them.

As though to prove him right, Trace's deep rumbling laugh echoed through the door.

RT scowled down at him as he made his way to the adjoining bathroom. Z held up his hand, hoping RT would help him up, but he got no assistance, which made him laugh.

He managed to get to his feet, pulled his jeans up, and then joined RT in the bathroom to clean up. A few minutes later, after fixing his clothes and cleaning the mess they'd made on the comforter, Z stood in the bathroom doorway and watched RT pull himself together.

God, the man was so fucking beautiful. Z could've simply stood there and stared at him. And to know that RT belonged to him… There was nothing in the world that was better than that feeling.

Before RT could sneak back out, Z pinned him to the wall, kissing him slow and deep.

"I hope you're up for round two when I get you home," Z told RT, cupping his face and staring into those intense crystal-blue eyes.

"I'm always up for round two," RT said roughly.

Z nodded toward the bed.

"At home, Z. I'm always up for round two *at home.*"

"Spoilsport," Z muttered, kissing RT hard once more and stepping back.

RT laughed, which was a damn good sign.

"Come on, let's go have dessert," RT said, reaching for Z's hand.

"Mmm, dessert."

"Is your mind always in the gutter?" RT asked as they made their way through the guest bedroom.

"Always," he assured his husband. "Double time when it comes to you."

RT stopped before he opened the door, his eyes going to the bed.

Z looked over, then grinned before releasing RT's hand and going to fix the comforter. "I assume Lilah will be doin' laundry this week?"

RT looked up at him. "God, I hope so."

Laughing, Z allowed RT to lead him back downstairs, where they found everyone sitting in the living room, having dessert and chatting it up. After filling a plate full of food, knowing he would pay for this later and have to spend two hours a day in the gym just to lose the ten pounds he'd likely gained since Thanksgiving, Z took a seat beside Hunter.

"What's up? Why the long face? Oh, wait … that's your normal look. Sorry, man."

Hunter discreetly gave Z the finger.

"How're things goin'?" Z inquired, chuckling.

"Good."

Didn't sound good.

Z noticed Hunter's gaze strayed over to Max Adorite, Hunter's brother-in-law.

"You heard from Dani lately?" Flinching as though Hunter was going to punch him, Z waited for a response.

He didn't get one. Well, not verbally, anyway. He got the Kogan death glare, the one that made a normal man's balls shrivel up inside him.

Not Z. He'd learned to deal with the Kogan death glare. Hunter and Conner had perfected that look over the years.

"So, what's the plan for New Year's?" Z inquired, figuring he'd given Hunter enough shit.

Hunter shrugged. "Don't know yet. Y'all?"

"We're thinkin' about checkin' out that club."

Hunter looked over his shoulder at Z. "Club?"

"Yeah," Z lowered his voice. "That sex club."

"That place Dylan and Alex were talkin' about?" Hunter inquired.

It was no secret that Sniper 1 Security was currently in talks with a small security company, CISS, looking to acquire them after one of the owners, Alex McDermott, had approached them a few weeks back. Turned out the company was having some financial hardships due to a string of events that hadn't gone their way. RT and Conner were seriously looking to acquire them, but had been in negotiations for weeks regarding how to handle it.

That wasn't the exciting part, though. At least not for Z. During their negotiations, Z had had the pleasure of meeting Alex, getting to know him on a more personal level. Turned out that Alex and his business partner, Dylan Thomas, had been silent partners in a previous club—a fetish club—that had closed down in recent years. They'd mentioned a new club—Devotion—and had extended an invite for their big New Year's bash.

Z was seriously trying to convince RT to go.

Hunter shook his head. "The day you get RT to go to a place like that, I'll kiss your fucking feet."

Z grinned. "You know how much I like a good dare."

Hunter chuckled. "I'd leave that place to the big boys, Z."

It was Z's turn to laugh.

Oh, he was a big boy, all right. No doubt about that.

AFTER THEY'D HAD DESSERT AND SPENT A couple of hours chatting with everyone, Ryan corralled Buddy and Z so they could get Buddy back to the nursing home before they sent out a search party.

The drive back was full of conversation and laughter, Buddy rehashing how much he'd enjoyed the evening. Ryan had remained relatively quiet, enjoying listening to Z talk in that animated way that Ryan loved.

It had been a good day.

And Ryan still had another surprise in store for Z tomorrow, one that he was looking forward to. Unbeknownst to Z, Ryan had managed to get Z's mother, brother, and sister to come to town for the holiday, agreeing to have lunch at their house to surprise Z. It hadn't been easy, due to everyone's schedule, but they'd managed to work it out.

Ryan was looking forward to surprising Z. He was also looking forward to round two tonight once they finally got home.

"Thanks for inviting me," Buddy told Ryan when they finally arrived back at the nursing home a few minutes later. "That was the best Christmas I've had in a long time."

"We're glad you could make it," Ryan told him. "And like my father said, you have a standing invite from here on out."

Buddy smiled, then patted Ryan on the back. "That means everything to me. Almost as much as giving you away"—Buddy looked at Z—"on your wedding day."

Z grinned, then placed a hand on Buddy's back, following him as he moved toward the doors that led to his wing of the home.

"Now, go tell your ol' man good night, then you boys go on home," Buddy told them when the electronic doors opened. "I'll be fine. I'm gonna go have a chat with Thomas, let him know all that happened tonight."

Ryan watched Z, noticed the way his eyes turned glassy for a brief moment, the emotion welling up there as it usually did. Ryan took Z's hand in his. "Let's go say good night to your father," Ryan told Z. "Then we'll go home."

Z nodded and allowed Buddy and Ryan to lead him to his father's room.

An hour later, Ryan stepped inside their house, but before the door closed behind him, he found himself plastered against the wall, trapped by Z's big body.

"Do you know how much I want you right now?" Z asked.

"You already had me once today," Ryan reminded him, sliding his hands beneath Z's jacket and pulling him close.

"Not enough," Z mumbled, pressing his lips to Ryan's. "Never enough."

Ryan moaned against him, allowing his tongue to slowly slide into Z's mouth, keeping the kiss gentle. It would be too easy to let things get out of control quickly. And since they always did, Ryan enjoyed these moments when he could leisurely explore Z, loving the deep moans and groans that rumbled in his chest.

"I love you," Ryan whispered against Z's mouth. "So much."

"Love you, too," Z whispered back, his hand sliding between their bodies and reaching for the button on Ryan's jeans.

Ryan grabbed Z's wrist. "Hold that thought," he mumbled against Z's lips.

Z pulled back, peering down at him.

Ryan took Z's hand and sidestepped him, then pulled him toward the kitchen. "I've got one last surprise for you."

"Ryan, you already got me the—"

Ryan silenced him with a hand over his mouth, then pulled him into the kitchen and took a step back, watching Z's reaction.

"What the hell is all this?"

Ryan laughed at Z's bewildered expression, watching as Z looked around the kitchen, taking note of all of the wrapped gifts sitting on the counter.

"You didn't think I picked up on your hints, did you?" Ryan asked, leaning against the wall.

Z glanced over at him, then turned away again, walking over to the counter.

Ryan, with Shelby's help, had wrapped all of the items and placed them where they belonged in the kitchen.

Z touched one of the wrapped items. "Let me guess, a Keurig coffee maker."

Ryan nodded.

"And a set of measuring cups," Z said, turning to the other items on the island.

Z looked over at Ryan. Ryan nodded again.

"Oven mitts?"

Ryan smiled.

"Why did you do this?" Z asked, still clearly confused.

Ryan moved closer and wrapped his arm around Z, pulling him in. "I was too worried that I wouldn't find the perfect gift, so I ordered all that stuff you circled in that ad. I thought maybe you could help me make lunch tomorrow."

Z's eyebrows lowered. "Lunch?"

Ryan nodded. "Just a small get-together. Trace, Marissa. Nothing big."

Truth was, Trace and Marissa weren't coming, but Z didn't need to know that. It provided Ryan with a good cover, so he went with it.

"Lunch. Tomorrow." Z looked around the kitchen again. "But I didn't get you anything else."

Ryan smiled up at Z. "And that's not the point. You're the only gift I need. The best one I could ever ask for."

A smile formed on Z's mouth and Ryan knew what was coming. Something dirty and salacious, and yes, that was another reason he loved Z so damn much.

"Well, I've got an idea," Z whispered, jerking Ryan to him. "And it involves you naked."

"I like where this is going," Ryan told him. Definitely liked where this was going. "Mind if I shower first?"

"As long as I can shower with you."

"Thought you'd never ask."

Z DIDN'T LINGER IN THE SHOWER WITH RT. He teased him briefly, washed them both, and then got out, tossing a towel to RT before slipping into the bedroom.

"Don't come out until I tell you," Z instructed, smiling when RT huffed.

Moving with purpose, Z snatched the box he kept hidden in the closet, retrieved the few items he needed, then set up the bedroom, lighting a few candles along the way. When he was finished, he took a step back and surveyed the room before telling RT he could come out.

RT walked out, naked as the day he was born, and Z took a minute to look at him. Smooth skin over sleek muscle. Damn, the man made him hard.

"Sit," Z ordered, pointing toward the chair in the corner.

RT looked at the bed, then over to the chair.

"No bed tonight," he told RT. "Gotta mix it up a little."

RT smiled, though Z could tell he was trying to keep from doing so. He moved slowly across the room, then lowered himself into the extra-wide, oversized upholstered chair RT sometimes used to read.

Once RT was settled, Z moved around behind him.

"What're you doin'?" RT asked when Z took one of his hands and pulled it over the arm of the chair, securing it to the Velcro tie that he'd looped under the chair.

Z didn't answer him, simply moved to his other side and secured that hand, too, ensuring RT couldn't move his arms.

"Blindfold or no blindfold?" Z asked, holding one in his hand just in case.

RT shook his head. "Wanna watch what you do to me."

Z was okay with that. He loved when RT watched him, loved seeing the expressions flitter across his face.

"Spread your legs," Z instructed, then knelt in front of the chair when RT pushed his knees apart.

135

Z started by kissing the inside of RT's thigh, slowly working his way up, keeping his eyes trained on RT's face as he licked and kissed him. When Z made it to his cock, RT relaxed in the chair, his focus between his legs.

Swirling his tongue around the head of RT's dick, he closed his eyes and hummed his pleasure.

RT grunted, his hips bucking slightly, but Z pressed down on his thighs, holding him in place while he laved him, keeping a slow, steady pace. He didn't want to rush. He wanted to savor every second.

"You taste good," Z told RT, sucking on the engorged head, teasing the hole with his tongue. Instead of taking RT in his mouth, Z placed kisses along the underside, moving downward. He briefly licked RT's balls, long enough to have RT's body going rigid.

"Z," RT hissed.

Z smiled, then resumed his feast, licking, sucking, tasting.

While he continued to play, Z retrieved the lube he'd stashed under the chair, then squirted a generous amount in his palm before lubing RT, stroking him slowly, leisurely while he sat at RT's feet and watched.

"Good?" Z asked, teasing RT more.

"So good," RT said through clenched teeth, his eyes darting from between his legs where Z was jacking him, up to Z's face, and then back down again.

Releasing RT from his grasp, Z got to his feet and took his own cock in his fist, stroking slowly and watching as RT's eyes glazed over. Z reached for RT's head, sliding his fingers through the wet, blond strands and pulling RT forward. He grazed the sensitive head of his dick across RT's lips.

"Open for me," he ordered.

When RT did, Z shifted his hips forward, pulling RT's head toward him and sliding past those smooth, warm lips.

"Suck me, Ryan."

Since RT couldn't use his hands, Z had complete control, and he used it to his advantage, driving his dick into RT's mouth slow and easy, forcing himself deep while he watched RT's face.

"I could watch you do this all day," Z told him. It was true.

For several more minutes, Z enjoyed the pleasure of RT's mouth, but when it became too much, he pulled back, not ready to come just yet. He released RT's head, then applied more lube to his hand, this time working his dick until he was slippery.

He had to get creative with his next plan, because the chair was low, and Z's legs were long, but he managed to work a couple of pillows beneath RT before he planted one knee on the chair, then grabbed RT's legs and worked his dick inside him, watching RT's face flush as Z fucked him slow and easy.

"Never tire of this, either," Z groaned. "So fucking tight."

RT growled, and it was obvious he was trying to control things, but being restrained, he was at Z's mercy. Just the way Z wanted him.

"Don't you dare come," Z warned RT.

RT narrowed his eyes at Z, a clear warning of his own, which made Z's balls draw up against his body. He was going to come and he was going to come soon.

But not yet.

Z pulled out of RT after long minutes, then crawled into the chair, straddling RT's legs. Thank God the chair was big or there was no way the two of them would ever fit on it, but that had been one of the reasons Z had picked this particular one. So he could do this.

As he sat astride RT, he reached behind him, gripped RT's thick cock, and guided it to his entrance.

"Fuck," RT growled when Z lowered himself onto him, taking RT inside him with ease.

"Ah, yeah." Z continued to watch RT. "You like when I ride your dick, don't you?"

RT groaned, his body tense, his hands pulling at the restraints.

"Need more?" Z asked, smiling at RT.

"You know I do," he ground out.

Z gave RT just what he needed, impaling himself on RT's cock, riding him hard and fast until they were both breathing hard. Z fisted his cock, stroking in time with the movement of his hips as he lifted and lowered himself on RT.

"You ready to come for me?" Z asked.

RT's ice-blue gaze lifted to meet Z's and he nodded.

"Come for me, baby. Come deep in my ass."

Z didn't slow, his thighs screaming from exertion as he continued to ride RT until Z saw the moment RT lost that hard-won control he was so often keeping a firm grip on. It was in these moments that Z felt like the king of the world, capable of robbing RT of that control, sending him over even if RT was the one fucking him into oblivion.

"Fuck... Z... Ah ... damn." RT's hips bucked and then stilled, his dick pulsing in Z's ass.

That triggered Z's release, and he gripped his cock tightly, shooting across RT's chest, which earned him another thrust from RT as he groaned again.

"Merry Christmas," Z whispered, leaning forward and kissing RT softly.

"Merry Christmas," RT said with a sigh, relaxing into the cushion and closing his eyes.

Best damn Christmas ever.

CHAPTER 10

The following morning, Ryan woke in an empty bed. He could smell food, which meant Z was already up, likely playing with his new toys in the kitchen.

The thought made Ryan smile.

Last night, after Z had rocked his fucking world, tying him to the chair, then fucking him like that… The thought made Ryan's dick hard instantly. It had been incredible. But curling up with Z, holding him while they drifted off, that had been beyond description.

Every minute he spent with Z reminded him of all the time he'd lost with the man. All the hell he'd put them both through, and he was forever grateful that Z had forgiven him for all he'd done. As far as he was concerned, he really was the luckiest man on the planet.

Turning his head to the side, Ryan looked at the clock, then bolted upright in the bed.

It was already eleven o'clock. How in the hell had he slept that late?

Jumping out of bed, he rushed to the shower, quickly soaped up and rinsed off, then brushed his teeth and got dressed. He did all of that before he checked his phone.

He'd purposely put it on silent last night, not wanting to ruin the surprise for Z if Reese or Jensyn texted him. And now, as he peered at the screen, he saw that they had.

They were leaving Cindy's house and heading their way. Based on the time he'd received the text, they should be there any minute.

"Shit."

Doing his best to appear calm, Ryan came out of the bedroom, forcing himself to move slowly. He'd been right, Z was in the kitchen, cooking something. All of the gifts that had still been wrapped last night had been unwrapped and placed in the spots Z wanted them.

"Mornin'," Z greeted, moving toward him and pulling Ryan in for a kiss.

Ryan was breathing hard by the time Z released him. "What was that for?"

"Can't a man simply kiss his husband because he wants to?"

"He could," Ryan said slowly. "But he usually doesn't."

Z grinned, placing his hands on his hips. "Ryan Jacob Trexler, I know what you're up to."

"You do?" Ryan was tempted to look around to see if he'd missed something. Or someone. But he didn't. Somehow, he managed to face off with Z.

"You forget who you're dealin' with," Z said. "I'm an elite security advisor. I can figure shit out."

"You can?" Ryan was a little lost. How the hell had Z figured it out? Granted, Z wasn't wrong. He was one of the best that Sniper 1 Security employed, but Ryan had thought he'd managed to keep it a secret.

"Yep."

Ryan waited for Z to elaborate, but he didn't.

Then the doorbell rang and Z's eyes widened. Ryan watched as he walked across the living room, saying, "I'm gonna be an uncle, I'm gonna be an— Mom! What are you doing here?"

Okay, that was not the sound of a man who'd figured anything out. Ryan released his breath and sagged against the wall as he watched Z pick up his mother, hugging her as he spun her around.

Z set Cindy on her feet and smiled down at her. "I thought—"

"You thought what, big brother?" Jensyn asked, stepping into the doorway before Z could close the door.

This was one of those moments, one of those memories. Ryan quickly grabbed his phone from his pocket and snapped several pictures of Z and his sister. Then more when Reese stepped inside. For a second, it looked as though Z was going to lose his shit.

Smiling, Ryan made his way to the living room, greeting Cindy, Jensyn, and Reese while keeping his eye on Z.

And Ryan knew then that the best gift to get Z was family. It was all the man needed.

Okay, so this explained the confused look on RT's face when Z had told him he'd figured him out. However, Z wouldn't have guessed that RT had been able to pull this off. He'd been thinking more along the lines of RT buying him the stuff for the kitchen so he could get more creative with meals.

RT had just given him the greatest gift in the world. His family.

Then again, RT had given him everything he needed already. His love, his support, his devotion.

"So, did it work? Were you surprised?" Jensyn asked as Z helped her out of her coat.

"I'd say," Z muttered.

"That man of yours … he's rather persuasive, you know that?" Reese said, handing his coat to Z. "I'm pretty sure he could sell ice to an Eskimo."

About that, Z had no doubt.

While RT led Z's mother into the kitchen, Reese and Jensyn not far behind, Z stood where he was, admiring the man he'd married. A year ago, Z never would've thought he'd be here. Not at this point in his life, happier than he'd ever been, and certainly not with the man of his dreams.

Yet here he was.

And to think, RT had been worried about what to get Z for Christmas. Only somehow, during all that worry, RT had gone above and beyond anything anyone had ever given him.

Ryan Trexler had given him memories to last a lifetime.

And in return, Z would give RT the one thing he would never give anyone else.

His heart.

Red's Jack Daniel's Pecan Pie Recipe

1 cup sugar

¼ cup butter (soft)

3 eggs slightly beaten

¾ cup corn syrup (light or dark Karo – we use light)

¼ tsp salt

2 to 3 tablespoons Jack Daniel's whiskey

1 tsp vanilla

3/4 cup chopped pecans

½ cup chocolate chips

1 9-inch pie shell- put tin foil around the edge of the crust so it doesn't get brown before the pie is done.

Cream sugar and butter, add eggs, syrup, salt, Jack Daniel's, and vanilla. Mix until blended. Spread pecans and chocolate chips in the bottom of the pie shell. Pecans will rise to the top. Pour filling on top of the mixture. Bake at 375°F for at least 40 to 50 minutes.

Note from Nicole:

This recipe was one that my husband's neighbor made every year for Christmas, and brought one to his family when he was growing up. When Steven and I were married in 2002, Red brought one for the judge who performed our ceremony as well as one for us. Every year since, I've been making them for our family and friends, and it has become one of the favorite holiday treats in our house.

Happy New Year

Luke McCoy, Sierra Sellers, and Cole Ackerley

from *Temptation* and *Devotion*

New Year's Eve

7:00 a.m.

Cole Ackerley felt the bed move, which must have been what had woken him up. According to the clock on his nightstand, it was seven o'clock, definitely the latest he'd slept in quite some time. Rolling over, he blinked the sleep from his eyes, smiling when he noticed Sierra and Luke lying beside him, both naked, blankets shoved off.

Technically, Luke was hovering above Sierra, her knees cradling Luke's hips as the big, beautiful man thrust slowly inside her. They looked intense, both seemingly lost in the other's eyes.

Content to simply watch, Cole ignored his dick as it went from firm to rigid within seconds. This was how he liked to be woken up every day, the two people he loved more than life right there at his side, making love because there was nothing else they'd rather be doing.

"God, baby," Luke crooned to Sierra. "You feel so good."

Sierra moaned, her hips rocking as she met Luke's gentle thrusts.

It didn't surprise Cole that Luke was once again buried to the hilt inside the woman they loved. After Sierra had given birth to Liam three months ago, and the doctor had insisted no sex for six weeks after the birth, Luke had once again panicked—something the man was notorious for. Not that Cole hadn't enjoyed the hell out of himself for those six weeks. That was one of the benefits of being in love with two people—there was always a backup. Or so Luke liked to tease.

However, since the day Sierra had been given the green light for sex, Luke had been making up for lost time. As had Cole. Only, it appeared Luke had beaten Cole to it this morning.

"Looks like we've got an audience," Luke mumbled, a smile in his voice.

Cole met Luke's gaze. "Don't stop on my account. I'm content right where I am." And it was true.

"Don't worry," Luke assured him. "I had no intentions of stopping."

Sierra's chuckle was husky and soft. Cole brushed his fingers over her arm when she reached for him.

Allowing his gaze to wander, he watched as Luke's thick cock slid out of Sierra, then slowly back in, the muscles in his back and ass flexing as he did. The man really was perfection in its finest form. At forty-two, Luke was definitely still in his prime.

"Luke," Sierra whispered urgently, her head tipping back as she dug her fingernails into Cole's arm. "Oh, God. I'm … so close."

Luke wasn't deterred, his cock penetrating her deeper with every thrust of his hips. Cole could see the strain on Luke's face, though. He was having a hard time holding back.

"Come for me, baby," Luke encouraged. "Come all over my dick. Let me feel you." His request was followed by a growl, and Cole could imagine what it felt like to have Sierra's sweet pussy clenching around him.

The bed began to rock faster as Luke picked up the tempo, lifting Sierra's leg and holding it against his hip, thrusting slow and deep while Cole continued to watch.

"Luke," Sierra moaned. "Harder."

Luke slammed into her.

"Faster," she pleaded.

Luke's hips picked up speed.

Sierra cried out, her back bowing as she succumbed to her orgasm. Cole's dick twitched, suddenly jealous that he wasn't part of it.

But before he could think about insinuating himself in the middle of it, there was a sound on the baby monitor, and Cole smiled to himself. Looked as though Liam was awake.

Not wanting Luke or Sierra to have to stop the fun they were having, Cole rolled out of bed, grabbed his boxers from the chair, and yanked them on, snatching his T-shirt next. Rubbing his hands over his jaw, then running his palm over his unruly hair, he slipped out of the bedroom, closing the door behind him.

He found Liam awake in his crib, his eyes open, staring up at the mobile dangling above the crib. His gaze slid to Cole, making his heart swell.

"Mornin', little man," he greeted his son after flipping off the baby monitor. "You're up early."

"Me, too, Daddy!" Hannah shrieked as she ran into Liam's bedroom.

Cole laughed as he turned around, snagging Hannah when she threw herself into his arms. Holding his almost-three-year-old daughter so she could peer into the crib with him, Cole grinned at Liam.

"Where's Mommy and Daddy-o?" Hannah asked excitedly.

Cole chuckled. They'd convinced Hannah to call Luke Daddy-o as a joke, but it had stuck, and since it helped to determine which of them she was talking to, they hadn't bothered to change it.

"Sleeping," he told her. "What do you say we get Liam dressed, then get you some breakfast?"

Hannah kicked her legs, forcing Cole to shift to keep from being rendered useless for the next five minutes. Placing her on her feet, he instructed Hannah to get him a diaper for Liam, something to keep her busy.

"All right, buddy," Cole told Liam. "It's time to get this day started."

_7:25 a.m._

"What time's your mom coming over tonight?" Luke asked Sierra after they'd showered and joined Cole and the kids in the kitchen.

While Cole cleaned up Hannah's breakfast, Luke held Liam against his chest, rocking his sweet little boy as they moved around the kitchen. Liam wasn't as small as Hannah had been at that age, but Luke wasn't a small man, either, which, if Liam was lucky, meant he would get Luke's height and not Sierra's. Based on what the doctor said, the newest addition to the McCoy-Ackerley family was well on his way to being above average in height. On top of that, Liam's eyes were losing the dark blue tint and turning green-brown like Luke's, which secretly made him happy.

"She said she'd be here by six," Sierra informed him. "Is that too late?"

Luke shook his head. "I'll need to go to Devotion earlier than that, if possible."

Since it was New Year's Eve and they had a ton of shit to get done, he needed to get down there before the doors opened and people started arriving. As for what he could do before, he didn't know just yet, but he would feel better if he were there.

"I thought I'd ride with Sam, Logan, and Eli," Sierra stated. "That way you and Cole can go make sure everything's set up."

"Works for me," he answered. He didn't want Sierra driving alone, but if Luke's brother was planning to take her, he couldn't argue that point. Luke turned to Cole. "What else needs to be done? Anything we're still waiting on?"

"I oversaw the decorating yesterday," Sierra noted. "And when I left yesterday afternoon, they were finishing up."

"I've got a last-minute liquor order coming this afternoon," Cole explained. "And I think Trent's waiting on a piece of equipment. But other than that, I think we're good."

Luke wasn't sure he wanted an explanation as to what Trent was up to. Trent Ramsey, one of the not-so-silent partners in Devotion, had been hell-bent on ensuring this was the New Year's party of the century. "Should I be worried?"

"About Trent?" Cole laughed. "Always."

"Good point." Luke cradled Liam's head. "But we're definitely good for tonight?"

"We're good," Cole assured him.

They needed to be. Luke had a lot riding on tonight. Not only did this need to be an epic New Year's party because that was what they were known for, but it needed to reflect the club's potential since they were in the process of securing more capital—by way of two more silent investors—for two additional clubs. It was still hard to believe that Devotion had maxed out the allotted memberships and still had an extensive waiting list.

Trent had been the one to propose the idea that they branch out, build another club in the Dallas area. And while they were at it, he'd suggested one in the Austin area, as well. The man never could get over the fact that Alluring Indulgence—the wildly popular resort owned by the Walker brothers—was homing in on their potential business.

Never mind the fact that Luke—as well as Travis Walker—had assured Trent that wasn't the case. Although AI catered to fetishes with their playrooms, it still had an entirely different feel than Devotion. However, Luke understood Trent better than he ever thought he would. In the few years they'd known one another, Trent had gone from being an overly obnoxious playboy actor to a man who had one thing on his mind—business. Well, business and a particular submissive who'd apparently caught his eye.

Speaking of.

"Do you have the guest list for tonight?" Luke asked Sierra.

"I do," she confirmed, toggling screens on her laptop, which was sitting on the bar in front of her.

Luke moved to stand behind her, giving the list a cursory glance.

Travis, Kylie, and Gage Walker-Matthews.

Zane and Vanessa Walker.

Brendon Walker, Cheyenne Montgomery.

Grant Kingsley, Grace Lambert, Lane Miller.

"Who are these people?" Luke asked Sierra, pointing to Grant Kingsley and company.

"Apparently Grace is Cheyenne Montgomery's cousin. Her family owns a ranch down near Austin. Brendon called and asked if we could extend them an invitation."

Fair enough. Luke continued down the list.

Logan, Samantha, Elijah.

Tag and McKenna Murphy.

Mistress Serena plus two.

Xander and Mercedes Boone.
Trent Ramsey.
Shane Gibson.
Clarissa Tinsley.
Kaden Walker.
Keegan Walker.

"I assume Kaden and Keegan are Travis's cousins," Luke mentioned.

"Yep," Sierra confirmed.

Phoenix Pierce, Mia Cantrell, Tarik Marx.

"Is that...?" Luke pointed to Phoenix's name.

"The owner of the Austin Arrows?" Sierra nodded. "The one and only. He called me up a couple of months ago, asking about New Year's. I offered an invitation."

Luke nodded. Made sense.

Trace and Marissa Kogan.
Ryan Trexler and Zachariah Tavoularis.
Conner Kogan plus one.
Maximillian and Courtney Adorite.

And that was the name Luke was looking for. Max Adorite, a potential investor, though Luke was still up in the air regarding that. Considering who Max was, Luke wasn't sure going into business with him was the right thing to do; however, he fully intended to entertain the notion by meeting with Max. He made a mental note to call Max in a couple of hours.

Leyton Matheson, Ashlynn Adorite, Jase Malone.

Luke pointed at Ashlynn's name. "Does her brother know she's coming?"

Sierra chuckled. "He does. She's a big girl. She can handle her own."

Luke didn't doubt that, but he wondered whether or not the club could handle them. It was no secret that Max's family had mob ties. Okay, so technically, by definition, they *were* mafia. Being that Max had personally reached out to Luke, inquiring about potential clubs in the area, Luke had given it some serious consideration. Then, after a lengthy conversation with Cole, they'd opted to see what the man was willing to offer. Hopefully, he'd find out tonight, or in the very near future.

Glancing back at the names, Luke skimmed farther down. It looked as though they had quite the list going. And based on some of the other names, those who would require complete anonymity, Luke knew that security needed to be beefed up tonight.

Which was just another thing on the long list of things to check off before the doors opened at nine o'clock.

It was definitely going to be a long day.

8:19 a.m.

SIERRA KNEW, BASED ON LUKE'S GRIM EXPRESSION, that he was beginning to get worried. The man was incredibly good at that. They'd been planning this party for nearly six months, down to every minute detail, including the complete overhaul of decorations in the main rooms, the updates and minor repairs to the private rooms, the finalization of the guest list, the ordering of food, liquor, and other necessities... They'd done it all, and she was pretty sure they'd thought of everything at this point, but she knew Luke would begin second-guessing everything.

That was the way he was.

Which was why she was grateful that Cole would be taking care of Luke today.

While she spent the day with the kids, then the evening getting ready for the party, Cole would take Luke to the club, keep him there, and ensure that everything was as perfect as they could make it. And she knew that when Luke got out of hand—which he was prone to do—Cole would also be there to bring him down a notch.

Not that she wouldn't mind seeing that. Cole had a special way of taking care of Luke, and she'd had the distinct pleasure of witnessing that on more than one occasion.

Sierra felt her face heat.

Cole's big chest pressed up against her back, his hands cupping her shoulders. "I know that look," he whispered against her ear.

"What look?" she asked, pretending not to know what he was talking about.

"The one that means you're thinking about sex."

Sierra chuckled softly.

"Keep it up," Cole continued, "and I'll take you to the bedroom and get my morning fix, too."

"Who says I don't want you to?" she asked. It was true, Luke and Cole managed to keep her in a heightened state of arousal at all times. Though the three of them had been together for three years and had two children together, their sex life hadn't dwindled in the least. Part of that was due to the fact that they practically lived and breathed sex all the time with the club and the various fetishes it involved. It didn't hurt that, at thirty-two, Sierra was in her sexual prime. As for Luke and Cole ... well, she was pretty sure they were and would always be in their prime.

Sometimes it still blew her mind that she'd ended up here, living this highly erotic version of life. Not that she was complaining. At all.

"I've got plans for you tonight," Cole whispered. "Big plans."

A ribbon of heat curled in her belly, making her squeeze her thighs together. She loved when Cole made promises like that.

"I plan to hold you to that," she told him.

Cole cupped the side of her face, turning her so that she was looking at him. When his lips met hers, she tasted the promise in his kiss.

A deep, rumbling growl came from behind her, and Sierra pulled back from Cole to find Luke studying them intently. She laughed, knowing what was going through his deviously dirty mind. He always enjoyed when she and Cole got intimate. It brought out the voyeur in him.

"Y'all better get to the club," she told them now. "I'm taking Liam and Hannah over to Alex and Ashleigh's for a little while to hang out with Riley." Ashleigh had been pleading for Sierra to bring Hannah over to play with Riley for the longest time, and now that she had several hours until the party, she figured it would be the easiest way to pass the time.

Hopping down from the barstool, Sierra took Liam from Luke, but not before Luke peppered his downy-soft head with kisses.

"Need me to do anything today?" she asked her husbands.

Luke looked at Cole, a sinful smirk forming on his lips.

"You know what I mean," she said, smacking Luke's arm.

"I think we're good," Luke told her, kissing her forehead. "But keep your phone with you in case we do."

"Will do," she said, locking eyes with Luke. "And I expect you to be good today."

"Baby, I'm always good."

The smirk he'd perfected over the years was out in full force. And she felt it all the way to her toes.

"Love you," she told them both.

"Love you, too," came the chorus from behind her as she slipped out of the room. Followed by Luke's gruff command, "Come on, we've got a ton of shit to get done today and not a lot of time to do it."

Yep, that was Luke. Already on edge.

It was definitely going to be an interesting day.

CHAPTER 2

9:23 a.m.

COLE KNEW AS SOON AS HE NOTICED Trent's fancy Lexus parked out in front of the building that things were going to get a little rocky. Okay, maybe he didn't *know*, but he certainly suspected. It was bad enough that Luke was on edge. Cole was used to that. But put Luke in a room with Trent Ramsey, and they made psychotic look like a leisurely Sunday walk in the park.

"What's he doing here? Isn't it too early for him to be out of bed?" Luke asked as they walked through the front door after Cole unlocked it.

Cole grinned. "Thought you'd be able to answer that one."

It was possible that Trent was there to take delivery of the equipment he was expecting—not that Cole knew what that was, nor had he asked. He honestly didn't want to know.

Truth was, Trent was a thirty-two-year-old man who had a penchant for blowing things way out of proportion. He'd done it as an actor—though that had garnered him a lot of attention, not to mention worldwide fame—and he still did it as the partial owner of Devotion. If Luke did what he said he was going to do and offered Trent his own club, Cole would be able to breathe easier.

Maybe.

They made it through the reception area, which was now decked out in all things sparkly.

"It looks like someone vomited glitter in here," Luke grumbled, making Cole smile.

It didn't look bad. A little over the top, maybe, but he figured that had also been the plan. The point of a New Year's Eve party was to celebrate the coming of a new year. A fresh start, a time to look forward to the unknown and leave the past behind you.

Cole followed Luke into the club proper, noticing there were a few lights on. A couple on the main floor and one on the second floor, in Trent's office.

"What's different?" Luke asked, glancing around, his tone alluding to the fact that he knew something was, just not what.

"I'd guess it's all the new furniture," Cole said, chuckling.

"The chairs," Luke said. "Where the hell did those come from?"

"My guess is that Trent went a little overboard." They were kind of cool, though.

Cole recalled seeing an ad from one of the furniture manufacturers they did business with. The chair was referred to as a yoga chair, but thanks to the design, it was quite useful when it came to various sexual positions. Looked as though Trent had thought so, too, because there were about twenty new leather chairs now interspersed throughout the main floor.

"That's what he bought?" Luke asked, sounding oddly relieved.

"Looks like it." Though Cole wouldn't put it past Trent to have other things on their way. The last time they'd had a major party, Trent had purchased several Sybian machines—which had honestly been a huge success.

Funny how Trent didn't refer to himself as a Dom, but Cole could see it. Maybe Trent wasn't interested in putting labels on himself, or possibly he didn't embrace the whole lifestyle the way Xander and Mercedes did because he was still in the public eye. Either way, it looked as though Trent had definitely found his niche.

"Y'all are here early."

Cole looked up to see Trent heading down the stairs. Unlike his usual attire of fancy suits and movie star hair, Trent was sporting sweat pants, a hoodie, and running shoes. His blond hair had that just-rolled-out-of-bed thing going on, and his light blue eyes had zeroed in on Luke—as they usually did when he'd done something questionable.

"What do you think?" Trent asked when he approached.

"I like the idea," Luke said, shocking Cole as much as he'd apparently shocked Trent. "Any other surprises I need to know about?"

Trent smiled, one of those smirks that his female fan base went crazy for.

"Not today, no."

"Good." Luke glanced at Cole, then back to Trent. "What else needs to be done for tonight?"

Trent frowned. "Nothing that I know of. I'm pretty sure this is the party to rival all. Hell, even Travis Walker is coming, which means it's gotta be better than what AI is putting on."

Cole covered a laugh with a cough. Trent had serious issues when it came to Travis Walker. It was obvious he liked the guy, but he didn't like the fact that Travis had made a name for himself in the same industry.

"His brother Sawyer is running point at the resort this year," Luke assured Trent. "Otherwise, I'm sure he'd be there."

Trent ignored the jab, and Cole's grin widened.

"I talked to Xander," Trent stated. "He said we can definitely utilize the cigar bar next week to meet with the potential investors. If you want, I'll contact Phoenix and Max."

Apparently, after seeing Phoenix Pierce's name on the guest list, Luke had sent Trent a text asking what he thought of him as an investor. Cole wasn't privy to Trent's response, but it was evident he thought the idea had merit. As for Max Adorite, Cole still wasn't sure how he felt about that one. Since Max was the boss of the notorious Adorite family, it seemed a little questionable—Max's clubs had been known to be raided by the FBI, and everyone knew that wasn't good for business. Not that Cole would question Luke. The man hadn't made it this far in life by making stupid decisions. If he was seriously considering Max as an investor, Cole knew he had his reasons.

"Great idea," Luke said. "I contemplated talking to them tonight, but I don't think it's the right time."

Trent nodded. "Agreed. So what brings you by so early?"

"It's my club," Luke said firmly. "I need to ensure everything goes off without a hitch."

Cole still didn't understand why Luke was all up in arms about this party tonight. They'd had several since Devotion opened its doors, but Luke was hell-bent that this be the best one yet. There was obviously something on his mind, and Cole wondered if it was really because he wanted to impress the potential investors, or if Luke was merely being Luke, or perhaps working another angle.

Problem was, when it came to Luke, Cole probably wouldn't know until it was too late.

9:48 a.m.

LUKE FINISHED WITH TRENT, THEN HEADED UP to his office, leaving Cole behind to do whatever he needed to do in order to ensure tonight's party had no hiccups.

Not that Luke was entirely worried; he simply had a reputation to uphold. Everyone expected him to be a little uptight. Well, a *lot* uptight was more like it, but whatever. Truth was, Luke knew that Cole and Sierra would see to it that everything was as perfect as it could be. And not only because they feared he would go off the deep end. That was just who they were, which was one of the many reasons he loved them.

And then there was the matter of him keeping everyone on their toes. It was something he enjoyed. Especially Cole. Though the man Luke loved more than life itself wouldn't coddle him, Luke did like the fact that Cole would put him in his place when necessary. Considering he'd spent the longest time pushing Cole away, only to find out that by giving in, he had finally found peace with himself, Luke looked forward to those moments.

In fact, he was hoping for one in the very near future.

But not yet.

A knock sounded on his office door, and he looked up to see Trent standing there.

"What's up?" Luke dropped into his chair, glancing down at his desk.

"Got a minute?"

He nodded, then looked up at Trent, watching him as he crossed the room.

"You seen the guest list?" Trent's tone was casual as he eased into the chair across from Luke.

"Yeah. You?"

Trent nodded. "Got any concerns with the Adorites showing up?"

Luke had several, but he wasn't going to mention that to Trent. First and foremost, Luke knew that Max Adorite was a businessman. Sure, the guy had his hands in some dirty dealings, but he did have some legitimate business, including Devil's Playground—one of Dallas's most popular nightclubs.

"Not really, no. Something I should be worried about?" Luke leaned back in his chair and regarded Trent.

"Other than him being a mobster?" Trent said snidely.

"Other than that."

Trent shook his head. "I've been thinking about him wanting to invest in the club."

"And?"

"And I think it's not a bad idea. In fact, I wanted to get your take on looking into a Las Vegas version."

"Las Vegas?" Luke couldn't deny that the thought had crossed his mind a time or two. Considering the clientele they could reach in a city known for sin, it wasn't a bad idea. "Who would run it?"

Trent shrugged. "I hadn't gotten that far. Just wanted to see what you thought."

Luke liked Trent. He liked the guy's business sense, his willingness to go to the extreme, to take chances when a lot of other people wouldn't. Didn't mean they always saw eye to eye, but Luke knew that was partly because they were so alike.

Not that he'd admit that to anyone. Ever.

"Let me think on it a bit. We'll get together next week. If you're really interested, put together a proposal. I'll take a look at it."

"Cool," Trent said, getting to his feet. "Need anything before tonight?"

Luke shook his head. "I think we've got it all covered."

Trent nodded as he turned for the door. Before he stepped out into the hall, Luke called his name. "Tonight's gonna be great," he told Trent. "Thanks for helping to pull it all together."

"Anytime. And I'll put something on the calendar for next week, and I'll get in touch with Max."

Luke gave Trent a quick nod, then glanced down at his desk. When Trent closed the door behind him, Luke tried to relax. Tonight wasn't about business—not entirely, anyway—and he needed to remember that.

Glancing at his watch, he noted the time. Ten o'clock. Roughly twelve hours before the night would be in full swing.

And he fully intended to be ready.

But first, Luke needed to check a few things and make a few calls.

So, that was exactly what he did.

Two hours later, just a few minutes before noon, Luke was sitting at his desk, facing the floor-to-ceiling window that overlooked the main floor below. The place was empty, but by ten o'clock tonight, it would be packed from wall to wall with a wide variety of people who appreciated an even wider variety of sexual fetishes. Even people who didn't quite understand what it was that compelled them just yet.

The guest list was proof.

As he thought back on that list and the new people who would embrace this world, he wondered what their first thought would be. Granted, coming to Devotion on New Year's Eve wasn't going to be a gentle introduction into the world, so if that was what they were hoping for, they needed to look elsewhere. Then again, the people who were coming to the club knew that, understood it even before they set foot into the place.

Still, Luke looked forward to seeing their reactions and to spending time with the diverse group.

Luke's phone rang, and he turned back around to face his desk, peering down at his cell. He smiled, then hit the talk button and put it to his ear.

"Hey, baby," he greeted his wife.

"Just checking in," Sierra said sweetly. "We're still at Ashleigh's. The kids are playing, and I'm hoping to tire Hannah out so she doesn't run my mom ragged tonight. You need me for anything?"

"I need you for a lot of things," he told her.

"Luke McCoy, you have a dirty mind. You know what I mean."

Luke chuckled. "We're good here."

"What'd you think of the decorations?"

Luke turned back to face the window. "I'm thinking you bought every speck of glitter they make."

Sierra laughed softly. "I tried. So that means you're good with it?"

"It's perfect, baby. Everything you do is perfect." And he meant that. Sierra and Cole had changed his life for the better—in every way. They'd given him Hannah and Liam, making an incredible life even better. They would forever be his saving grace. All four of them.

"Aww," she said. "You're buttering me up, Mr. McCoy. What devious sexual things do you have planned for me tonight?"

"I'm still thinking on that." He had plenty of ideas, but it would depend on where the night led them.

"Well, when I get there, I'll give you a few ideas I've been tossing around," Sierra teased.

"Looking forward to it."

"I've gotta go round up Hannah. Sounds like Ashleigh's got her hands full. See you tonight."

"Love you," he told her.

"Love you right back."

With that, Luke hung up the phone and stared out the window once more. Time to get back to business.

12:10 p.m.

"ARE THEY BOUNCING OFF THE WALLS YET?" Sierra asked Ashleigh when she rejoined them in Ashleigh's living room.

"Almost," Ashleigh said with a smile. "How's Luke?"

Sierra grimaced. "He actually sounded ... calm."

Ashleigh chuckled. "I like how that confuses you."

"I know, right? I should be happy." She *was* happy, but still, she couldn't deny that she was a little thrown off to hear Luke so at ease. By now, she expected him to be ranting at anyone and everyone who would listen. Perhaps he didn't have anyone to order around if the club was empty. She hadn't bothered asking if anyone else was there. She doubted they were. Most of their friends were married at this point, so spending New Year's Eve day at the club—when nothing was going on—probably wasn't on their agenda.

Only Luke. And Cole.

And maybe Trent.

"Who wants a snack?" Ashleigh asked the girls.

"Me! Me!" Hannah and Riley sang.

"So what are your plans for tonight?" Sierra asked Ashleigh when they followed Hannah and Riley into the kitchen.

"We're gonna hang out right here. I invited my brother over for dinner, so I figured we'd eat, put Riley to bed, maybe watch the ball drop on television."

Sierra knew that Ashleigh's brother, Dylan, was a recovering alcoholic. For as long as she'd known him, the man had drowned his sorrows in liquor, but from what Ashleigh had told her, he'd recently come to realize that the bottom had dropped out of his world completely, and it was time for some action. As for what that meant for Dylan's future, Sierra didn't know, but she was glad to hear he was focusing on himself.

"That sounds like heaven," Sierra told her friend. Although she loved going to the club—more so now that she didn't go that often—she still looked forward to those nights spent at home.

"I'm sure it will be. That is, if I can keep Alex and Dylan in line. They tend to get a little competitive when they're around one another."

"What's Xavier doing tonight?" Sierra asked, referring to Ashleigh's grandfather, who just so happened to be Sierra's stepfather. Sierra smiled at that. It wasn't easy to think of him as her stepfather, although she loved the man to pieces. Xavier had married Sierra's mother six months ago, not bothering to tell anyone other than Sierra, Ashleigh, and Dylan before he did. They'd wanted something simple and easy for their nuptials, so they'd all obliged them. But not without throwing them a lavish wedding reception afterward, which had come as a total surprise to them both.

"He'll be at home. You know him. Pops insists that he's too old to party on New Year's."

At eighty-three, Sierra understood why.

"I would take the kids to *their* house," Sierra told Ashleigh with a wink, "but I think they'd drive him up the wall."

"Probably," Ashleigh agreed, doling out sliced bananas and milk to the girls.

Liam's abrupt wail called a halt to their conversation.

"He hungry?" Ashleigh asked.

"Yep. It's lunchtime for him. Mind if I…?" Sierra pointed toward the living room.

"Not at all."

1:37 p.m.

Sierra was exhausted by the time she got Hannah and Liam back to the house. As soon as they stepped in the door, she put Liam down in his crib, hoping he would stay asleep for at least another hour. Hannah wasn't quite as easy. Being fiercely independent, she didn't do naps anymore, but they had started allowing her to watch television for an hour in the afternoon, to help her calm down a bit.

"What do you wanna watch?" Sierra asked her daughter.

"*Paw Patrol!*" Hannah squealed.

Sierra put her finger over her lips in the universal sign for quiet. Hannah grinned sheepishly, then grabbed her hand and pulled her. Sierra followed her to the living room, then turned on *Paw Patrol*, which would keep Hannah occupied for at least half an hour.

More than enough time for Sierra to relax.

She was tired, but no more than any other mom on the planet. Probably less than some even. But she still needed a few minutes to regroup.

And she intended to do that right now. With a little nap.

CHAPTER 3

2:03 p.m.

COLE COULD HEAR THE YELLING FROM DOWNSTAIRS, and he knew exactly where it was coming from. Only he didn't know who the hell Luke was yelling at, but he fully intended to find out. They had roughly six hours until people started arriving at the club; there was no way Luke could go off the deep end already.

With a sigh, Cole pushed open Luke's office door, coming to a halt when Luke slammed down the phone, his hazel eyes slamming into Cole's face.

"What do you want?" Luke barked.

Cole studied his husband momentarily. "Figured I'd come see whose life needed saving."

Luke spun around and faced the window, huffing as he did.

"What's the problem?" Cole asked, closing the office door behind him and locking it for good measure.

No one else was at the club, but Cole knew better than to invite trouble. The last thing he wanted was for some unsuspecting person to walk in and witness what would be coming next.

"Nothing for you to worry about."

Cole shook his head in disbelief, but Luke couldn't see him. He wanted to smile, but he managed to keep that to himself. For the past … probably a year … Luke had been having tantrums very similar to this one. He would fly off the handle, only Cole never knew who was at the receiving end of his tirade. Which made Cole believe that there wasn't anyone at the other end.

And yes, he was on to Luke's game. Not that he minded, because the outcome was always worth his while.

Always.

"Sit," Cole ordered.

Luke pivoted around to face him, his eyes hard.

"You heard me," Cole snapped. "Don't make me tell you again."

As was usually the case when there wasn't a legitimate fire needing to be put out, Luke slowly lowered himself into the desk chair. Had there been a real issue, Luke would've continued his tirade.

Didn't look as though there was a real problem, other than Luke needed someone to give him a little attention. Generally, Cole would be the one to come and soothe Luke's frayed nerves, going to his knees before this impossible man, sucking his cock just to get his mind off his troubles because it was something they both enjoyed immensely.

Not today.

Today, Cole had something else in mind.

As he moved closer, Cole worked his belt free, then undid the button of his jeans, but he stopped working his clothes free as soon as his feet stopped, coming to stand directly in front of Luke.

"Who was on the phone?" Cole questioned.

Luke frowned. "It's nothing."

Cole wondered how much truth there was to that statement. However, he had no intention of calling Luke to the carpet. If he wanted to continue these games, so be it.

Moving around behind Luke, Cole placed his hands on Luke's tense shoulders. Faking it or not, the man's muscles were knotted. He began kneading until Luke relaxed, exhaling deeply as he sank back into his chair.

"Don't get too comfortable," Cole told him, smiling to himself.

"Why's that?"

"Because I've got the perfect way for you to take your mind off your troubles."

"Is that right?" Luke didn't sound convinced.

Pulling his hands from Luke's shoulders, Cole worked his jeans open all the way, took his cock in his hand, and then moved back around to stand in front of Luke.

His husband's eyes widened slightly when his gaze settled on Cole's rock-hard dick.

"Suck me," Cole instructed, keeping his tone firm.

"Isn't that typically my line?" Luke's eyes lifted to meet Cole's.

"Not today, it's not." Cole nodded downward. "Take my dick in your mouth, Luke."

The way Luke's eyes flashed with heat told Cole that he'd been right. The man was expecting this. And Cole was more than willing to deliver.

When Luke began to reach for Cole's cock, he tsked. "No hands," Cole told him. "Only your mouth."

Luke peered up at him again, his mouth opening slightly.

Cole brushed the head of his cock against those smooth, firm lips, inhaling sharply as he did. "Just like that. Now close your lips around me."

Luke's mouth encircled him, his tongue easing over the engorged head, and a shiver raced down Cole's spine. The man really did have a wicked fucking mouth.

It was true, Luke McCoy enjoyed being in control, but Cole knew that there were times when he wanted that control stripped away from him. And yes, Cole was the perfect person for the job.

"Suck me," Cole demanded, keeping his voice low. "Suck me like you mean it."

Luke released Cole's dick from his mouth. "Be careful what you wish for."

Cole smiled. "Baby, I always wish to see my dick tunneling in and out of your mouth. Your threats mean little to me. Now suck me."

Luke took him in his mouth once again, working him the way only Luke knew how, and Cole's eyes threatened to roll back in his head. He managed to maintain his control, sliding one hand into Luke's hair, holding his head in place, then cupping Luke's jaw with his other hand.

"That's it," Cole murmured. "Let me fuck your mouth. The same way I'm gonna fuck your ass when I bend you over your desk."

A couple of years ago, those words would've never come out of Cole's mouth. But now … watching Luke's eyes glaze over, Cole knew that was exactly what Luke had been hoping for.

But not yet. He wanted to feel the warm suction of Luke's mouth for as long as he could.

And when he could take no more, he would do exactly as he'd promised.

2:19 p.m.

LUKE HONESTLY NEVER THOUGHT HE WOULD BE where he was now. It'd taken him so long to finally realize—or accept, as was probably the better way to look at it—that he would appreciate being on the receiving end of someone else's commands. In fact, it wasn't until Sierra and Cole had come into his life that he'd realized there was something he'd been missing all along.

Granted, the only person he took commands from—when it came to sex, anyway—was Cole. And he intended for it to stay that way.

Ever since that first time... Damn. The memory of that day made his dick throb against his zipper, his need ratcheting up another notch. Thinking about what Cole had done to him, how he'd made him feel... It had been better than he could've anticipated.

He remembered it as though it were yesterday.

"I want to feel you," Luke bit out. "I don't need the damn toy, I fucking need you. Right now."

"I want you inside me," Sierra whispered close to his ear as she ran her hands up over his shoulders, then into his hair. "I want to feel you when Cole takes you."

There wasn't even a second of hesitation before he shifted, ramming his cock inside of her, heavenly warmth enveloping him.

"Cole. Please. Now," Sierra murmured.

At least they were on the same page.

Seconds felt like hours as Cole slowly—so fucking slowly—worked his cock into Luke's body.

"I need this. I need you," Cole whispered.

Sierra's hands came up to slide down Cole's cheek as he leaned forward, his chest resting against Luke's back.

The pleasure was intense. So intense, Luke wasn't sure he would survive it.

Planting his hands on top of Cole's, which were flat on the mattress, Luke twined their fingers together and turned his head to look at the man he loved.

"I love you," Luke whispered. "I need you."

Cole began rocking his hips, driving deep and retreating slowly. The pleasure was intensifying, but he needed more. So much more.

"Cole," Luke groaned. "Make me come. Please make me come."

"Come for me," Cole ground out. "I need you to come for me, baby."

And that was exactly what Luke did.

And now, here they were, Cole once again taking the reins. Luke needed to feel him, needed Cole to be lodged to the hilt in his ass, robbing him of his senses and leaving him blinded by the pleasure.

"So fucking good," Cole ground out, reverently sliding his palm over Luke's cheek as he pulled his cock from Luke's mouth, continuing to stare down at him with so much love in his eyes it made Luke's heart constrict. "Stand up."

Luke got to his feet without argument.

Cole proceeded to remove Luke's belt, unbutton his slacks, then force them down his thighs.

"Turn around."

Luke did as instructed, unable to argue, even if he'd wanted to.

The sound of a drawer opening made him smile.

"Put your hands on the desk."

Bending over, Luke planted his palms flat on the desk and widened his stance as much as he could with his slacks around his legs.

Cool lubricant slid down over his asshole, and the next thing he knew, the head of Cole's cock had breached him, sucking the air from his lungs. The foreplay was obviously done, and Luke was fine with that. He ached for Cole, needed him more than he needed anything else at the moment.

Luke clenched his teeth as Cole pushed into him, forcing the thick head past the tight ring of muscle. He forced himself to relax, taking a deep breath as he kept his hands planted firmly on the desk.

"So tight," Cole muttered. "So fucking tight. You know how good it feels to be inside you?"

Luke had an idea because he had the same thoughts when he was buried inside Cole. But this… This was a pleasure he'd come to crave, to need as much as he needed to claim Cole himself.

"I'm gonna fuck you now," Cole told him.

Luke didn't say a word. Dropping his head, he began pushing back against the intrusion, his cock desperate for attention, but he knew better than to touch himself.

Cole's fingers bit into his hips, and Luke closed his eyes, relishing the fullness, the erotic grind of Cole buried inside him, his thick cock brushing his prostate and making his dick swell.

Cole was the only man Luke had bottomed for, the only man he would ever bottom for. He loved him, and the feeling of him deep inside his body was a connection that he'd long ago accepted that they both needed.

Closing his eyes, he groaned as Cole pushed inside, withdrew, then slid in again. Over and over, Cole fucked him so perfectly, giving him exactly what they both needed until Luke knew he was going to come. There was nothing he could do to stop that.

"Harder," Luke growled. He needed more, needed everything Cole was willing to give him.

Cole slammed into him, pulling out, then slamming home again. His pace quickened, his thrusts more urgent as he pounded into him. The sound of flesh against flesh echoed in the office, mingling with their deep breaths and the involuntary groans of pleasure.

"Fuck, Luke," Cole whispered harshly. "I'm gonna come in your ass, baby."

Luke's cock jerked.

Cole slammed into him several more times before his hips stilled, his dick pulsing in Luke's ass. But it wasn't over, because Cole reached around him, gripping Luke's dick firmly and jacking him off until Luke was biting back a strangled cry, his release barreling into him.

"Aww, fuck … Cole…" Luke groaned, dropping his head as he bucked his hips, driving himself into Cole's hand. "Oh, fuck."

"Let go," Cole commanded.

Luke came hard and fast, a smile forming on his lips.

3:09 p.m.

SIERRA SAT AT THE KITCHEN TABLE, HOLDING Liam in her arms as she watched Hannah devour some apples. She felt oddly refreshed after a full one-hour nap. How she'd managed that, she wasn't sure, but she definitely wasn't going to question it. Hannah had kindly woken her to ask if she could have an apple. As though the sweetness of her tone wouldn't have been enough, Hannah had followed it with a kiss and a whispered, "I love you." No way could Sierra resist that.

"So what are you and Grandma gonna do tonight?" Sierra asked her daughter.

"Play with stickers!" Hannah squealed excitedly.

Her daughter had taken to stickers months ago. Thankfully, she'd gotten out of the habit of putting them all over people, preferring now to decorate the sticker books Luke and Cole had bought her. It was rather amazing that stickers could keep her occupied for hours on end.

"I bet your daddies bought you a new sticker book," Sierra said. "But you have to be super good to get it."

As though they sensed she was talking about them, Sierra's cell phone rang. She grabbed it from the table and hit the talk button.

"Hey," she greeted Cole.

"Hey, baby," he said. "Things good there?"

"Yep. Hannah's having a snack and Liam just ate, too. How are you?"

"Good. Things are all settled here."

"By things, are you referring to Luke?" she asked with a chuckle.

"Yep."

"Did he pull that thing again?" Sierra and Cole were on to Luke's little game of pretending to be worked up to the point of needing something to calm him down. Sure, there were times when it was clear he was nearing the breaking point, but they'd long ago been able to determine which moments were real and which were fabricated.

Not that they intended to let him know they were on to his game.

"He did," Cole said softly. "Took good care of him."

"Wish I could've watched," Sierra said softly.

"Me, too," he replied. "I think we're gonna come home for an early dinner, help with Hannah and Liam while you get ready."

"That'd be great." Not only would she appreciate the help but she wouldn't mind seeing either of them. "Should I cook?"

"No, we'll take care of that."

"Okay. What time?" Sierra looked at the clock.

"Around four?"

"Works for me. See you then."

"Love you," Cole said.

"Love you, too."

Sierra disconnected the call.

"Was that Daddy? Or Daddy-o?"

"Daddy," Sierra told Hannah.

"Where's Daddy-o?"

Sierra smiled, still amused that Hannah had started referring to Luke that way. Not that Luke minded; in fact, Sierra was pretty sure he enjoyed it. "With Daddy. They're at work."

"Are they coming home?"

"In a little while."

"What time?" Hannah asked, morphing into the grown-up version she liked to pretend to be from time to time.

"Four o'clock," Sierra explained. "When the first number on the clock is four."

"Okay." Hannah shoved her last piece of apple into her mouth. "Can we watch more *Paw Patrol?*"

Sierra tried not to let Hannah watch too much television, not wanting to get in the habit of leaving her unattended—because it would really be easy for Sierra sometimes—but she figured it couldn't hurt. That would burn some of the minutes between now and the time Luke and Cole came home.

And then, when they did, Sierra was looking forward to a long, hot bath before she had to get ready for the night.

4:12 p.m.

ON THE WAY HOME FROM DEVOTION, COLE and Luke had tossed around the idea of what to have for dinner. When they'd come to the conclusion that steaks were on the menu, they'd stopped by the grocery store, grabbed what they needed, then headed home. Because the temperature was relatively mild, Luke had suggested Cole grill, and he'd easily agreed. He didn't mind, and it gave him a chance to spend some time with Hannah. She'd long ago insisted that she be able to help, so they'd worked out a way to make that happen without allowing her to get too close to the grill.

His daughter had become incredibly independent in recent months, and though Cole found it endearing, he knew that meant they had to keep extra eyes on her. She was sweet, but mischievous all the same, and almost always insisted that she was the one in charge.

And in order to keep her from making the rules, their grilling routine had become streamlined out of necessity.

While Cole readied the grill, Luke prepared the steaks, then put them in plastic containers, allowing Hannah to bring them out to him, one by one. After taking the meat and flopping it onto the grill, Cole would send the empty containers back inside, and Hannah would help Luke rinse them and put them in the dishwasher. While Cole kept an eye on the steaks, Luke helped Hannah make chicken nuggets and macaroni—her favorites—to pass the time. Then, when the steaks were ready, Cole would put them in another container, wrap it in a towel, and she would deliver it to the table.

Cole loved watching Hannah, how excited she got to do something as mundane as making dinner. The little girl stole his heart every time he looked at her. Especially when she got a burst of excitement and got sidetracked, dancing around the kitchen, as she was now.

"I'll take that," Cole told her, retrieving the plastic container from her grip and placing it on the table.

"Dinner's ready," Luke called to Sierra, who was playing with Liam in the living room.

While Luke got Hannah situated in her chair, Cole went to the living room to assist Sierra. Helping her to her feet, Cole wrapped his arm around her shoulder and kissed her on the top of her head. God, he loved this woman, this family he'd been blessed to have. He still thanked God every single day for allowing him to live this incredible life. Sometimes it seemed surreal.

"I've got him," Cole told Sierra when she went to pick up Liam. "What's up, little man?" Cole crooned to the newest addition to their family. "Wanna watch us have dinner?"

Carrying the little boy into the kitchen, Cole settled him into the bouncer and then sat down to enjoy another meal with the loves of his life. Today was the last day of 2015, the last meal they would share this year. It wasn't that he was a sentimental man, but he had learned long ago not to take anything for granted. So, while everyone dug in, Cole took an extra minute to watch them, smiling as he did.

5:08 p.m.

ONCE DINNER WAS FINISHED, LUKE CLEANED UP, loaded the dishwasher with Hannah's help, then allowed her to wipe down the counters before they joined Cole and Liam in the living room while Sierra snuck off to take a bath.

He tried not to look at his watch, but it wasn't easy. Although he was enjoying spending time with the kids, keeping his thoughts from straying was beginning to get difficult. He was counting down the minutes until they left, thinking about all the things they needed to do between now and then.

The kitchen was clean. Sierra was getting some time to herself. Hannah was reading a book—or pretending to, anyway. Liam had been fed. The only thing left was for him and Cole to shower and change.

"Relax," Cole whispered, glancing over.

"I'm trying," Luke assured him. He really was, but his mind was awhirl with all the things he might've missed. The doors would open in a few hours, and he damn sure didn't want to be left scrambling at the last second.

He mentally ran through the guest list, wondering if he should've thought of anything else, but came up blank. When his cell phone buzzed in his pocket, he damn near flew off the couch. Looking over, he noticed Cole laughing at him.

"Daddy-o's a nut," Cole told Liam.

"Hello?" Luke said into the phone after stabbing the screen.

"Hey, it's Trent."

"What's up?" Luke asked, trying to sound relaxed and not at all jumpy.

"Wanted to let you know that I got a call from Phoenix Pierce. He wants to know if we'll have some time to talk tonight. Maybe before the party."

Once again Luke glanced at the clock, as though more than three minutes had passed since the last time he had. "Yeah. What time?"

"Can you be there by seven?" Trent asked.

"We'll see you then," Luke assured him, then disconnected the call.

"Trent?" Cole asked when Luke dropped his phone on his leg.

Luke nodded. "Phoenix Pierce wants to meet."

"Investor, right?" Cole's attention never left Liam.

"Yeah. I think he's definitely interested."

"Sounds like it."

"We need to meet him at the club at seven."

Cole nodded in agreement. "What time is it now?"

"Five twenty."

"You wanna keep an eye on them while I go shower? I'll use the guest bathroom. Then we'll trade?"

Perfect. And Veronica would be there by six, which would leave Sierra plenty of time to get ready while her mother was there to watch the kids.

Shit.

Now Luke needed to…

"Don't worry about it," Cole said, handing Liam over to him. "I've got your proposal ready and waiting in your office at the club. You have nothing to fret about. It'll be fine."

Yeah. It would. Luke knew that. Didn't mean he wasn't going to *fret* about it, anyway, as Cole liked to put it.

When Cole leaned down and kissed him, Luke relaxed immensely, giving in to the gentle brush of Cole's lips against his own. The man always knew how to get him to relax.

Didn't matter that three minutes after Cole had left the room, Luke was pacing the living room.

6:17 p.m.

SIERRA EMERGED FROM HER BEDROOM WEARING HER robe, not wanting to put her dress on just yet. She was surprised to find Luke and Cole standing in the living room, talking to her mother, both of them dressed to the nines.

Lord. Have. Mercy.

As she looked at those two men, her breath lodged in her chest momentarily. Luke, with his midnight-black hair and striking hazel eyes, looked intimidating in his tuxedo, while Cole, with his blond hair and devastating blue eyes, looked the picture of class and elegance. They were different but equally stunning.

"There she is," Veronica said when Sierra stepped into the room. "I thought your husband was going to lose his mind."

Sierra didn't need her mother to clarify which husband she was referring to. She could practically see Luke vibrating as he attempted to keep his feet rooted to the floor. If she had to guess, he'd probably worn a rut in the hardwood already.

"Something wrong?" Sierra asked, looking up at Luke.

"No. Trent called. Phoenix wants to meet before the party. We need to head over to the club now."

Sierra nodded. "I'm riding with Logan, Sam, and Eli. Y'all didn't need to wait for me."

"But we wanted to," Cole said, grinning from behind Luke.

With a smile of her own, Sierra pulled Luke's head down to hers and gave him a quick kiss. "I'll see you in a bit."

"We'll be waiting," Luke assured her. "Love you."

"Love you," she replied, moving over to Cole and kissing him quickly. "Keep him calm."

"He'll be fine," Cole said. "He's cool when it comes to business. This is probably the best thing that could've happened."

"I'm sure it is."

Both her men kissed the kids good-bye, then dashed out the door without looking back.

When they were gone, Sierra turned to her mother. "Mom?"

Veronica's blue eyes met hers, her eyebrow lifting in question.

"Can you help me with my hair?" Since her hair now hung down to her butt, it wasn't easy to curl it herself.

"Sure."

"And I'll probably need your help with my dress."

"Is something wrong with it?"

"Not at all," Sierra told her. "But I fully intend to blow their minds when I see them next. I want to make sure the only thing they think about for the rest of the night is me."

"I'm sure you won't have a problem pulling that off."

Sierra hoped not. It had been a long time—or it seemed that way, anyway—since she'd dressed up. Being pregnant with Liam, she hadn't been able to wear heels, and now, tonight, she had the first opportunity to glam herself up.

And she fully intended to go all out.

After all, she wanted to make sure Luke and Cole spent the last hours of this year—and all of next year—thinking about her. And only her.

CHAPTER 5

6:59 p.m.

COLE RISKED HIS LIFE TO GET LUKE to the club by six o'clock, but they made it—only breaking a few traffic laws in the process—and that was all that mattered. When they pulled into the parking lot, he noticed that all of the valets were already set up out front, gearing up to move cars once guests started to arrive in an hour.

Sixty more minutes before the night got underway, and Cole was beginning to wonder if Luke was going to survive until then. Thank God for the meeting, that was all he knew. It would provide the perfect distraction for a man who was getting himself worked up for absolutely no reason.

However, he had to give Luke props because he had managed to refrain from giving Cole hell on the way there, even now as the clock turned to seven and Cole pulled up in front of the club. But before he'd even managed to put the car in park, Luke was out the door, walking inside without looking back.

Cole smiled to himself, climbing out of the car, shaking his head.

After handing the keys to the attendant, Cole went inside, greeting Candace, the woman who manned the reception area. She had her work cut out for her tonight, but it appeared she was getting ready for the event, so he attempted to pass through with a wave, but she caught him before he could.

"You ready for this?" she asked, turning to face him.

"Aren't I always?"

"Is he?" Candace chuckled, nodding toward the door, where Luke had disappeared.

"I'm sure he'll relax."

"Maybe after a couple of drinks," she said.

"Drinks. Why didn't I think of that?"

Candace smiled. "I'm sure it'll be fantastic."

Cole nodded. "Let me know if you need anything. Though I doubt we'll need it, we've got extra security coming in."

"I saw that."

Security was one thing they took seriously. On any given night, there were two bouncers at the front doors, then more managing each of the exits and several standing guard on the floor. Due to the nature of their club, it was crucial that they didn't let anything get out of hand. And since they'd have a few unknowns at the club tonight, he and Luke had agreed they needed to beef things up.

"See you later," Cole told Candace before pulling open the door. After a quick pass through the main floor, checking the bars to ensure they were being set up, Cole poured Luke a drink, then met up with him in his office, where Trent and three others were already waiting.

"I'd like you to meet my husband, Cole," Luke said to the others when Cole approached. "Cole, this is Phoenix Pierce, his wife, Mia, and his husband, Tarik."

"Nice to meet you all," Cole responded, shaking the hand of each person, noticing that someone—hopefully Trent—had thought to get them drinks, which was a good thing. He didn't mind being the gofer, but he had his hands full with Luke, or he probably would've thought ahead.

Handing Luke the tumbler of scotch, Cole discreetly studied Phoenix and his better … thirds… *Is that how the saying goes when there are three?* Mia was a pretty blonde with ice-blue eyes, the perfect counterpoint to the fierce-looking, dark-haired Tarik, a man who obviously was responsible for handling Phoenix's protection. The guy looked like he was ex-military, but Cole honestly had no idea.

Cole didn't know much about Phoenix, other than recognizing the name due to the man's public persona. He was a prominent Texas businessman, not to mention the owner of the Austin Arrows—Austin's NHL team.

"Please, sit." Luke gestured toward the table and chairs set up in the corner of the office, where they occasionally had meetings such as this. Rarely, though. In fact, this was the first time since they'd opened Devotion that they were actually having this particular conversation.

Expansion.

That in itself was a big deal, especially after Luke had abruptly closed down The Club at Club Destiny a few years ago when there was a threat to their client list. The man definitely didn't put up with a lot of shit, and he certainly didn't trust many. So for him to consider branching out and putting trust in others once more said a lot about how far he'd come in the past couple of years.

"If you'd like, I can provide you with my business proposal," Luke offered.

"If you don't mind, we'd like to keep this casual," Phoenix replied. "I really just wanted to introduce you to Mia and Tarik."

Casual. That was a good thing. If Luke got started discussing business, he likely wouldn't stop, and Cole would be forced to rein him back in once people began to arrive. He glanced at his watch. They didn't have long.

And while he was interested in where this might lead, Cole knew that no decisions would be made at this meeting. He and Luke had discussed what Luke expected to get out of tonight, and basically, he was looking for reassurance that Phoenix was seriously interested. Whether or not that meant they went through with this was still to be seen.

So, until then, Cole decided to sit back and listen. And next week, once the new year was underway, he'd worry about the logistics. Until then, this was basically to appease Luke.

Something Cole had found himself doing quite frequently lately.

And with great pleasure.

7:47 p.m.

BASED ON THE BRIEF CONVERSATION THEY'D JUST had, Luke decided that he liked Phoenix. He was a good guy. Professional. Intelligent. All the qualities Luke was looking for in a business partner.

And as far as Luke was concerned, Phoenix was definitely the smarter choice in investors when it came down to Phoenix or Max, though he was still kicking around the idea of working directly with Max Adorite. He'd given considerable thought to Trent's suggestion about opening a club in Vegas, and he was fairly certain Max would be the perfect partner in that venture. His only concern regarding that was the fact that Max was a known mobster. His money wasn't exactly clean—most of it, anyway—and getting in bed with the guy, so to speak, meant taking a risk that Luke had to be sure he was willing to take.

Needless to say, Phoenix's interest was a good thing.

It was clear that Phoenix was a keen businessman, too. Since the Austin Arrows were kicking ass again this season, a seemingly new trend since Phoenix had taken over the team when his father had passed away roughly two years ago. But what impressed Luke the most was Mia and Tarik. Those two knew what they wanted, and if Luke wasn't mistaken, Phoenix wasn't the one looking to invest in a club; they were.

And he was good with that. Which even surprised him.

Leaning back in his chair, Luke watched the three of them as they talked to Trent, noticing the way both men doted on Mia, probably without realizing it. Luke knew the feeling. There was something about a woman—*your* woman—that automatically brought out protective instincts in a man. Luke and Cole felt the same about Sierra, and a lot of the time probably looked much like the threesome sitting across from him now.

"Have you been to a club like this before?" Luke asked, not directing the question to anyone in particular.

Mia shook her head, then glanced over at the men on each side of her.

Phoenix didn't answer, nor did Tarik, which made Luke laugh at the same time Mia asked, "When?"

Phoenix's arm slid around Mia. "Not since we've been together."

"That's good to know," she teased. "Except I'm wondering why you didn't bring me."

Tarik's dark eyebrows lifted and Phoenix grinned.

"I think we've ruined her," Phoenix said, his emerald-green eyes landing on Luke's face.

179

Luke's phone rang on his desk and Cole moved to answer it. When he hung up, he watched as Cole returned to the table.

"We've got early arrivals," Cole informed them, coming to stand behind Luke.

"Are you guys ready to see how crazy things can get?" Trent asked, getting to his feet. "Why don't I take you downstairs and get you set up with some fresh drinks. Then I'll show you around."

"It was great to meet you," Luke told Mia and Tarik directly, realizing that was exactly what Phoenix wanted. "Hopefully you'll enjoy yourselves tonight, and we'll reconvene next week to see where we go from here." If Phoenix was interested in investing in the club, Luke got the sense that everything would be handled during the week and mainly over the phone.

So tonight's impromptu meeting had been about Mia and Tarik.

And Luke was going to keep that in mind because it said a lot about the man he'd hopefully be doing business with in the future.

7:55 p.m.

"HOLY SHIT," SAMANTHA SAID WHEN SIERRA OPENED the front door and greeted her friend. "Where did you get that dress? You look incredible."

Sierra hugged Sam, then took a step back.

"You'll never believe that I found it on clearance."

"It's fabulous, but probably more so because it's on you," Sam said, still looking her over. "Your men are going to go nuts when they see you."

Sierra grinned. "That's the plan."

"Are you ready?" Sam asked. "I'm not trying to rush, but Logan and Eli are waiting in the car. I think they're ready to get this night underway."

"I'm ready," Sierra confirmed. "Let me grab my clutch."

Sierra strolled into the living room to find her mother sitting on the couch with Hannah in her lap. They were watching some holiday cartoon and getting ready to wind down for the night.

"I'm heading out," Sierra told them, moving close and kissing Hannah on the head.

"Be careful," Veronica told her.

"Always. And if you need anything at all, call. If you can't reach us on our cell phones, you can always call the club."

Veronica smiled, one of those grins that told Sierra she was used to doing this and knew how it went.

"Love you," Sierra told them both, grabbing her clutch and heading back to meet Sam in the foyer. "I'm ready when you are."

A minute later, Sierra was in the backseat with Sam, with Logan at the wheel and Elijah riding shotgun. They said their brief hellos, but then Elijah and Logan continued with a conversation they'd been having when Sierra climbed in.

"How's Luke?" Sam asked, keeping her voice low.

"He's doing much better than I expected," Sierra answered with a chuckle. "Doesn't mean it'll last all night, but I have to say I'm pleasantly surprised."

"Don't be," Sam said sweetly. "I think the man knows that he has you and Cole there to keep things in order so he doesn't have to stress quite so much."

True. He didn't. Only Sierra and Cole knew that he did anyway.

And sometimes, as they'd learned, he did it on purpose.

Which was why Sierra and Cole had something special in store for the man tonight.

Something they were all going to enjoy.

CHAPTER
6

8:25 p.m.

COLE REMAINED CLOSE TO LUKE AS GUESTS began arriving. He greeted the people he knew and was introduced to some he didn't. One thing he noticed right off was that the guest list was diverse. Everyone from political powerhouses, A-list actors, small business owners, right down to the average, everyday rancher.

And of course, the Walkers. Some of them, anyway.

"Good to see you again," Travis Walker greeted with a firm handshake.

"Same to you," Cole returned, smiling at Kylie and Gage—Travis's wife and husband. "How's the family?"

"Never better." Travis pulled Kylie up next to him.

"And Kate?" Luke asked, shaking Travis's hand in greeting, then hugging Kylie and shaking Gage's hand.

Travis's grin grew bigger than Cole had ever seen it. "She's perfect. And it looks like she's going to be a big sister in the near future." Travis placed his hand protectively over Kylie's belly.

"That's fantastic," Luke inserted. "Congratulations."

"I hear congrats are in order for y'all as well. How're the kids?"

"Doing well," Cole told him. "And how's AI?"

"Good," Travis told him. "Filled to capacity."

"That's expected," Cole told him. "It's quite impressive."

"Thanks." Travis looked around. "The same can be said for this place. So tell me, is it true? You're looking to branch out some?"

"That's the rumor," Cole confirmed, glancing over at Luke.

Kylie placed her hand on Travis's chest. "You promised we weren't talking business tonight."

Travis smiled. "She's right. I did promise, so we won't keep you," Travis said. "But hit me up next week, would you? I've got an idea of my own if y'all are interested."

Cole nodded at the same time Luke said, "Will do. Glad you could make it. Let us know if you need anything."

Travis, Kylie, and Gage moved on toward the bar, and Luke moved to stand closer to Cole's side.

"You doing all right?" Luke asked.

"That's my question for you," Cole teased, looking at him. He was cool and calm, and handsome as hell.

"So far, so good." Luke's eyes widened suddenly. "Holy fucking shit."

Cole turned to see what or who Luke was looking at, and his gaze landed on the absolute most stunning woman in the world.

"Sierra," Cole muttered. "Where the hell did she buy that dress?"

"I don't know, but I'm buying stock in that fucking company," Luke said, his arm around Cole's shoulder as they moved toward her.

"Hi," Sierra greeted with a grin.

"Hi," Cole said, suddenly tongue-tied.

His wife was wearing a very short, nearly indecent silver dress that molded to her body as though it had been designed for her. Perhaps it had; he didn't know. It'd been a while since she'd dressed up, mainly because of the pregnancy and all that was going on in a household with children. They didn't get the opportunity to go out much, and when they did, it was generally for a quick bite to eat. Nothing that would warrant her to dress up.

She looked phenomenal.

"You look good enough to eat," Luke whispered, moving in and taking one of her hands in his.

"This ol' thing?" she teased, glancing down.

The heels adorning her feet glittered in the light, catching Cole's eye as he soaked up the sight of her.

"I can't wait to get you out of that," Luke muttered. "Or maybe I'll leave it on you. Either way…"

What he said, Cole thought as he continued to eye Sierra.

"Whatever we do, we're keeping the shoes on," Cole told them.

Luke peered down at her feet. "Definitely."

Cole glanced behind him, noticing plenty of others looking Sierra's way, as well, likely admiring her because she was by far the most beautiful woman in the place.

A surge of pride expanded his chest.

Because this exquisite, gorgeous woman belonged to them.

And them only.

8:31 p.m.

LUKE WASN'T SURE HE COULD CONTINUE GREETING the guests as they arrived. Hell, he wasn't sure he'd be able to focus on much of anything tonight. Not with Sierra looking like she did. She made his mouth water, his hands itched to touch her, and he suddenly couldn't concentrate on anything else.

"Luke?" Sierra said, but he couldn't stop staring. He wanted to slide his palms over her thighs, then up beneath that indecently short skirt to see what she wore beneath.

Someone cleared their throat, and Luke pulled his gaze up to meet Sierra's face. She was nodding over his shoulder.

Luke turned around, coming face-to-face with Brendon Walker.

"Luke," Brendon greeted, holding out his hand. "You know my better half, Cheyenne Montgomery."

"Nice to see you again," Luke told the famous country music star. "I'm glad you both could make it."

"Thank you for having us," Cheyenne replied in that soft country drawl that most of America was acquainted with. "I'd like to introduce you to my cousin, Grace Lambert."

Luke held out his hand to Grace.

"It's very nice to meet you, Mr. McCoy," she said in a thick Texas drawl. "These are the rowdy cowboys in my life, Grant Kingsley and Lane Miller."

"Please, call me Luke." Luke shook their hands as well, trying to be a good host, but it wasn't easy when the only thing he wanted to do was turn around and ogle his wife for a little while longer.

"Glad you could make it," Cole said, clearly stepping in when Luke lost his manners.

"Thank you for extending an invitation," Grant said. "We've heard a lot about this place."

"Good, I hope," Sierra added.

"Of course," Grace said with a smile. "Looks like tonight's gonna be the party of the year."

"That's the plan," Sierra told her.

"Then it's a good thing we were invited."

Luke looked over to see a set of identical twins standing beside Brendon.

"You must be cousins," Luke said, offering them his hand.

Brendon turned to the two dark-haired men standing beside him. "These are my cousins, Keegan and Kaden."

"Nice to meet you."

"The pleasure's ours," Keegan stated. "Nice place you have here. Very interested in checking it out."

Luke chuckled when Kaden's gaze followed a couple of women who walked by. There were quite a few single ladies in the house tonight.

"If we can get you anything, just let us know," Cole offered.

"Thanks again," Brendon said, nodding his head, then taking Cheyenne's hand in his and leading the group toward the nearest bar.

"Is it just me or does the Walker family all look the same?" Sierra muttered.

"Hadn't noticed," Luke said, once again staring at Sierra. "Can't get past the dress."

Sierra's eyes held his and her smile was radiant. "Thank you."

"No, thank you," he said, pulling her against him.

"We ready to kick this thing off yet?" Cole asked, placing his arm around Sierra's waist.

"Ready as ever."

After a quick look around the room, Luke noticed things were getting into full swing. It didn't usually take long before clothes started falling off, and it looked as though tonight wasn't an exception.

He glanced back at Cole and Sierra.

Yep, definitely going to be the party of the year.

And it was going to involve a very naked Sierra crushed between him and Cole in the very near future.

9:44 p.m.

THE LOOKS ON LUKE'S AND COLE'S FACES were what women everywhere longed to see, and Sierra couldn't deny seeing them like that made her body heat to astronomical degrees. And when Luke had had difficulty greeting the guests, that only added fuel to Sierra's internal fire.

For the past hour, Sierra had been standing with her husbands, greeting the guests one by one as they came into the club, while the only thing she really wanted to do was to prowl the room and see what was going on. Although she'd spent several minutes talking to friends who had arrived to celebrate the new year with them, she'd opted to stay close to her men.

Still, she didn't mind checking out what was going on.

Yes, there was a voyeur lurking beneath the surface, something she hadn't realized until she'd met Luke years ago. And now, as the party was getting underway, she was eager to join in the festivities.

"Drink?" Cole offered, placing his hand around her waist.

"I'd love one," she told him, allowing him to guide her over to the bar as Luke engaged in conversation with Max and Courtney Adorite.

"You look breathtaking," Cole whispered against her ear after he'd ordered her drink.

"You don't look so bad yourself."

Cole's big hands slid down her back, over her ass, coming to rest on the backs of her thighs. She could feel the rasp of his thumbs as he teased between her thighs. Part of her was tempted to spread her legs a little to give him better access, but she refrained. Although she wasn't necessarily opposed to public exhibitionism, they had learned long ago that no amount of security would be able to keep people from doing things they shouldn't—such as snap photos and threaten to sell them to the tabloids. And for that reason alone, the three of them had agreed that they would use discretion when at the club, unless the guests were limited to their closest friends.

Granted, they didn't always hide out, and they wouldn't promise to, either, but on nights like this, when there were extra guests, several of whom they didn't know all that well, they knew they had to be cautious.

"Do you know how much I want you right now?" Cole mumbled against her ear. "I want to put you on this bar, spread your legs, and drive my tongue into your pussy."

A lightning bolt of heat slammed into her. She absolutely loved when Cole allowed his dirty mouth free rein. Truth was, he didn't do it often. Unlike Luke, Cole was somewhat shy, though he'd shed some of that in the years they'd been together.

"Then what would you do?" she asked, taking her drink when the bartender pushed it toward her.

"Mmm." Cole's fingers twined into her hair, wrapping it around his fingers as he tugged her head back so she was forced to look up at him. "After I made you come with my mouth, I'd pull you down into my lap and let you ride my cock until you were screaming my name."

"And when do we get to make this a reality?" Sierra asked, glancing over her shoulder to see Luke still conversing with Max and Courtney.

"Once all the guests have arrived," he told her.

"That's too long," she said, smiling up at him.

"Don't I know it."

But something else Sierra had learned over the years—mainly thanks to Luke—was that patience definitely was a virtue.

And tonight, she would have to hone hers because, as she glanced at the door, she noticed more people pouring in.

CHAPTER 7

10:27 p.m.

Now that the party was in full swing, Cole stayed with Sierra and Luke, enjoying the conversation and drinks. So far, so good as far as no issues or concerns arising, and he hoped that it remained that way for the rest of the evening.

"Is that…?"

Cole turned to Sierra, then followed her line of sight to see that she was looking at RT and Z in a corner, making out like teenagers. It was almost amusing considering how straight-laced Ryan Trexler was. But Cole knew that the atmosphere prompted people to do things they didn't usually do. Such as have sex in public.

Then again, if people weren't curious, he doubted they would be there in the first place.

"RT and Z," Luke confirmed. "I have to say, I'm rather impressed."

Sierra looked up at Luke. "Impressed that they're making out?"

"That they're letting loose."

Cole was impressed, as well, but he was fairly certain that both men could still tell you where every person in the room was, what they were wearing, and possibly how many drinks they'd had already. It was how they operated. They might be indulging in a little PDA, but he knew it wouldn't go much further than that. Those two just weren't the type.

"Looks like Trent's new furniture is being broken in tonight," Luke noted.

Cole had noticed that, too. In fact, he'd made a mental note to get one of their own to try out at the house.

"Now, that's hot," Sierra said with a whistle.

Cole turned once again, noticing his wife was staring at Xander and Mercedes Boone. The power couple had forgone the opportunity for one of the glass rooms tonight, instead choosing to go with the flow—Xander's words. And it looked as though they'd found their flow, all right. Cole could imagine how their nights were planned. Since Mercedes was a Domme, and Xander was a Dom, the two were a very unlikely pair, but they'd somehow found their way.

Cole pulled Sierra against him. "Are you ogling Xander?"

Sierra smiled up at him over her shoulder. "Have you seen that man?"

Cole laughed. Okay, so Xander was fairly impressive. Six foot six, two seventy-five… The man was massive, towering over most people in the room. And now, shirtless, with Mercedes kneeling before him, he was definitely a sight to behold.

"Are *you* ogling Xander?" Luke asked Cole.

Cole chuckled. "Maybe."

The atmosphere was definitely starting to get to him. His blood was pumping faster as he took it all in. Watching as some couples got down and dirty on the main floor, while others continued to talk and mingle. But no matter what they were doing, everyone seemed to be watching everyone else. And those who'd lost their clothes were being watched the most.

"Well," Luke said, cupping Cole's face in one big hand, "I can definitely think of something to take your mind off that man."

"Here?" Cole asked, releasing Sierra and turning to face Luke.

Luke shook his head, which didn't surprise him. Public exhibitionism was great and fine, hell, Cole even enjoyed it from time to time, but tonight was not going to be one of those nights. He had absolutely no desire to share Sierra or Luke with people he didn't know.

Cole glanced at Sierra. She nodded.

"I've got an idea," Cole told Luke, taking both their hands and leading them toward the stairs.

"Where are—"

Sierra stopped, placed her free hand over Luke's mouth, effectively silencing him. "Tonight, Mr. McCoy, you don't get to ask the questions."

"But—"

Sierra shook her head. "Shh. I promise, we'll take good care of you."

And Cole definitely intended to do just that.

10:54 p.m.

LUKE WASN'T SURE HOW THIS HAD HAPPENED, but here he was, in his office, watching Sierra and Cole intently, wondering what the hell they were planning to do to him. A couple of years ago, he wouldn't have budged from the main floor, insisting that he keep an eye on things.

When it came to Cole and Sierra, he'd long ago resigned himself to doing things he'd never thought he would do. Like sneak up to his office in the middle of a New Year's party.

When Cole took Luke's hand and led him over to the windows that overlooked the floor below, he willingly moved with him. Reluctance didn't play a part in his feelings at the moment. Anticipation, sure. Desire, definitely. Anxiety … maybe just a little bit.

But Luke trusted them, knew they wouldn't hurt him in any way. That was part of what love was. The ability to put yourself in someone else's hands and trust that they will take care of you. He knew from experience that these two would take good care of him.

Sure, it had taken Luke a long time to get to this point in his life. He'd been almost forty when he'd fallen in love for the first time. But since the day he'd met Sierra, he'd known something was different about her. She had changed him, given him the opportunity to open his eyes and see what was important, including his feelings for Cole.

"Put your hands on the glass," Cole instructed.

Luke did, placing his hands on the glass on either side of his head, leaving about three feet between him and the window. While they moved around behind him, Luke watched the people below. Things were getting interesting at this point. The chairs Trent had invested in were getting good use, and he didn't mind watching. Not at all.

He noticed Trace and Marissa Kogan standing by the bar, laughing and talking with Travis, Kylie, and Gage. Luke didn't expect any of them to participate in public sex, but they didn't seem to mind what was going on around them. In fact, Grant, Grace, and Lane—the people Cheyenne had introduced him to—were going to town on one of the sofas behind Travis and his entourage. And that, he hadn't exactly expected. The sweet little cowgirl seemed much too innocent to be kneeling in front of the bigger cowboy—Lane—his dick tunneling in and out of her mouth while Grant stroked Lane at the same time. But they seemed to be enjoying themselves.

Then, of course, Mistress Serena and her two male subs were in one of the glass rooms. She had one strapped to a St. Andrews cross—facing the cross—while the other kneeled behind him, rimming his asshole with his tongue. Of course they had an audience, raptly watching from outside the room, including Max and Courtney Adorite, who were talking to Phoenix, Mia, and Tarik.

For a brief moment, Luke wondered what they were talking about, but that thought quickly fled when Sierra's arms came around his waist, her deft little fingers working open his belt.

He managed to keep from speaking while she worked his slacks open, then did the same to his shirt. Within minutes, she'd disrobed him completely, leaving him standing there naked, once again with his hands planted on the window.

The people below couldn't see him, but for a brief moment, he wished they could.

Unable to stifle a groan, Luke closed his eyes when Sierra's mouth blazed a trail of fire down his spine, her soft fingers moving over his skin as she teased and tormented him before coming to stand in front of him.

"You've been a naughty boy, Mr. McCoy."

Luke grinned. "You think so?"

"I definitely think so," she said, taking his cock in her small hands and fisting him, stroking him slowly.

Another groan escaped him.

"Turn around," she instructed.

Luke let his hands drop to his sides, then turned around to see Cole was naked as well, his lean, muscular body on full display. Sierra, however, was still wearing that sexy dress and those fuck me heels. He secretly hoped she didn't take off either because, although she was the most impressive thing he'd ever seen when she was naked, she rocked that dress like no one else could.

As he watched, Sierra hopped up onto the edge of Luke's desk, facing him. She kept her legs demurely closed initially, but then her hands slid down her thighs, and she spread her knees, giving him a fucking incredible view of her soft pink folds. She wasn't wearing any panties, and he found that hot as hell.

"Cole," Sierra called.

Cole moved around to stand before her, the muscles in his back flexing as he placed his hands on her knees, shouldering his way between her thighs as he went to his knees before her.

Sierra smiled when Luke met her gaze.

"You get to watch," she said.

"Watch what?" he prompted, wanting to hear her go into detail about what he was about to witness.

"Watch him lick me," she said.

"It would be my pleasure."

Never having been one to follow the rules, Luke took a step closer, coming to stand directly behind Cole. He gripped his cock in his fist while he watched Cole's head dip between her thighs. Sierra moaned, her eyes rolling back as Cole's tongue darted out and slid through her slick folds.

That was when Luke got an idea. A better idea than this one, even.

"Wait," Luke said. Holding out his hand to Sierra, he paused until she reached for him.

Hiding his smile of victory, he helped her off the desk, then took a seat in his chair, pulling her down on top of him, her back to his chest.

"My turn," Luke growled. "Cole, come here."

Cole willingly turned around so that he was kneeling between their legs. Luke had adjusted Sierra so that his cock was visible between her thighs, right there in plain sight for Cole to see.

"Make her come," Luke instructed. "With your mouth."

He stifled a groan when Cole's big hand wrapped around his dick, stroking him slowly as his warm breath fanned the swollen head. Unable to look away, he watched over Sierra's shoulder as Cole's mouth descended, his tongue stroking Sierra's smooth flesh as she sat in Luke's lap, her hands gripping the arms of the chair.

"You like that?" Luke whispered in her ear. "You like when we both give you what you need?"

Luke reached between her thighs, separating her folds with his fingers, giving them a better view of Cole's skilled tongue caressing her engorged clit.

"Tell me, Sierra," Luke encouraged. "Do you like it?"

"Yes," she said on a breathless sigh. She slid her fingers into Cole's hair, holding his head between her legs. "I've been waiting for this."

It had been a while since the three of them had played together. Due to busy schedules, Liam's birth, the holidays … an endless list of reasons … they hadn't had a chance to be together like this.

But tonight, even though there were people downstairs, it was all Luke wanted, all he needed. These two people.

Right here. Right now.

11:12 p.m.

"God, baby," Luke crooned in her ear, "you are so wet."

She definitely was. It was pure heaven to have Cole between their legs. He'd started alternating between licking her pussy and sucking Luke's rigid cock. His tongue was doing incredible things to her while she sat on Luke's lap, to the point her body was humming.

If she hadn't been overwhelmed by pleasure, she would've said something about Luke taking control of the situation. She'd had a few ideas of her own, but she should've known that Luke McCoy wasn't an easy man to control. But, on the flip side, she enjoyed this so much more. Loved the way he took over, intensified her pleasure by focusing on her.

There were times when she didn't feel as desirable as she'd once been, but never when she was with these men. They always made her feel like the most beautiful woman in the world, their desire for her unwavering. It only ratcheted up her need for them.

Luke's fingers released her pussy lips, his big hands gripping the insides of her thighs as he spread her legs wide.

"Lick her," he grunted to Cole. "Fuck her with your tongue."

Cole obliged, his tongue sliding inside her as Luke shifted her, allowing Cole better access.

"Let him see your tits," Luke grumbled in her ear.

Sierra pulled the top of her dress down, freeing her breasts, and Cole's hungry gaze slid up her body. The dress was now bunched around her waist. Knowing that Cole enjoyed it when she participated, Sierra cupped her breasts, squeezing them, teasing her nipples while he slipped two fingers inside her, his lips wrapping around her clit, sucking until the sensation was nearly too much.

"I want you to come," Luke said, his voice laced with gravel. "Then I want to slide my dick into your sweet little ass while Cole fills your pussy. Can you handle that, baby?"

Sierra nodded, trying to process what he was saying, but the words were merely filler at this point. She was overwhelmed by sensation, her body tightening as her climax loomed.

"Luke … Cole…" She couldn't hold back any longer; her orgasm crested, then exploded. She cried out, her body convulsing as Cole continued to lick and suck, his fingers curling until they were brushing her G-spot, making brilliant flecks of light dance behind her closed eyelids.

She thought he would send her over again, but Cole slowly eased his fingers from her body, and she opened her eyes to see him laving Luke's dick, his eyes locked on them.

"Fucking perfect," Luke growled. "Love watching you suck me."

While he did, Cole reached behind him for the desk, retrieving a tube of lubricant. Sierra fought to catch her breath as she watched Cole lube Luke's dick, preparing him so that he could fill her ass the way he'd promised.

When Cole got to his feet and planted his ass on the edge of the desk, Sierra wondered what they had in mind, but it didn't take long for her to figure it out. Luke stood, lifting her as though she weighed nothing. She reached for Cole, wrapping her legs around his waist, her arms around his neck. He was holding her weight off him while Luke guided Cole's cock into her pussy.

Sierra eased down on him, Cole's hands gripping her ass tightly. She couldn't move in this position, but Cole easily lifted her, lowered her, his cock filling her so exquisitely. She felt Luke's warmth at her back, knew he was getting ready.

And then his cock was nudging her asshole while Cole stilled, the muscles in his arms flexing as he held her between them. Sometimes she wondered how they came up with these positions, but she never complained. They knew what they were doing, knew how to pleasure her in ways she'd never imagined.

"Relax, baby," Luke whispered against her ear as the thick head of his cock breached the tight ring of muscles.

Sierra took deep breaths, relaxing as he slid deeper, her body so full it was uncomfortable at first. Cole began moving beneath her, filling her, and she realized that Luke was holding her, as well. And then they were both thrusting their hips upward, filling her at the same time, then resuming an alternating rhythm. Someone's thumb—she didn't know whose—pressed against her clit, circling the bundle of nerves until she was panting, her head spinning as the pleasure intensified.

She reached for Luke, her hand curling around his neck behind her while her other arm ringed around Cole's neck, holding them both to her as they fucked her roughly, their combined grunts and groans echoing in the oversized office.

"Ah, Sierra," Cole mumbled. "That's it, baby. Squeeze my dick."

Her inner muscles clamped down on him as he fucked her.

"God, Sierra," Luke groaned. "So fucking tight. Gonna make me come."

She wanted them to come. At the same time. Wanted them to fill her, to claim her in a way that only they could do.

That thought triggered her orgasm, brilliant sensation racing out from her center, making her mind spin as she gave herself over to her release.

More grunts followed and she knew they were close. Their combined thrusts jarred her, but she held on to both of them until their rough groans turned to possessive growls as they slammed into her once more, then twice. On the final thrust, they both roared in unison, hard bodies surrounding her as they came.

It was the perfect way to end the year, once again crushed between the two men she loved, filled by them, loved by them, consumed by them.

CHAPTER 8

11:43 p.m.

AFTER GREETING GUESTS FOR THE FIRST TWO hours of the night, Trent had taken to the shadows as he normally did. Being in the limelight, especially at events like tonight, wasn't high on his priority list. He knew that because of who he was—one of the most sought-after actors on the market at the moment—he often drew unnecessary attention.

And when it came to Devotion, attention wasn't necessarily a good thing. People who came to places like this enjoyed their anonymity, and the last thing they wanted to worry about was the paparazzi stalking someone else and them getting caught in the crossfire.

That had happened to him before and he'd learned his lesson.

But this place… Devotion… This was his sanctuary. A place he actually found offered him a purpose, and he wasn't only talking in a sexual sense.

So, tonight was about enjoying the scenery, making sure people were enjoying themselves, and that the potential investors for what he hoped would be his own club in the very near future were getting what they needed.

Luckily, that seemed to be the case tonight. Which was how he found himself with a few minutes to spare before the countdown to midnight began.

Call him a glutton for punishment or whatever, but there was one particular woman he was in search of. He'd already seen Clarissa Tinsley once tonight, but as usual, she seemed to be avoiding him.

Glancing around the room, taking a few minutes to admire the writhing, sweaty bodies engaged in a wide variety of sexual endeavors, Trent sought Clarissa out once more. He had noticed she had come with Xander and Mercedes Boone tonight, and not with Shane Gibson, a Dom she'd once been involved with. Why that had made him feel better, Trent didn't quite understand, but he knew that foreign feeling was worth pursuing, at least for one night.

He scanned the room, moving from one face to another.

There.

Squinting to see through the dimly lit club, Trent locked his eyes on Clarissa's sexy, petite body, her long chestnut hair that hung down her back in thick waves. He had the sudden urge to wrap his fists in her hair and pull her in so he could claim her mouth.

As though she sensed his attention, her honey-gold eyes lifted to meet his, and he stopped for a moment, trying to feel her out. Would she welcome his advances tonight? Or would she push him away the way she had in the past?

It wasn't that Trent minded the games—it was refreshing, actually—but with Clarissa, he got the feeling he had to play this just right or she would run far and fast in the opposite direction.

A deep, rumbling voice echoed through the space. "Everyone, we've got ten minutes until midnight."

Ten minutes was just enough time for Trent to get in place, so he stopped by the bar, grabbed two flutes of champagne from the many that had been set out, then headed for Clarissa.

Without saying a word, he invaded her personal space, locking his eyes with hers as he held out the glass for her to take.

Her bright brown eyes widened as she stared up at him, but she didn't take the champagne he offered.

"What do you want?" she questioned softly.

Trent smiled, never looking away as he said, "You."

Unlike a lot of women who would've jumped at the opportunity to be pursued by him, Clarissa glared at him, a frown obscuring her beautiful features.

"Sorry, not interested."

Oh, she was interested, all right. He knew it and she knew it. If she wanted to play hard to get, Trent was game. He didn't mind one fucking bit, because he knew what Clarissa Tinsley wanted from him.

The woman he'd set his sights on was submissive, and that fact called to a very dominant, very possessive side of him. She wasn't looking for a man who would bend to her will; she wanted a man who would stake his claim. But, again, Trent knew there was a very delicate balance here. There was a vast difference between being dominant and being controlling. She didn't want someone who wanted to control her.

And Trent... He didn't want to control her.

But he definitely wanted to dominate her. In every fucking way possible.

CLARISSA FELT THE HEAT IN TRENT'S IRIDESCENT blue eyes, and it took every ounce of her self-control not to give away anything that she was feeling. For so long, she'd wanted this man, only she didn't think he could give her what she needed.

It was true, she was a submissive, and she wasn't looking for just any man. She wanted a Dom, a man who could tend to her every need.

That was the reason she'd been with Shane for so long, only their relationship wasn't intimate by design. Sure, there was sometimes sex involved because that was the nature of the lifestyle, but for the past six months, Clarissa had put a halt to that.

And this man—with his otherworldly good looks, his light blue eyes and dark hair, chiseled jaw and prominent chin—was the reason she'd been abstaining.

"Five minutes!" someone announced, referring to the countdown to midnight.

Clarissa swallowed hard when she realized Trent wasn't moving. He wasn't the least bit intimidated by her, and that made her body all the more aware of his.

"You're interested," Trent said, his tone firm. "You can deny it all day long, but I know better."

They continued to stare off with one another, but Clarissa couldn't seem to back down. Part of her wanted to lower her eyes, to show him that she was willing to submit to him, but something kept her from doing so.

The space between them seemed to be growing smaller and smaller, and Clarissa realized Trent was moving closer. She instinctively took one step back and found herself pressed up against the wall.

"Two minutes!"

Clarissa barely heard the words, her heart was pounding so loudly in her ears. And it had nothing to do with fear and everything to do with anticipation.

Trent turned, and for a moment, Clarissa thought he was going to leave her, but he simply put down the champagne glasses, then turned back to her, this time closing the gap between them entirely.

He was tall, which required her to stare up at him, her body now trapped between the wall and his impressive chest.

She sucked in a breath when Trent cupped her face in his big, warm hands.

"I'm going to kiss you, Clarissa. The way I've wanted to kiss you for so fucking long."

Her head nodded, without her permission.

A small smile tipped the corners of his beautiful mouth.

"One minute!"

Swallowing hard, Clarissa closed her eyes when Trent leaned in, his mouth hovering directly above hers. She could feel his breath against her lips.

"Tell me you want this, Rissa."

Oh, she wanted this, all right.

She sucked in another breath, fighting to keep her hands at her sides.

"Tell. Me."

The dominance in his tone had her eyes opening, meeting his gaze once more, but she couldn't find the words.

"I won't kiss you until you do," he said. "And I'm not asking. I'm telling. I want to hear you say it."

"I want it," she whispered.

"What? What is it that you want?"

"I want you to kiss me," she admitted, her body vibrating, her stomach doing a series of somersaults.

"You know when I do it's only going to be the beginning, right?"

She hoped that was the case.

"They say that the person you kiss at midnight is the one you'll be with in the coming year. Can you live with that, Rissa? Because that's the promise I'm making."

Clarissa nodded.

"Ten!"

"Nine!"

"Say it," Trent demanded.

"Eight!"

"Seven!"

"Six!"

"Five!"

"Last chance," Trent growled.

"Four!"

"Three!"

She nodded again. "Yes. I can live with it."

"Two!"

"One!"

While everyone screamed, "Happy New Year," Clarissa found herself giving in to Trent's kiss. He cupped her face firmly, his lips sliding over hers, claiming her mouth in a way she'd never expected. She reached for him, trying to pull him closer, although they were already touching. She opened her mouth when his tongue coaxed its way in, tangling with hers as a rough rumble vibrated in his chest.

His kiss was unlike anything she'd ever known, anything she'd ever expected.

And Clarissa knew in that moment that this next year … she would learn some things about herself that she'd never expected.

All because Trent Ramsey had claimed her at midnight.

CHAPTER
9

New Year's Day

12:00 a.m.

"Happy New Year," Luke whispered, his arms around Cole as they held Sierra close to them. They shared a kiss, separately, then together, sealing the deal for the year.

They'd rejoined the party only thirty minutes ago, never leaving one another as they'd anticipated the countdown to midnight, and here they were, together.

"I love you," Luke whispered against Cole's ear. "More than I can ever express."

It was true, Luke wasn't sure he'd ever be able to express to either of them just how much they meant to him, but he certainly was putting forth the effort. Each and every day.

Were there some games involved? Like him pretending to go off the deep end just to get their attention? Sure. But most importantly, it was never devious, because when it came to these two, every minute he got to spend with one or both of them was what he lived for.

Cole pulled back and met Luke's gaze. Luke could see in Cole's eyes that he knew Luke loved him unconditionally. It'd taken time to get to this point, but once they'd arrived, he knew there was no going back. Ever.

"I love you, too," Cole replied, then they both looked down at Sierra, who was smiling up at them.

"I love you, too, baby," Luke told her at the same time Cole did.

Sierra's grin widened as she stared up at both of them. She was leaning against Cole, her hand clutching Luke's jacket. "Happy New Year," she said. "To another amazing year."

"And many more," Luke told them.

The traditional New Year's song began to play, and everyone was hugging one another and laughing, which, for Luke, was the best part of this party. Their family and friends were here—a lot of them, anyway—celebrating the beginning of another fabulous year. And though some people were rooted in tradition and would be making resolutions, Luke only planned on one thing.

Spending 2016 with the people he loved, the people who meant the most to him.

His family.

CHAPTER 10

9:33 p.m.

COLE FELT AS THOUGH HE WERE WALKING around in a fog. He was past the point of exhaustion. Between the party at Devotion last night—which had lasted until after four this morning—and then spending the day with the kids and having dinner with Logan, Samantha, and Elijah, he was wiped out, ready to hit the pillow and not wake for at least eight hours.

"There you are," Sierra greeted him when he walked into the bedroom.

"Here I am," he conceded, watching her through bleary eyes.

"Get on the bed," she said sweetly. "I'll give you a back rub."

Oh, hell. A back rub sounded like pure heaven at this point.

He didn't even bother to strip off his sweat pants, but he managed to yank off his shirt before he flopped onto the bed, facedown.

Sierra crawled over him, straddling his ass, her soft, cool fingers sliding over his back, drawing a contented groan from him. He loved when she massaged him. He heard the shower turn off as he lay there, moaning in earnest when Sierra began kneading the muscles in his shoulders.

"It's been a long day," Sierra said softly.

"Definitely." Cole didn't bother turning his face, his nose still buried in the mattress. He was too damn tired to move.

"You should relax a little."

"Trying."

After Logan, Sam, and Elijah had left, Cole had cleaned the kitchen and managed to take a quick shower while Luke put Hannah to bed and Sierra tended to Liam. Now both kids were sound asleep, the house was quiet, and Cole was ready to curl up next to Sierra and Luke and sleep until morning. Except he didn't want Sierra to stop what she was doing, because her magical fingers were stirring his fatigued body to life despite the fact he could hardly keep his eyes open.

"He asleep?" Luke's deep voice reverberated through the room.

"Not yet," Cole mumbled, turning his head and getting an eyeful of Luke's naked body. "You walk around like that and I don't think I'll be able to sleep."

Luke grinned and Sierra chuckled, her elbow now digging gently into his knotted shoulder muscle.

"I can think of something that might help him sleep," Sierra told Luke from her perch on Cole's back.

"I can, too," Luke agreed, his eyes meeting Cole's. "Turn over; let her massage your front."

Oh, hell. Cole knew exactly where this was going.

"Unless you're too tired," Sierra whispered in his ear.

He was never too tired for what they were proposing.

Never.

9:47 p.m.

LUKE WATCHED COLE AS HE ROLLED OVER onto his back, the muscles in his upper body flexing beautifully as he did. Just watching him move made Luke's dick hard.

That and seeing Sierra sitting there, wearing Cole's T-shirt and a smile.

"We should get him out of his clothes," Sierra said. "I can massage him better that way."

Cole moaned, making Luke laugh.

Without hesitating, Luke stripped Cole's sweat pants from his body, tossing them onto the floor. He turned to Sierra. "Your turn."

"Me?" Her eyes widened in mock surprise.

"Definitely need you naked," Cole told her, pushing her T-shirt up.

Sierra sighed heavily, another smile breaking free. "Fine."

Her shirt quickly joined Cole's sweat pants on the floor.

"Keep massaging him," Luke commanded.

Sierra straddled Cole's waist while Luke grabbed the tube of lubricant from the nightstand drawer, then moved to the end of the bed. He placed one knee on the mattress, then leaned down and kissed Sierra's neck. She tilted her head, giving him better access. He trailed his lips down her back, moving her hair out of the way as he did. When he reached the dimples just above her ass, he bent down, gripped Cole's cock, and gently licked over the swollen head.

Cole groaned, his hips bucking upward, nearly sending Sierra tumbling off him.

"Be still," Sierra instructed Cole with a laugh.

"Not easy when he's sucking me," Cole retorted, his hands fisting in the blankets.

Luke devoted his full attention to Cole, licking, sucking, laving his balls while Sierra continued to rub his chest and arms.

"Feel good?" Sierra asked.

Luke couldn't see Cole's face, but he could imagine him lying there, eyes closed, mouth partially open. The mental image made his dick thicken.

"So fucking good." Cole thrust up against Luke's hand. "Come here," Cole groaned, and Luke looked up to see Sierra shifting, moving forward until she was straddling Cole's head.

"Oh, God," she hissed, her hands gripping the headboard.

Luke stroked the velvety, hard length of Cole's dick while he watched Sierra ride Cole's mouth. She didn't seem to be in a hurry, but neither was Luke. Although he couldn't imagine going to sleep until the three of them had come, he was still tired. It'd been a long couple of days, but this was one of those moments that he couldn't pass up, no matter what.

He managed to work his way up onto the bed, inserting himself between Cole's thick thighs as he sucked Cole's dick. He forced Cole's legs back, then proceeded to suck Cole's balls into his mouth one at a time, then both, giving them all the attention he could.

His dick throbbed with anticipation, desperate to feel the tight clasp of Cole's body, but he managed to keep himself in check. Tonight was about Cole.

Sierra cried out, her body drawing tight. "Cole! Oh, God. Right there … right there … don't stop. Oh, fuck … please don't stop."

Luke kept his eyes on Sierra as she continued to sit astride Cole's head, her hips thrusting as she rode Cole's mouth, letting him fuck her with his tongue. It was a beautiful sight, one Luke would never tire of seeing. One of his favorite pastimes was watching the two of them together. They were so damn sexy, so fucking beautiful, sometimes it hurt to look at them, and when they were together, Luke couldn't get enough.

"Cole!" Sierra screamed as she pressed down against Cole's mouth, her body shuddering as she came.

When she rolled off Cole, curling up next to him, Luke released Cole's dick from his mouth and smiled.

"You ready for me?" he asked Cole as he knelt between his legs, reaching for the lube.

"Always."

And wasn't that the most beautiful word in the English language?

Luke squeezed a generous amount of lube onto his fingers, then gently slid them over Cole's taint, going lower, dipping one finger inside his asshole, then two. He never took his eyes off Cole's face, watching him as he began gently thrusting two fingers deep inside.

"Have I told you how much I love watching this?" Sierra whispered.

Luke grinned over at her. "A few times."

"It's so damn hot."

That was exactly how Luke felt about watching the two of them together. He didn't know what it was, wasn't sure why he enjoyed it, but he didn't question it. He had the best of both worlds, he wasn't going to deny it.

Sierra reached for Cole's cock, stroking him at the same slow pace that Luke was fucking Cole's ass with his fingers, dipping a third inside, then back to using one.

"Luke," Cole groaned, his eyes closing briefly when Luke purposely brushed Cole's prostate. "Don't tease."

Because Cole instructed him not to, Luke teased Cole for a while. One finger, two, three. Back to one. He repeated the process, continuing to go slow while Sierra leisurely jacked Cole's rock-hard cock.

"You want me to fuck you?" Luke asked Cole.

"Yes." The single word came out on a breathless moan.

"And you want to watch me fuck him?" Luke asked Sierra.

"Desperately."

Luke grinned. "In case I'm too tired after this ... I love you both."

"Love you, too," came the chorus.

Forcing Cole's legs closer to his body, which caused Sierra to switch positions so she could continue to stroke Cole, Luke added more lube, coated his cock, then lined up so he could ease inside Cole. Pinning him with his gaze, he sank into Cole, drawing in a deep breath as he did, the warmth of Cole's body stealing his breath.

"Fuck, you feel good," he mumbled, dropping his gaze to where their bodies were joined.

"Need you ... to fuck me..." Cole ground out, his head tilted back. "Now!"

Luke didn't need to be told twice. He pushed into Cole, retreated, pushed in again. Keeping his movements slow and easy, he worked his way inside, and once he was settled all the way, he pulled out and then slammed home.

A sexy rumble came from Cole's chest.

Luke continued, impaling Cole, bending him in half while Sierra snaked her hand between their bodies, continuing to jack Cole off while Luke fucked him for all he was worth.

Cole met his eyes, determination and love reflecting back at him. It was so damn beautiful.

Luke changed the angle, pounding downward into Cole's ass while he held himself above him. "Gonna make you come," Luke bit out, fucking Cole hard and fast.

Cole didn't respond, the muscles in his neck tightening as he forced himself into the mattress, angling his hips so Luke could hit that sweet spot.

"Fuck... Fuck..." Cole closed his eyes and Luke continued to watch him. "Gonna... Oh, fuck, Luke... Gonna come."

"Come for me, baby," Luke commanded, grinding his teeth together in an effort to hold back.

Cole grabbed a pillow and covered his face, a dull roar sounding from beneath it. He came hard, which triggered Luke's release. He slammed into him again and again, shallow, deep, letting go as he filled Cole's ass.

"Yep, that was definitely hot," Sierra said from beside him.

Cole tossed the pillow away and they both looked at Sierra. Luke couldn't help it, he laughed at the same time Cole did, forcing Luke to retreat from Cole's body.

"Glad you enjoyed it," Cole teased.

"Always."

And there was that word again.

10:42 p.m.

WHILE LUKE AND COLE DISAPPEARED INTO THE bathroom to clean up, Sierra grabbed her discarded shirt from the floor and pulled it on. She slept naked a lot of the time, but with Liam's sleep schedule, it didn't necessarily make sense. Then again, when she tried to go to bed with clothes on, Luke usually insisted that she remove them.

That didn't stop her from trying, simply to get him to remove them.

Hmm. It seemed as though she had a game she played, too. Not much different from the one Luke engaged in, pretending to be on the verge of a meltdown just to get a response from them.

The thought made her smile.

Maybe that was how they kept their marriage spontaneous.

It made her wonder what game Cole might play. Or if he merely enjoyed playing theirs.

"You ready for bed yet?" Cole asked, grinning down at her as he pulled the blankets back.

When he crawled into bed, she curled up against him, resting her head on his chest.

"You know Luke's gonna make you take the shirt off," he said softly.

"I know."

Cole chuckled and kissed the top of her head. "I love you, Sierra."

"I love you, too. So much."

Luke joined them a moment later. When he pulled the blankets back on his side of the bed, Sierra could feel the heat of his gaze against her back. A rumble escaped his chest as he said, "The shirt needs to go."

Sierra smiled to herself as she worked the shirt off, then tossed it at him.

Luke turned off the lamp and crawled into bed, his warm body spooning hers as he crushed her between him and Cole.

"Love you," Luke stated, his voice already raspy with sleep.

"Love you, too," they both said in unison.

"Happy New Year," Luke rumbled, getting settled as he moved his hand so that it rested on Cole's chest.

Sierra placed her hand over his, then Cole rested his on theirs.

"Happy New Year," Cole mumbled, sounding half-asleep.

Another smile formed on her lips as she lay there, surrounded by the men she loved.

She'd made it through another year and was already embarking on the next, knowing she was truly blessed. She had two beautiful, healthy children, two amazing husbands, a fantastic group of friends and family.

What more could a girl ask for?

And now, as she drifted off, she wondered what the next year would bring.

Fall Festival

Zane

"Whose idea was this, anyway?" Zane grumbled to anyone who would listen, although he realized no one really was listening to him. Not unusual.

"Hush," V told him, squeezing his arm gently. "You're gonna have fun and you know it."

Zane smirked, unable to help himself. He was actually looking forward to the fall festival that they'd been roped into attending, but he knew everyone would expect him to protest a little. It was what he did, especially now that Travis was so freaking happy all the damn time. His oldest brother used to be the one to bitch and moan at every turn, but now he was just … happy. It was kind of freaky.

Speaking of Travis...

"Where is Travis, anyway?" Zane asked, glancing over his shoulder at Braydon and Brendon, who were following close behind with Jessie in tow.

"He was helpin' Mom and Pop with their crap," Braydon informed him.

"What crap?"

"They've got a booth this year," Brendon said.

"What kind of booth?" Zane asked, spinning around to face his brothers.

"No idea. They wouldn't tell me."

Zane looked around at all the people milling about. Every year Coyote Ridge put on a fall festival, and it seemed that no matter what, the entire town generally made an appearance. Granted, Zane wasn't usually amongst those in attendance because he frequently found a reason to get out of it. Not this year.

No, this year, Kaleb had insisted that they attend for Mason's benefit. Since it was his nephew Mason's first festival, Zane hadn't been able to argue. Now that he was there, he was wondering where the others were.

"There's Kylie and Gage." Jessie pointed in the direction of her sister. The rest of them turned to follow where she was looking. Sure enough, Kylie and Gage were making their way over, and it looked like Gage had already made a stop at one of the concession stands.

"Turkey leg? Seriously?" Zane asked his brother-in-law. "And you didn't think to get me one?"

"You're a big boy. Get your own," Gage said with a devilish grin. "Anyway, I got this one for my wife."

"I bet you did," V stated. "Kinda makes me question why you haven't bothered to share it with her yet."

"I'm holding out for funnel cake," Kylie said. "He can have a turkey leg, but Travis is probably gonna have somethin' to say about him not waiting for him."

"What kind of booth are Mom and Pop settin' up?" Zane asked, hoping someone could enlighten him. Why he wanted to know, he couldn't say for sure, but he was incredibly curious.

"Pies," Kylie said with a mischievous grin.

"Like, apple pies?" Jessie questioned, but even Zane could tell Jessie was in on the joke.

"Yes. Sort of." Kylie nodded her head, her eyes wide.

Oh, hell.

"Who's helpin' them with this booth?" Zane asked, not sure whether he wanted to hear the answer to that question.

As though on cue, his cell phone rang. He snatched it from his pocket and looked at the screen. It was his dad.

"What's up?" Zane greeted his father, his stomach churning because he suddenly knew exactly what the phone call was about.

"Your mother and I need you to come help us with the booth."

"Why?" Zane asked, knowing he should've just kept his mouth shut. "I thought Travis was helpin' out."

"He's done his part. Now it's your turn."

"My turn? Why not Kaleb? Or Sawyer? Or Ethan?" Zane looked at the twins. "Or the twins? Why's it have to be me?"

"You won the coin toss. Now get over here, boy."

Zane shoved his phone back in his pocket when his father disconnected as he peered around at his family. They were all looking at him knowingly.

"Son of a bitch," he grumbled.

A chorus of laughter erupted, and then he was being ushered away from the concession stands by Braydon and Brendon. When he tried to dig his heels in the dirt, Gage lent a hand, and he had no choice but to keep moving forward.

"Y'all just remember that payback is a bitch."

"We know. Why do you think you won the coin toss?" Gage asked, chuckling.

"Me? What the hell did I do?" Zane tried to think about the last stunt he'd pulled, and no matter how hard he tried, he couldn't come up with anything.

This was not going to be good. He could feel it now.

Travis

"Is he on his way?" Travis asked his father when the old man disconnected the call.

"Yup," Curtis replied, a small smile curving the corners of his lips.

"'Bout time," Sawyer added. "He's gonna be pissed, y'all know that, right?"

"He'll get over it," Beau chimed in.

Travis glanced at Ethan, who was standing beside Beau, the two of them looking more content than Travis had ever seen them.

"You lucked out this year," Travis told Ethan.

"Me? What the hell did I do? I've been good all year long," Ethan said, his serious tone belying the grin he couldn't seem to hide.

"Right. And what's the new definition of good? I'm gonna need to make sure I'm up on this new terminology," Sawyer said smartly.

"Careful," Ethan warned Sawyer. "As I look around here, I think I can count at least two dozen women who'd love to see you in Zane's place."

Sawyer turned and looked around as though trying to eye those women Ethan was referring to before looking back at him. It wasn't hard. There were literally about two dozen who had Sawyer in their sights. The guy was a fucking chick magnet.

"Probably. Not gonna happen, though," Sawyer said confidently.

"It might," Curtis added. "You never know."

Travis laughed, trying to hide his grin when he noticed Brendon, Braydon, and Gage pushing Zane toward them, Kylie, Jessie, and V walking a few steps behind them, grinning wildly.

"What is goin' on?" Zane asked when he approached, his eyes widening when he looked at the table that had been set up and the stand behind it. "Oh, hell no. No way, man."

"Watch your mouth, boy," Curtis growled. "There're ladies present."

"Yes, sir," Zane mouthed. "But seriously. Y'all cannot do this to me."

"We can. And we did. You're up," Travis said, gesturing toward the booth.

"I thought y'all said this was somethin' to do with pies."

"It is," Travis confirmed, stepping back out of the way, allowing Zane to see the boxes that were stacked behind him.

"What are those?" Zane asked, confused.

"Pies. Just like we promised," V confirmed.

"So why do I have to do that?" Zane pointed to the dunking booth that they'd set up behind the table.

"It's our new marketing strategy," Sawyer answered Zane. "We figured we'd sell more pies if we let each person who buys one get a chance to dunk you."

Zane's forehead wrinkled and he glowered at all of them. Travis had to admit, the idea had been rather brilliant. Unfortunately, he didn't get to take the credit for coming up with it.

"Whose idea was this?" Zane questioned, looking at each of the faces staring back at him.

"Mine."

Travis laughed as their mother stepped forward, taking full credit for coming up with the idea. And she had, too. Granted, she hadn't nominated Zane to be in the booth, but they'd all figured he needed some payback for something.

"Why me?" Zane asked, pouting.

V moved up beside him, wrapping her arm around him as she smiled.

"Actually…" Lorrie paused, causing all eyes to turn to her. "Every one of my boys is gonna get a chance in that booth today."

Zane smirked.

Travis frowned.

"Hold on a minute," Travis addressed his mother. "That wasn't the deal."

"And how do you know that?" Lorrie countered. "If I remember correctly, you boys didn't help us make those pies."

Travis looked at Kylie. She was smiling sweetly, apparently enjoying this new turn of events.

"We all got together and had a discussion," Kylie informed him. "While we were making pies."

Damn.

He wasn't sure how he was going to be able to get out of this one.

Ethan

Ethan watched the others, trying to figure out just how he had managed to get pulled into this.

"Hey, wait a minute. I did help make those pies," he said, ignoring Beau, who was laughing over his shoulder.

"You're right, you did," Lorrie replied. "Which is why we've nominated Beau to go in your place."

Ethan laughed, looking back at Beau. He laughed harder when the smile on Beau's handsome face immediately fell, and he sputtered something unintelligible.

"I like that idea," Ethan said.

The look Beau gave him offered his own brand of retribution, and Ethan laughed but managed not to say anything. He could take anything Beau had to dish out. And he'd gladly take it, at that.

"So, I'm first, huh?" Zane asked, his expression reflecting just how unhappy he was with that idea.

"Yep. You're up," Gage told him.

"And how did you get out of having to do this?" Brendon asked Gage.

"Lucky, I guess," Gage replied.

Ethan wondered just how he could go about changing that. In all fairness, if Beau had to get dunked, Gage should have to, as well.

Watching Zane as he moved toward the booth, Ethan listened to the chatter around them. They'd drawn a crowd, there was no doubt about that. Then again, he wasn't sure there was a person in Coyote Ridge who wouldn't want to take a chance at sending one of his brothers into a pool of water. Honestly, the idea of selling pies— all of the money from those sales would go to the church—and giving the purchaser the opportunity to dunk one of them had been rather brilliant. He kind of wished he'd been part of that discussion. But at least he wasn't going to have to be in the booth.

Zane made his way up the steps after discarding his boots and his hat, handing them to V while she giggled uncontrollably.

"You better watch yourself, woman," Zane told V, smiling. He glanced around to ensure their mother wasn't in hearing distance before he continued, "Paybacks are a bitch. And honey, you're first on my shit list."

V laughed. "Bring it on, cowboy," she taunted.

"Oh, sweetness, I plan to."

Zane took his seat, his feet dangling above the water as he stared down at the tub beneath him. All eyes were on him, including Ethan's.

Lorrie placed the sign on the table, reflecting the price of her homemade apple pies and the fact that all money was going to the church. Curtis then stepped up beside her and announced just how it worked. Within seconds, a line had formed, at least thirty people deep. First person in that line was… Of course. Beau.

Ethan watched the man he loved as he handed over a few dollars, not taking a pie, though. Apparently he was willing to pay for the opportunity to dunk Zane, leaving the pie for someone else to buy. Ethan never took his eyes off Beau, although he wanted to watch his brother go down. He just couldn't seem to tear his gaze away from the hottest cowboy he'd ever had the pleasure of laying eyes on. And to think, Beau was his.

All his.

Beau wound back, verbally taunting Zane for a moment before he launched the ball at the target, hitting it right in the center. The next sound was Zane's big-ass body hitting the water, followed by hoots and hollers from the crowd gathered around. Ethan found himself clapping and hollering right along with them. He was tempted to go right up to Beau and kiss him, but he settled for standing next to him, their arms touching, while he listened to the deep, resonating tone of Beau's voice. That was about as good as Ethan got with public displays, but the point was, he was with Beau, and honestly, that was all that really mattered.

Kaleb

Watching Zane take a quick dunk in the booth and now Braydon making his way in, was sending Mason into a fit of giggles. Kaleb tightened his grip around the little boy as he laughed at his brothers, enjoying the hell out of their misery. Granted, he knew he would be going up there soon, but that was a small price to pay, especially if it put a smile on Mason's face like the one plastered there now.

"Are you havin' fun, buddy?" Zoey asked Mason, coming to stand beside them.

"He's lovin' it," Kaleb told her.

"Just wait till it's your turn. He's gonna love seein' his daddy in there."

"We're waitin' to see Uncle Trav, aren't we, Mason?"

Travis, who was standing just a couple of feet away, shot Kaleb a menacing glare. Too bad the crinkles at the corners of his eyes gave away his amusement.

The line was moving at the table now, everyone purchasing a pie, but really, Kaleb believed they were more interested in their chance to dunk one of them in that booth. Heaven knew there were plenty of reasons for the town's residents to want to see it. They were a rough-and-tumble bunch, had been all their lives, and this was probably the first time their neighbors had been given a chance to get them back.

Three people made an attempt to take Braydon down, but each of them missed. That was when Kaleb noticed Sawyer had snuck into the line, sweet-talking a couple of girls so he could get in front of them. Sawyer handed over a wad of cash to Lorrie before taking one of the balls and making his way to the pitching line.

"Man, this is so not cool," Braydon hollered from behind the Plexiglas.

"It's payback," Sawyer said evenly.

"Right. And just remember, you're next."

Sawyer, who had played baseball in high school, reared back and threw the ball, hitting the target in one shot, sending Braydon into the water with a loud yell and making Mason giggle and squeal in Kaleb's arms.

It only took a minute for Braydon to drag himself out of the water, completely drenched, and for Sawyer to get into position. Kaleb glanced over at the table to see who the lucky person was going to be, and that was when he noticed Kennedy Endsley whispering something to the person at the front of the line, smiling brightly when the guy allowed her in front of him.

She handed over money, but rather than take one ball from the table, she took three.

"You worried you can't get it in one shot?" Sawyer asked her from the booth.

"It's just a precaution," Kennedy said smoothly.

Kaleb's brothers joined him, all of them standing together, including Zane and Braydon, who had towels around their necks.

"Come on, Kennedy!" V shouted. "Take him down!"

The group laughed as Sawyer narrowed his eyes on Kennedy, promise of revenge in his eyes. Funny how he tried to look ominous, but even Kaleb could see the heat in his gaze when he looked at the pretty vet.

"You ready?" she taunted Sawyer.

"As I'll ever be, darlin'."

Kennedy threw the first ball and missed. She immediately geared up to throw the second. She missed with that one, as well. She was smiling and giggling as she got ready with the third. Just when she pulled her arm back to throw the ball, she stopped, running forward and nailing the target with her hand, sending Sawyer into the water.

Kaleb laughed at Mason's little-boy giggle while the rest of the crowd hooted and hollered about Sawyer going down.

"It's your turn," Zoey said softly, pulling Kaleb's attention down to her.

"Let me guess, you're gonna buy a pie."

"Oh, no, I've got others to do that for me."

Kaleb glanced over at the line of people to see none other than Zoey's father at the front, sitting in his wheelchair with a wide grin on his face.

Lovely.

Just fucking lovely.

Curtis

Curtis handed one of the balls to Zoey's father as Kaleb made his way into the booth. For the last couple of minutes, Curtis had been chatting with Carl while they waited for Kaleb to take his turn. Although Carl happened to be quite fond of Kaleb, Curtis couldn't blame the guy for wanting to take a shot at sending him into the water. Hell, he couldn't blame any of these people, which was why, when Lorrie had informed him of her plan, he'd gotten right to work on securing a dunking booth for the occasion.

Not only were they bringing in a lot of money selling off all the pies that Lorrie and the girls had worked so hard on these last few days, but everyone seemed to be enjoying themselves. And that was the highlight of the day. Even though Zane had grumbled about going first, Curtis had seen a glimmer of excitement in his youngest boy's eyes.

Yeah, his boys were definitely good sports.

No matter how much trouble they liked to cause, they were still good kids.

Once Kaleb was in place, Carl made an attempt to take him down. He missed, but he laughed when he did, moving back out of the way so the next person could take their chance. Curtis glanced over at his grandson, noticing Mason was alight with excitement as he watched his daddy in the booth. His little-boy giggle had everyone laughing.

Finally, Kaleb went down after three more tries, and then it was Travis's turn. Of course, Curtis's oldest boy moaned and groaned the most, but he still made his way inside. When he was getting settled, Gage came over and tried to sweet-talk his way into the line, but Curtis intervened.

"I've got this one," Curtis told Gage.

"Pop."

Travis's warning went in one ear and out the other, sort of the way all the warnings that he'd dished out to them over the years had.

"Yes, son?" Curtis asked innocently.

"What are you doin'?" Travis asked, his deep, gruff voice reflecting his irritation.

"I'm donatin' to a good cause. What does it look like I'm doin'?" Curtis asked, taking his spot on the line.

"Well, I hope you don't miss," Travis goaded.

"Boy, I've been waitin' for this my whole life."

"Of course you have. Doesn't mean you're gonna…"

Travis's sentence trailed off when Curtis reared back, sending the ball heading right for the target. A second later, Travis was in the water, and the crowd was cheering.

"Beau, your turn, boy," Curtis said, watching Beau and Ethan as they stood together on the sidelines observing the action. As he thought back to all the shit that had happened earlier in the year, Curtis couldn't help but smile at his son. It was about damn time Ethan had come out of his shell, living life rather than just existing. Funny how it'd taken Beau to get him there.

Whatever works, Curtis thought to himself.

Backing away from the pitching line, Curtis made his way over to his wife. She was currently standing near the table with Jessie and Zoey, trying to take money and make change as the line in front of them continued to grow.

"Looks like the boys may have to take another turn in that booth," Lorrie told him.

Glancing over his shoulder, Curtis laughed as Beau got into position, Ethan already in place to take him down.

"I'm sure they'll be up for it," Curtis told them.

"We could call Jared and Jaxson," Lorrie suggested.

"Oh, they're already on their way. Did you think I'd let them miss out on the fun?" Curtis replied. "This is a family event, after all."

"So does that mean you're gonna take your turn up there?" Lorrie asked sweetly, placing her soft hand on his arm.

"Do you want me to go up there?" he asked her. "'Cause you know I will."

"I think it's only fair," came the rough voice from behind him. Curtis glanced over his shoulder to see Travis. He was rubbing the towel over his sodden clothes.

"Fair, huh?" Curtis joked.

"Yes, sir," Travis said, just as Braydon, Zane, and Sawyer came over to join them.

"I'm first," Zane shouted.

Arguing ensued between the boys as they all fought over who would get to take him down. Curtis didn't mind one bit. If they wanted to send him into a pool of water as payback, more power to them. He could be a good sport if they were.

"Fine. I'll go after Brendon," Curtis told them.

They all turned to see Brendon climbing in while Beau grabbed a towel and dried himself off.

"But then y'all have to go again."

"Fine," they all agreed easily.

Sawyer chuckled, his gaze traveling past Curtis, so he turned to see what his son was looking at, and that was when he noticed Cheyenne Montgomery making her way to the front of the line. Of course, she was being mauled by her obvious fans until Ethan—the only one who wasn't wet at this point—made his way over and helped her through. Once she was at the front of the line, she handed over some money and took one of the balls.

"Seriously?" Brendon shouted from inside the booth.

"Yes, sir," Cheyenne hollered back.

"Hold up!" Brendon called back, reaching for the hem of his shirt and lifting it over his head, tossing it out of the booth before turning his attention back to the beautiful young woman standing there watching him. "Okay. Do your worst, honey."

A chorus of applause erupted from the other ladies in the line, obviously showing their appreciation for Brendon, who was now shirtless.

Lord, have mercy, Curtis thought to himself. That boy was in over his head.

Beau

Beau couldn't help but laugh when Brendon removed his shirt in an apparent attempt to torment Cheyenne. He had to give her credit, though, she was doing a good job of pretending she wasn't affected by the guy. Pretty good, just not good enough. Her eyes were still traveling over Brendon's shirtless form as he sat there staring back at her.

"There's gonna be a riot," Jessie said, laughing.

"That should be a new rule," someone from the crowd yelled. A female someone. "They have to do it again. With their shirts off."

Beau glanced over at Ethan, finding him staring back at him. "What?"

"Nothin'," Ethan said softly.

"That look says a helluva lot more than *nothin'*," Beau retorted.

"I was just thinkin' maybe she's right. I wouldn't mind seein' you up there without your shirt on."

Ethan's words were spoken so low Beau hardly heard them. But he *had* heard them, and his body heated instantly. "Is that right?"

"Yep," Ethan said quietly, turning his attention back to Brendon up in the booth.

Beau smiled to himself.

Yeah, he loved this man with everything that he was. And he loved how Ethan continued to open up more and more as time passed.

"You ready?" Cheyenne provoked Brendon, who was still staring at her. She was taking her own sweet time as she stood there, tossing the ball into the air and catching it with her other hand.

"Ready as I'll ever be," Brendon replied.

If Beau wasn't mistaken, there was a world of innuendo in those few words. Brendon was ready for a lot more than just to have that woman dunk him in a pool of water. Maybe one day they'd figure out how to make that work. And if not, maybe they'd quit torturing one another.

Cheyenne made her first shot.

And missed.

Brendon's grin grew wider, more wicked as he watched her.

"That kinda sucked," Brendon told her.

Travis stepped up behind Cheyenne, handing her another ball. Beau noticed that Ethan's oldest brother was holding at least five more in his hand. Well, if she didn't make it with one of those, she could always pull the same stunt Kennedy had.

The excitement grew as the crowd spurred on the country music superstar. With each pitch, she missed, but no one seemed to care. No one except for Brendon, who hadn't taken his eyes off Cheyenne since she'd walked up.

"All right," Cheyenne said firmly. "I'll stop playin' around now."

"Playin' around, huh? Is that what you call that?" Brendon shouted.

"It is," Cheyenne said, changing her stance and focusing on the target.

This time, when she pulled back, she threw it underhanded and nailed the target instantly.

"By the way, did I mention I played softball?" she asked when Brendon sputtered as he got to his feet in the pool of water.

Based on the look he shot Cheyenne, he hadn't known that.

Beau laughed.

As did everyone else.

Travis

Now that all of his brothers had taken their turn in the booth—with the exception of Ethan, who had somehow managed to weasel his way out of it—Travis was ready to watch his father go down. They'd turned the tables on them when Lorrie mentioned they would all be taking turns, and since paying her back wasn't an option—she was their mother, after all—Travis would settle for the next best thing.

Taking their father down.

Not that Travis really minded the change in events that had occurred. Granted, he wasn't going to let everyone else know that. As it was, he continued to get sideways glances from his brothers all the damn time. He still couldn't believe he'd really made that much of a change since he'd given in to his love for Kylie and Gage, but maybe he had.

"Your turn, ol' man," Travis told his father. "If you're lucky, I'll get you out on the first shot."

"Let's just hope you've got it in you," Curtis replied.

Suddenly, a chant started from the ladies in the crowd. "Shirt off! Shirt off! Shirt off!"

Travis laughed, thinking about his father up there without his shirt. The guy was in his sixties, but he was still in his prime.

"Ladies," Curtis addressed the group before stepping into the booth. "I'd gladly take my shirt off for you, but I'd really hate to make my boys look bad."

Everyone laughed. Everyone. Including Lorrie and the girls. The old man was something else, there was no doubt about that.

When Curtis got in place, Travis went over to the table, handed his mother some more money, and took one ball. That was all he was going to need.

"You're goin' down, Pops," Travis told his father.

Curtis glanced down at the water beneath him and then back up to meet Travis's gaze.

"That's kinda the idea."

Travis smirked.

He noticed Kylie, Jessie, Zoey, V, and Cheyenne were all looking at him. Their gazes were darting back and forth between where he stood and the target in front of him. That was when he felt someone move up beside him.

Sawyer had joined him, smiling at him as he tossed a ball in the air.

On his other side, Kaleb stepped up.

Beside him was Ethan.

Then Zane.

Braydon and Brendon stepped up on Sawyer's other side.

They were all tossing a ball in the air, catching it, and then repeating the motion as they stared up at Curtis, who was now grinning from ear to ear.

"Ready when you are, boys," Curtis said, his gaze locking with Travis's briefly.

Joining his brothers, he tossed the ball into the air once and then pulled his arm back as they all did the same, still watching his father intently.

And then…

Smack!

Curtis went down into the water, everyone laughing, some people doubled over because Curtis certainly hadn't been expecting that.

He stood up, water dripping from his face and hair, eyes wide as he looked around to see just what had happened since none of them had thrown the ball.

Travis watched as his mother walked over in front of the booth, smiling at Curtis.

"Y'all seemed to forget that I was supposed to get a turn," Lorrie told him.

And when Curtis looked down at his wife, Travis saw the love the man had for her shining in his eyes. It was the same love Travis had seen reflected in his father's eyes for as long as he could remember.

As Travis glanced around at his brothers, their significant others, his nephew, and now his cousins who had just walked up, he felt the love overall. Even as they stood there dripping wet after being plunged into water for a good cause, despite their grumbling, the joy of being together was still there.

And he knew, without a doubt, that the reason for it all lay in the love that those two people had for one another. His parents.

Love like that came along once in a lifetime.

He could see the same love between Kaleb and Zoey, Zane and V, Ethan and Beau. He could also sense it was there somewhere for Braydon, Sawyer, and Brendon. He looked forward to watching theirs unfold sometime in the near future.

But now, as Travis glanced over at Kylie and Gage, he smiled. He didn't have to wait any longer for his once-in-a-lifetime. He'd already found it. He'd just happened to find it times two.

STAY TUNED

This was my first year doing this, and I have to say, it was so much fun. It took far less time to get pulled back into the stories than I thought it would. I hope you enjoyed spending the holidays with them as I did.

If you enjoyed *Naughty Holidays 2015*, please consider leaving a review.

ACKNOWLEDGMENTS

While writing is a solitary task, it's not a completely solo project. Because of that, I'd like to thank those who've assisted in one way or another.

As a side note, I received no compensation for these acknowledgments, so they are in no particular order.

My family: I'd like to thank my family for not looking at me like I'm completely out of my mind when I am lost in thought (translated to: having a silent but animated conversation with one of my many muses). Thank God for unconditional love.

Chancy and Amber: I truly enjoyed writing these stories, and your input made the experience even more delightful! Thank you so much for being a part of this journey—I really couldn't have done it without you.

You, the reader: I can honestly say this book would not have been written if it weren't for your persistence. The fact that you love my characters enough to want more is humbling (and intensely gratifying). So thank you. Thank you for reading, thank you for writing a review, and thank you for hopping on social media and telling your friends about the book. You're cool like that.

ABOUT NICOLE EDWARDS

New York Times and *USA Today* bestselling author Nicole Edwards spends her days stringing words together to make complete sentences. Sometimes not. Her best friend is coffee, and she has a love/hate relationship with sarcasm. She's been accused of having a filthy imagination, which she admits is true.

Nicole lives in the suburbs of Austin, Texas. She proudly claims one husband, three grown children, and three bosses (better known as the dogs). When she isn't writing, watching football or hockey, or keeping her bosses happy, you can probably find her with a book in hand.

BEFORE YOU GO!

Now that you've read one of my books, I'd like to think we can consider ourselves friends. And since friends usually hang out, I want to let you know where you can find me.

If you've got a minute or two, I hope you'll visit my website - **www.NicoleEdwards.me** - to find exclusive content you won't find anywhere else, including my Ramblings of a Writer Blog, Sneak Peeks, the Walker Family Tree, A Day in the Life character stories, exclusive giveaways, and more. If you'd like to be part of the VIP crowd, you can join Nicole Nation (free and easy to do) and get access to more cool stuff, like the option to join my review team if you're so inclined.

Don't forget to sign up for **Nic News** ... This is my newsletter, a.k.a. where the good stuff is. The best part: it's sent directly to your inbox. And because I know how difficult it is to manage your email, you've got a couple of options. When you sign up, you can choose to get the bare minimum: announcements for preorders and new releases. Or you can go all in and get those plus fun stuff like the Nic Newsflash, as well as giveaways, sales, etc. Either way you go, I only send out a couple a month, so I promise not to spam your email.

Oh, and I can't forget my **Naughty & Nice Shop**! This is where you'll find signed books and fun merch. There's plenty of naughty and nice options to go around.

Last but not least, if you're on Facebook, you should check out my reader group: **Nicole Nation**. This is where I interact with my friends. You can ask me questions, play fun weekly games, celebrate during release week, and enter exclusive giveaways!

You can also follow me on:

Facebook
/Author.Nicole.Edwards

Instagram
/NicoleEdwardsAuthor

TikTok
/@nicoleedwardsauthor

BookBub
/NicoleEdwardsAuthor

By Nicole Edwards

THE WALKERS OF COYOTE RIDGE
Kaleb

Zane

Travis

Holidays with The Walker Brothers

Ethan

Braydon

Sawyer

Brendon

Curtis

Jared

Hard to Hold

Hard to Handle

Beau

Rex

A Coyote Ridge Christmas

Mack

Kaden & Keegan

Trey

Rafe

Violet

Brantley Walker: Off The Books

All In
Without A Trace
Hide & Seek
Deadly Coincidence
Alibi
Secrets
Confessions
Bounty
Off Course
Chain Reaction
To Have and To Hold
Missing Pieces
Smoke and Mirrors

The Jamesons Of Coyote Ridge

Hot Chocolate Wishes
Rough & Dirty

Austin Arrows

Rush
Kaufman

Club Destiny

Conviction
Temptation
Addicted
Seduction
Infatuation
Captivated
Devotion
Perception
Entrusted
Adored
Distraction
Forevermore

DEAD HEAT RANCH
Boots Optional
Betting on Grace
Overnight Love
Jared *(a crossover novel)*

DEVIL'S BEND
Chasing Dreams
Vanishing Dreams

MISPLACED HALOS
Protected in Darkness
Salvation in Darkness
Bound in Darkness

OFFICE INTRIGUE
Office Intrigue
Intrigued Out of The Office
Their Rebellious Submissive
Their Famous Dominant
Their Ruthless Sadist
Their Naughty Student
Their Fairy Princess
Owned

PIER 70
Reckless
Fearless
Speechless
Harmless
Clueless

PRIMAL INSTINCTS
Chase (Volume 1-3)
Capture (Volume 4-6)
Claim (Volume 7-9)

HEROES & HAVOC
(Sniper 1 Security, Devil's Playground, Southern Boy Mafia)

Wait for Morning
Beautifully Brutal
Without Regret
Never Say Never
Beautifully Loyal
Without Restraint
Tomorrow's Too Late

STANDALONE NOVELS
Unhinged Trilogy
A Million Tiny Pieces
Inked on Paper
Bad Reputation
Bad Business
Filthy Hot Billionaire
RULE

NAUGHTY HOLIDAY EDITIONS
2015
2016
2021

www.ingramcontent.com/pod-product-compliance
Lightning Source LLC
Chambersburg PA
CBHW060423180626
46817CB00007B/2648